What the critics are saying...

5 cups! "*Ms. Ladley* does a fantastic job of transporting the reader into the world of the bordello with a science fiction twist that works wonderfully. I was absolutely unable to put this one down..." ~ *Keely Skillman for Coffee Time Romance*

5 Angels! "...the perfect blend of erotic romance and science fiction...*Ms. Ladley* has a wonderful sense of dialogue and humor that will have you laughing out loud." ~ *Tewanda for Fallen Angel Reviews*

5 Stars! "A steaming sci-fi romance with adorable characters and a fascinating setting...The love scenes are sizzling hot, sometimes a bit kinky and they'll leave you breathless." ~ *Tina for Mon Boudoir*

4½ Stars! "From the vividly described settings to the distinctive characters, this tale by *Titania Ladley* is compelling from start to finish...this couple really heats up the pages with their spirited and diverse sexual adventures. The storyline is uniquely original and inventive, and the unpredictable twists will stun readers." ~ *Amelia Richard for eCataRomance Reviews*

4 Stars! "The sexual attraction is amazing…If you like a hot and sexy paranormal, then this is the book for you." ~ *Ann Lee for Just Erotic Romance Reviews*

"Scorching is the best way to describe *Moonlite Mirage*…The sex is so scintillating and descriptive...It was great to see such a taboo, yet amazing place as the Bunny Ranch be the focal point for this book... Pleasure will be found by all who read this enchanting story!" ~ *Courtney Michelle for Romance Reviews Today*

Moonlite Mirage

Titania Ladley

An Ellora's Cave Romantica Publication

www.ellorascave.com

Moonlite Mirage

ISBN #1419952099

Edited by: Briana St.James
Cover art by: Syneca

Electronic book Publication: December, 2004
Trade paperback Publication: September, 2005

Warning:

The following material contains graphic sexual content meant for mature readers. *Moonlite Mirage* has been rated *E-rotic* by a minimum of three independent reviewers.

Ellora's Cave Publishing offers three levels of Romantica™ reading entertainment: S (S-ensuous), E (E-rotic), and X (X-treme).

S-e*nsuous* love scenes are explicit and leave nothing to the imagination.

E-*rotic* love scenes are explicit, leave nothing to the imagination, and are high in volume per the overall word count. In addition, some E-rated titles might contain fantasy material that some readers find objectionable, such as bondage, submission, same sex encounters, forced seductions, etc. E-rated titles are the most graphic titles we carry; it is common, for instance, for an author to use words such as "fucking", "cock", "pussy", etc., within their work of literature.

X-*treme* titles differ from E-rated titles only in plot premise and storyline execution. Unlike E-rated titles, stories designated with the letter X tend to contain controversial subject matter not for the faint of heart.

Also by Titania Ladley:

Jennie In a Bottle

More Than Magick (Anthology)

Me Tarzan, You Jewel

Enchanted Rogues (Anthology)

A Wanton's Thief

Moonlite Mirage

Heather —
Thanks for your
support!
Best wishes!
Titania Ladley

To the Reader:

Some time ago, Dennis Hof, the charismatic owner of the world-famous Moonlite BunnyRanch bordello near Carson City, Nevada, invited me to tour his unique business for research purposes. I'd come with the notion—or rather, the question—of whether or not love and romance could be found in a "house of ill repute". During my four-day stay, I embarked on a mission to unearth that which most people might argue could never be found in such a place. As I explored the vibrant establishment and interviewed Dennis, his lovely Madam Suzette and a bevy of gorgeous, real-life call girls, I began to feel the distinct aura of sensuality, class and, yes, love.

In MOONLITE MIRAGE, you will be given a clear picture of the brothel's physical layout. Please note that this is a work of fiction, and though most descriptions of the Ranch itself are accurate, some rooms (for instance the Orgy Room) are mostly fictitious in description. Keep in mind that all characters and events are purely imaginary, and none are even remotely based on actual people or occurrences.

Be aware, too, that in being a work of fiction, safe sex is not depicted in MOONLITE MIRAGE. However, The BunnyRanch and its associates always practice and encourage the use of condoms during all sexual encounters.

Note that at the end of this work, you will find a word-building glossary of Dorjanian language terms to further enhance your reading pleasure. I hope you have fun reading MOONLITE MIRAGE as much as I enjoyed researching and writing this paranormal, sci-fi, erotic romance.

Yes…there is love and romance in the air, you just wait and see!

Astere!

Dedication

To my wonderful editor, Briana St. James, I extend sincere thanks for seeing value and promise in my work. Your sharp editor's eye and friendly, very knowledgeable guidance are priceless gifts I'll treasure forever. You will always be dear to my heart.

To my husband, Dan, I pledge undying gratitude and a lifetime of endless, moonlit love. Thank you for maintaining faith in me even when I had none in myself—without you, I'd be lost. With all my heart and soul, I will love you to the ends of the earth.

And last but certainly not least, this is for you, Mom. You taught me the strength to carry on, to persevere in times of challenge, times when it seemed there would never be moonlight in the tunnel of life. In you, I saw a mirage of hope, a mirage that formed into a real foundation of love, bravery and almighty grace. I love you dearly!

Acknowledgements

To Dennis Hof, owner of the Moonlite BunnyRanch: Thank you for extending to me such a warm and hospitable welcome, and for allowing me free rein of your empire. The research opportunity was greatly appreciated and has served to enrich MOONLITE MIRAGE, to bring more genuine detail to this erotic romance story. I had a most memorable stay and will never forget your generosity.

To Madam Suzette: My trip would not have been complete without your enthusiasm, patience and kindness. Thanks for offering all those helpful resources, and for inviting me to join in on the parlor fun. The elegant, sexy, all-girl tea party has stayed with me as one of the fondest memories of my trip.

Sam: What a wonderful asset you are to the BunnyRanch. Thank you for coordinating my stay, for conducting it with such friendly helpfulness, and for keeping in touch over the last year or so. This book would not be possible without your interest, support and creative business mind.

To all the gorgeous Bunnies: Wow! I can't thank you enough for allowing me to spy and interrupt your intriguing jobs. You each possess a distinctive beauty and charm that makes the BunnyRanch that rare, sought-after, classy destination to fulfill secret fantasies. A special thanks to those Bunnies who took time out of their busy schedules to grant me such fascinating interviews.

A warm thanks to Raelene Gorlinsky, Managing Editor, Ellora's Cave Publishing, Inc. I will always appreciate your help and kindness in the many stages of this project. You went above and beyond the call of duty, and your efforts will never be forgotten!

Chapter One

Rolf Mahoney was fit to be tied—literally.

He didn't know how it had happened, but when he awoke, he was naked and secured to the bed like an animal.

And he was alone.

Where in the fuck am I?

He scanned his foggy memory. It took a moment, but he gradually remembered where he was. *Ah, yes.* His flight had arrived late into the night, and he'd finally been whisked by limo to the Moonlite BunnyRanch, the world-famous legal bordello near Carson City, Nevada. Exhausted, he'd been shown to a bungalow behind the busy establishment, and had collapsed on the bed.

It was the last thing he remembered.

"What...?" He rolled his head from side to side. There was a nightstand on either side of the bed and a mirrored dresser near the bathroom door. He raised his head and peered across the room toward the door that led into the living room. He could see his luggage grouped just where he'd abandoned it near the overstuffed white sofa. Soft music played from a stereo somewhere in the next room. Rolf shook the grogginess from his head at the sudden whiff of a sweet, seductive perfume. He could have sworn it tapped him on the shoulder and zinged beneath his nose.

"Hello..."

He jerked at the husky voice and yanked against the silk tied about his wrists and ankles. "What the hell?"

"No, not hell," the voice replied with a girlie giggle. "Paradise."

Yes. Most men considered the BunnyRanch an Eden, but there must be some mistake, he thought. He wasn't here for play. He was here on business.

"Okay, okay, so I shouldn't have had that last cocktail on the plane. As a result, I'm having a bizarre dream…in paradise, as you claim." He couldn't see her, and that made him feel all the more foolish, in addition to his vulnerable spread-eagle position. He moved his gaze across the ceiling, into nooks and crannies. "I give up. Where are you? Where's the hidden camera and audio speakers?"

"Speakers? Camera? There's no speakers or camera." There was a distinct breeze as warmth blanketed him. Womanly pressure slid over his bare skin, down to the sensitive flesh of his penis.

Then he lost it. An involuntary moan escaped him when the sensation of a wet mouth closed over him. He looked down between his spread legs. *There was nothing there!* Yet he could feel the tongue swirl around the head of his cock, and his body responded with a swift hard-on. His balls drew up in anticipation of that paradise in question. Never before in his entire thirty-three years had he received a blowjob by force. Granted, it was every man's dream, but he just couldn't allow it because *he* controlled his life, *he* called all the shots. No, this forced seduction by a…a ghost, or whatever the fuck it was, just wasn't going to fly with his ego. Oh, it may very well be a dream, but even in his dreams, Rolf Mahoney always practiced discipline over things in his life.

"Goddamn it! Stop it right now!" he growled through clenched teeth. "Just stop it!"

The heat was wrenched from his cock and he sucked in a breath as cool air assaulted the moist, half-hard length of him.

"Is there something wrong, Rolf?"

She said it softly in his ear. He could feel the heat of her breath on his cheek. Why couldn't he see her?

"How do you know my name?"

"Everyone here knows who you are," she said in a tone to imply his question had been silly. And an object that felt suspiciously like a tongue snaked into his ear. Next came the sensation of strong teeth clamped on his earlobe.

A spontaneous fire coursed its way from his ear to his sex. Rather than go soft, as he'd hoped it would, it hardened to full steel capacity. He throbbed with need, but he ignored it and called upon his prior military training. *Discipline. Mind over the needs of body and flesh. Gratification is not allowed.* He rehearsed it in his mind, but it was no use. Have I been drugged? he wondered suddenly.

"Untie me. Now."

"I can't do that," she purred, and her mouth, wherever it was, covered his. His eyelids fluttered shut.

He sighed then, and concentrated on the tactic of learning everything about his invisible enemy. Her hands were soft pads of fire that moved up and down the inner flesh of his forearms and biceps. The energy of her form covered him like an X, her legs spread as his were. Her mouth moved over his in a deadly kiss of temptation, and she tasted of an exotic flavor he'd never before experienced. He squinted, and still, he could not see her. Yet, she was there. She moved a flat surface—was it her abdomen?—over his stomach in an erotic dance. His cock—damn the traitor—played along and rose each time her V went high enough for it to almost slide into her dampness.

He tore his mouth from hers. "You're going to fuck me—and technically, without my consent, aren't you?"

"Mm, yes, *technically,*" she whispered. To underscore her words, she aligned him with her slit. Alluring and seductive, she moved herself in a circular motion and coated his dick with her juices. "But your words of affirmation or declination mean nothing. It's your body that talks to me, that says yes."

"I didn't come here for this." He refused to agree with her valid point. Mixing business with pleasure was a no-no in his life. And he resented the fact that the BunnyRanch offered him this bizarre encounter when he'd never once requested it—if it was, in fact, real.

Her legs spread wider and she lowered herself so that just the head of his penis penetrated her. Pre-cum oozed from the tip and lubricated her further. He could vividly imagine the sensation of shoving it completely to the extreme depths. Ah, yes, now *that* would be paradise!

He shook his head and fought the direction of his thoughts. *No, don't think of it, Rolf. Concentrate on…on…spring training. Yes, baseball season's beginning! All that promising talent they've moved up from the Minors and—and all those interesting stats…and…and…* Oh, she definitely *did* possess some awesome stats and measurements of her own! He clamped his teeth together and groaned. Rigid restraint loomed barely out of his grasp. If he could just distract her, maybe he could take control. Then maybe, just maybe, he *would* continue with this little game, only he'd be the one to hold the rulebook.

"Yes. You're here because of the movie," she replied, and her weight slid down, causing her pussy to close over him by mere maddening centimeters.

He hissed and his ass muscles tightened. "You know…all about that?" he asked around gasps and moans.

"But, of course I do," she said in a soothing tone. And she took in another half-inch of him. "The whole BunnyRanch is excited to have a famous Hollywood producer here. Believe me, as you roam the Ranch and try to choose the woman you want to play the part of that special call girl in your movie, you're going to be pampered like you've never been before."

Her mouth was on his again, but he tore free of its enticing flavor. "I told you…" He growled as her sleek passage released him then instantly took him back in again. "I didn't come here for this."

"Oh, but I did," she murmured. "I did."

"Who *are* you?" He couldn't take this torment any longer. This was cruel and unusual punishment. If it turns out not to be a dream, he'll damn well let the owner know that he doesn't appreciate it one bit—as soon as he's freed.

Bit by bit, the pressure on his cock was released and cold air assaulted its full length. By way of a nonverbal answer, she gradually appeared to him in a cloud of mist. She hovered over him in full human form, yet he could see right through her, as if she were a spirit. Her hair was a soft fluff of silky whiteness with startling streaks of golden blonde, and he itched to be released so that he could run his fingers through it. Within the perfection of the heart-shaped face, multi-colored eyes stared back at him. They were breathtaking and glistened like a conglomerate of emeralds, rubies and sapphires. In the center, the pupils were the shape of stark-white, four-pronged stars. They shimmered like finely cut diamonds, mesmerized him with their gentle twinkle. Struck by the beauty and unusual colors, he stared in wonder. His anger fell to the wayside, forgotten, and the thud of his heart thumped softly, almost blissfully, in his chest. After a long, quiet pause, he tore his gaze from hers and passed it ever so slowly down the length of her as she hovered mere inches above him.

That body...whew! What absolute perfection it was! He longed to reach up and yank her down so that the fullness of her ample breasts pressed against his chest. The sleek plane of her belly taunted his gaze and drew it down toward the beautiful juncture of her sex. His dick, erect and shimmering with her cream, was positioned just below the clean-shaven lips of that gorgeous pussy.

And that very dick had lost its pathetic battle.

She smiled gently at him, even as she lowered herself and took in an inch of his length. His breath caught, but he waited for her next words before he exhaled. "I'm Zoey," she murmured, finally answering his question.

Zoey? He rather liked the sound of her name. It was unusual, just like the dream he was in, just like her.

"Well, Zoey, honey, I'm delighted to finally meet you. However, I—oh!" he cried out when she slammed herself fully upon his rod. "Jesus…holy…sonofa—"

It was no use. For the first time in his life, he'd lost control, and there was no getting it back. She moved over him in the perfect rhythm, hovered and swished in a dance of seduction. Juicy sex lips stroked him like a practiced mistress. Her mouth found his, and, as if this weren't enough for her, she pinched his nipples ravenously and plucked until they hardened like his cock. Fire shot to his loins. He pulled against his restraints and attempted to buck her upward, but she held on expertly, and rode him violently. Then her mouth found the crook of his neck. She pressed her hands down on his inner forearms while her teeth nipped his flesh, and he moaned aloud when she suckled his skin into her mouth. Her tongue twirled around and sent ripples of gooey heat to his manhood. As if she could feel the blood settle there, she clamped her female folds tighter around his rod, and moved to devour another section of his neck with her mouth.

Moist fire engulfed him. Never before had he been brought to such extreme levels of lust in such a short time.

This was completely maddening! How to resist such a forceful, sweet, ravenous fuck? His eyelids grew heavy and his head thrashed from side to side. The orgasm was building, and there was no stopping it. And just when he thought it couldn't get any more torturous, she tore her mouth from his neck and lifted his head to her chest. Upward she stretched until she could force one of her hard nipples into his mouth. He was starved for it. She'd pushed him over the edge of reason, and there was no way he could resist it now. He took it between his teeth, and she hissed out her pleasure. While the tip of his cock pounded the depths of her sticky hole, her nipple and part of her breast fucked his mouth. He laved his tongue over every inch of the sweet flesh, and then he tore his mouth from it and rooted until he found the other.

"Oh!" she screamed. "Yes! Yes, I'm coming!"

Her hips moved at an unbelievable speed, and he marveled at how tight her involuntary, orgasmic spasms were around his length. He'd never felt such a fierce reaction to his cock in his entire life! He longed to wrap his arms around her and steady her violent response. But there was no control in this mating—at least not on his part. The volcano rumbled deep within his loins. Lava-come bubbled and roiled. Then the force went completely out of kilter. It exploded like never before. Rolf cried out, over and over, as he shot his scorching juice into her core.

There was a long quiet moment following their release where she stilled above him. Then she gently pulled her breast from his mouth and collapsed upon his chest.

He could hear his heart thud behind his breastbone, feel it thump, and he dragged in a ragged breath to soothe the discomfort. Calm now, Rolf closed his eyes and inhaled the unique floral scent of her.

And everything went black again.

*****

An electrical zap shot through her.

Nidus *stores ninety-one point three percent complete.*

The *compubot's* monotone transmission message registered in her brain's *datochip*. Ah, so it wouldn't be long. A few more *fleks* out of the man, and she would be ready to return to Dorjan—that is, if the *portalship* is healed of its malfunctions by that time. Barring any complications, she would be out of his life before he even had a chance to realize he'd been under siege by dream-travel.

He would only remember vague snippets of their encounter, and somehow, the thought disappointed her. Though he wouldn't recall her name or her face or anything specific about her, he would remember that he'd had a very erotic "dream".

But she, on the other hand, would have every nuance, each curve and plane of his form, every sense of him etched into her mind.

Zoey Fabiyan studied him for a while longer. As she did so, she untied him and prepared to return to her body. She ran her hand through the thick midnight hair, shivering at the memory of those misty blue eyes penetrating her soul. Captivated, she trailed a finger down the straight nose, across the interesting lips, lips she longed to kiss yet again.

Her palm brushed the slightly stubbled jaw line. She normally didn't care for hair of any length on a man's face. But somehow on this particular male, the shadow of it was unique and very becoming while coupled with the strong jaw.

And his body! Wow! The powerful build and excellent stamina were reminiscent of the male species of her world. Zoey dragged her hands down the wide, smooth chest, across the rippled abdomen. Warm, tight flesh tantalized her palms, making her long to press her tingling breasts along the tanned plane. She thirsted to taste that firm skin again, and unable to resist, she pressed a gentle kiss to his navel.

He let out a long breath just as her perusal shifted lower. Then there was his *ketka*! It had fit perfectly within her passage. Closing her hand over the soft girth of it, a hot goo warmed her sex. Thick and long, his impressive tool had delivered a potent batch of spermatozoa to her *nidus* chamber, where it joined all the other samples she'd collected since her arrival at Earth's BunnyRanch weeks ago.

But there was something unique about this particular Earthling, something that had caused an instant disinterest in all other males. Zoey clamped her lower lip between her teeth. Such indifference worried her, since mating random males in vast quantities was the encouraged norm for a Dorjanian female. This strange interest must be kept under control, she thought as she abruptly released his cock. It must not become an obstacle while she performed her duty.

Her mission had moved along without complication—until tonight. She sighed at the thought of adding further confusion to her delicate assignment, and gathered her spirit form into a tight ball. Closing her eyes, she prepared herself for the swift journey to retrace her spatial path back to her combination office-apartment at the front of the Ranch.

She had settled at the BunnyRanch after her *portalship* had delivered her here to the Nevada region, a place where her research had indicated heavy coupling activities in comparison to other areas of this planet. While Dorjanians and Earthlings were very different in some ways, they were extremely congruent sex partners. Their *gametes* were compatible, and could thereby produce similar enough offspring if cross-mated.

Answering an ad for an accountant, she'd sidled her way into the business so that she could accost the many male Earthlings who frequented the establishment in search of soul-altering sex. She hadn't wanted to bring undue attention to herself and become a flashy, high-paid call girl. Being an accountant onsite allowed her strategic geographical dream-travel access to the men while not drawing unnecessary interest to herself when it was time to vacate and return to Dorjan. And the *compubot* portion of her genetic makeup, via the *datochip* in her brain, had easily briefed her on Earth mathematics and accounting principles so that she fit perfectly within the position.

The goal was to collect compatible male seedlings for storage within her *nidus*, and return it to her home for immediate dispersion to those women who were of the breeding season. Dorjan, a fraction of a light-year away and within another solar system, was nearly an extinct planet, and it was solely up to her to remedy the male-mortality crisis. Within the last galaxy *manoyear*, ninety-one percent of Dorjan's male population had been stricken with a rare and deadly disease. Most of the remaining nine percent clung to life, unable to mate. Dorjan was in danger of eventual extermination, which was why Zoey, a highly skilled *astrolage*, had been chosen to travel to their primitive sister-planet to harvest *genetoid* material.

Zoey took one last look at him as he slumbered peacefully. Ignoring the strange tug in her breast, she turned and traveled through space and walls and structures until she popped out into the cool, moonlit April evening beyond the enclosure of Rolf Mahoney's assigned bungalow. She rather liked the Nevada terrain with its majestic rise and fall of the horizon, the dark gray Sierra Nevada Mountains capped with snow. Before her, the land was barren with sandy, dry soil. Sagebrush dotted the landscape as it climbed upward toward the mountainous peaks…toward the solar system of her home. She inhaled the raw scent of soil upon the wind, so very similar to that of Dorjan's natural fragrance.

As she traveled behind the BunnyRanch, she caught the melody of song and laughter, passion and ecstasy. A man and a woman embraced in a spa of steamy water on the rear patio. Off in the far distance, in the still of the night, she could see a group of three wild mustangs as they galloped across the open, moon-soaked field, and if she perked her *audiotrap* just so, she could hear the thunder of their hooves upon the hard ground. Wistful and homesick, it made her long for her *stallisor*, the Dorjan species equivalent in features to Earth's equines, yet far more enormous and powerful.

Zoey moved on until she approached the front of the building, then she forced her altered mass through the glass of the window. She unrolled and floated to the floor then glided to her physical body where it lay unmoving beneath the covers of her bed. The re-joining process was always painful following dream-travel, and she clamped her eyelids tight and braced herself for the transition. With a sharp intake of breath, she leapt into her body and refilled its space.

Her eyes fluttered open. She stared across the room at the desk and scattered sofas and chairs. Moonlight slanted in through the windowpane and bathed the space with a bluish glow, much like a Dorjanian summer-solstice night. She thought of the great weight that was on her shoulders. The *portalship* had successfully delivered her here to her destination, but as she'd neared Earth, the panel had indicated several major malfunctions. Still, she had had no word from Raketar or King Luran's fleet. Had the *portal* been repaired? Would it be ready in time to transport her back to Dorjan?

She pushed the thought to the back of her mind. It was useless to ponder its implications. Instead, she curled onto her side, bunched one fist beneath her chin, and drew in a long breath. The spicy scent of his cologne remained vivid in her memory, almost as if he were still in her arms. Flashes of his solid body moved through her thoughts. Her clit hardened instantly, and warm moisture soaked her *pless* between her legs. She pressed a hand to her abdomen where his seed was stored safely in her *nidus*.

But the tender gesture brought dread and fear back to the surface.

If the *portal* had been damaged beyond repair, she would be forced to become an Earthling, to never return home. Even more disturbing was the knowledge that his fertile stores would die within her.

And so would all of Dorjan.

Chapter Two

Rolf had risen before dawn the following morning. Bleary-eyed and restless, he'd immediately called for the limo. There was other business to attend to while in town, and he'd intended to see to it while he was here. Now, hours later, he felt himself go hard as the car neared the BunnyRanch. He glanced out the window and made every distracted effort to study the charcoal and smoky, white-tipped peaks of the Sierra Nevadas.

But it was no use. *She* was there in everything he saw, everything he did. Her image was fuzzy, yet he sensed her clearly in his soul. The mountains were her breasts, the ride in the plush limo brought to mind her smooth and seductive lovemaking, and the meeting he'd had not an hour ago had put him into a rigid state of drowsiness in which it seemed he could smell her again, feel himself inside her.

And that had been downright embarrassing when the executive producer of his upcoming movie, who happened to have a second home in the Carson City area, had adjourned the budget meeting in an abrupt manner after he'd spied Rolf's spontaneous hard-on. God, it'd been humiliating. He'd felt like a pimply teen trying to slouch down in his seat at school to hide his unruly cock!

He pressed his lips together and settled back into the black leather seat as the driver maneuvered closer to his destination. Hopefully, the madam would have the lineup all perky and ready for him to examine this morning. The Moonlite BunnyRanch had a reputation as the top-notch bordello in all of Nevada, and he fully expected to find the perfect hooker to cast in his movie. It was an unconventional method of casting, he knew, but Rolf had exhausted all other means. He'd been through take after take, rehearsal after rehearsal, and still, every single actress had struck him as ordinary. And he didn't want an ordinary actress for this particular project.

He wanted the real thing.

He wasn't going to waste any more of his precious time or hard-earned money for the artificial. He needed a real hooker, one who would exude sleaze and sex appeal and a lack of inhibitions onto the big screen. Oh, they could teach her all the behind-the-scenes stage cues, lingo and camera angle tricks, he thought as the one-story building came into view.

But no actress could portray a prostitute like a real one could, that he was certain of.

Just outside the structure's perimeter, they approached an open gate with a sign that read *Warning. Sexual entertainment ahead 300 yards. If this offends you, please turn around.*

Rolf chuckled to himself. Though he wasn't residing at the BunnyRanch for the week to satisfy his own pleasure, he would most definitely not be offended. He'd had his share of sexy, accommodating women. And he intended to have many more.

That is, after this trip was over.

He didn't need a woman to fulfill any fantasies at the moment. His dreams—thank you very much—had done a fine, bizarre job of that already. Rolf lifted a hand and stifled a yawn. He'd slept like the dead before and after that vivid dream, yet he was still exhausted. He focused on the passing terrain as he struggled to recall her name and face, but they eluded him. Instead, her honeysuckle scent, the satiny touch of her skin, the sweet warmth of her perfect body, all rose to taunt him. And, son of a bitch, there was no forgetting the tight heat of her pussy as it had spasmed around his cock!

He sighed and absently rubbed his growing arousal. No, he insisted silently. Getting laid wasn't on his list of priorities at the moment.

Sleep was—and the discovery of the perfect woman for the part.

The limo pulled onto the paved parking lot. It came to a rolling stop before a wrought-iron gate. The driver climbed from his seat and opened the rear door, then stepped back to allow Rolf to emerge.

"Your briefcase, sir," the man said sternly, his dark gray uniform impeccably pressed and speck-free. "Would you care for me to take it on back to your bungalow, or would you like to handle it yourself?"

Rolf stepped forward, reached into his trousers pocket, and drew out a jeweled money clip. He slipped a crisp one-hundred-dollar bill into the man's hand. "No, thank you, Jonathan," he replied as he clutched the briefcase. "I can take it from here."

"Thank you, sir. Very much appreciated." He slipped the bill into his jacket pocket.

They strolled up to the gate together. The chauffeur pressed a large button set within the bars.

A reply buzzer sounded. The iron entrance swung open. Rolf followed the driver up the short walk to a tinted glass door. As they waited for admittance, a movement caught his eyes and he jerked his gaze to scan the long white complex. Two windows down from the door, red velvet curtains parted, held apart by an elegant, slim hand.

And his eyes rose to meet hers.

He swallowed the thick lump of excitement that clogged his throat. Her eyes were an unusual shade of blue—or were they green or lavender?—like a sea nymph with gemmed irises. Her flaxen hair, a long cascade of waves and layers, framed her finely boned face before falling to rest behind her narrow shoulders. He imagined—no, he prayed—that its length reached the curve of her ass.

Though the window was somewhat filmy, he could see her from the hips up. She was lithe yet curvy, and her stance spoke of a sort of irresistible mixture of sophistication and sensuality. She wasn't clad in lingerie or a seductive, dick-zapping costume as one might expect at a bordello, but her snug white blouse left little to the imagination. Rolf rubbed one palm over his thigh and briefly caressed his crotch. He watched as her eyes narrowed, and she licked her cherry-red lips almost insolently. His gaze traveled down the slim column of her neck to the generous cleavage that oozed from the gape of her garment.

He shifted his stance. His suit trousers grew rather tight as a vision haunted him. It flashed before him and took the place of the woman. He was fucking…*her* again, the witch in his dreams. He didn't know who she was, why she haunted his thoughts and his sleep, but he saw the foggy image of her there for just an instant in the window.

"Who is that woman?" he croaked to the driver.

The man, still awaiting entry into the establishment, shot Rolf a look of pure confusion. "What woman?"

"There, in the…window," he added softly. But she was gone.

The driver shrugged and chuckled. "There're lots of women here, sir. If you can't find that particular one, there's plenty more where she came from. The right amount of money can get you just about anything you want."

He merely grunted a reply. *I don't want more. I want* her.

"Welcome to the Moonlite BunnyRanch, Mr. Mahoney." A pretty redhead in a skintight blue mini-dress slowly pulled open the glass door and stepped aside to allow him entrance. "You're quite the early riser—so sorry to have missed you this morning. But we trust you slept well in your bungalow last night," she cooed.

The driver turned after delivering his passenger to the door, and quietly retreated.

At the sweet voice, Rolf shook the disturbing image from his head and made a quick recovery.

"Well…hello, beautiful." His gaze moved seductively over her voluptuous body. Had he determined that he wasn't here for a woman? "Early, and not a moment too late," he mumbled, and added a low whistle for good measure as he stepped through the doorway.

She had the manners to blush. "Right this way, sir. We've been preparing for your visit for some time now, hoping to make you feel as at home as possible during your decision-making process."

He examined the room—empty of patrons at the moment—as she led him directly into the cozy yet elegant parlor. Though he'd passed through late the night before, he'd sported a bad case of jetlag and had merely allowed himself to be led to his cottage. But now…now that he was suddenly alert and ready for the task at hand, he took his time and inspected his surroundings. There was the heavy scent of enticing perfume and sex along with the aroma of various mixed cocktails. The room stood complete with a fireplace, mirrored walls, butterscotch sofas and a long bar in the lounge set beyond an arched doorway. It was lit seductively by various neon lights and soft, yellow sconces placed strategically between the mirrors. And, naturally, he thought with amusement, there was a gold strippers' dance pole positioned in the center of the room.

The young woman continued. "Madam Ivana has groomed her most prized ladies. And all with you and your movie in mind."

"I'm already feeling very much at home," he assured her as he eyed her fine ass. Alluringly, it peeked from below the wickedly short dress as she bent to fluff the pillows on the sofa.

She gestured to the area she'd just readied. "Please. Sit. And what would your pleasure be?"

Legs feeling suddenly rubbery at the purr to her voice and the deep décolletage she presented him, he collapsed onto the divan and sank into the heavenly softness of it. "Uh, martini, dry. No olive, please."

She winked at him, and for the first time, he noticed the deep brown of her eyes, like decadent dark chocolate bonbons, he thought. "Coming right up," she said huskily before crossing to the bar.

She waited patiently for the bartender to prepare the cocktail then brought it to him upon a tray. Deliberately, she pressed the glass into his hand and held it there for a brief moment. Her eyes bore into his. He could smell the seductive aroma of her perfume.

"You know," she crooned as she trailed a French-manicured nail over the back of his hand. "If you don't find what you're looking for when Madam brings the lineup to you"—she leaned in closer and the warmth of her sweet breath caressed his cheek—"I'm available for whatever your desires might be, Mr. Mahoney."

He growled low in his throat. The woman was good, he thought, as he studied the way her eyes devoured him.

But she wasn't good *enough*.

She didn't have the look, the mysterious depth of appealing sexuality he sought. She didn't have that underlying…something—he couldn't quite define it. Oh, she'd definitely be good for an afternoon romp in bed, he admitted, but not as the wounded yet deviant, eye-catching call girl he wanted to cast for his movie, *Scarlet Angel*.

And not even his hardened rod could steer him away from his course.

"I'll certainly keep that in mind," he said over the rim of the glass.

"Well…" She inhaled with a bit of a tiger's growl, exhaled softly, and ran her hands down the length of her curves. "I'll inform the madam of your arrival. But, in the meantime, if you should decide what it is you're looking for, the name's Gypsy. I'll be around tending to this and that if you should decide on some fun."

He cleared his throat as she spun on her heel in departure. She turned back and asked, "Was there something else you required?"

He shifted in his seat. The warmth from the blazing fireplace seemed to suddenly smother him. "There was a young lady…a beautiful, exotic woman looking out the window when I arrived."

"Window? What window?"

Rolf had no idea where he was going with this, but there was no ditching the inquiry at this rather blatant moment. He was committed now that this Gypsy stood before him like an eager servant awaiting her master's every whim. "As I was admitted into the main door just now, it was, oh, two, three windows down to the left of the door." He stood and raised a hand, holding it parallel to the floor. "She was about so tall, rich blonde, streaked hair, big…" He cupped his palms in front of his chest.

"Tits?" Gypsy supplied.

"Yes, big breasts. Could you maybe find out who she is and add her to my lineup?"

She winked. "But, of course, Mr. Mahoney. After all, you have arrived at the world-famous BunnyRanch where fantasies are indulged, all wishes granted." He caught a snap of something volatile in her dark eyes. "I will see what I can do and inform the madam."

She spun on her heel with an almost angry whirl. Then he watched her slink away as the clip of her stiletto heels echoed down the corridor. And, with each fading step fall, he was filled with anticipation at seeing the woman in the window once again.

With a sigh, he collapsed back onto the sofa. He glanced about and made note of the elegance of the room. It was so damn nice to command the best! People kissed his ass simply because they knew his bank account oozed with excessive funds. He loved the power—and, yes, he *was* arrogant, he knew. But he'd never forget what circumstances he'd sprung from. And that was precisely why this movie was so important to him.

He tossed back the remainder of the martini and set the glass aside. Settling into the soft cushions, he drew in a deep breath, closed his eyes and propped his head against the wall.

He would just rest his eyes for a bit while he waited for Madam Ivana's delectable lineup.

*****

Zoey darted from the window and paced in the confines of her office. Ledgers and invoices lay forgotten upon her wide desk as her heart thudded against her ribs. The computer had long since enabled its screensaver and scrolled a blinking list of all of Ivana's precious girls.

"*Mama Luna,* he saw me!" she said aloud to herself. And there was no mistaking it. He was the man she'd gone to late last night in dream-travel.

It was Rolf Mahoney.

"Think, Zoey, think. What are you going to do?" She crossed her arms under her breasts and spun back toward her desk. But she couldn't concentrate on a plan, and could only think of *him*. She sighed and collapsed in her desk chair. Images of his naked, sprawled body flooded her mind. She closed her eyes and imagined the warmth of his mouth as it claimed the swell of her bosom, and washed over her like a Dorjan ocean tide. With vivid clarity, she could recall the taste of his passionate kisses, the corded muscles of his chest against the palms of her hands, her own wetness as it coated his steely shaft with her excitement. She inhaled and could almost smell the earthy scent of him.

Her eyes flew open.

"No! Stop it this instant! You can't see him, and you can't let him know who you are. Not outside of dreams." Her hand dropped to caress her abdomen. She thought of Dorjan and how the whole planet depended on her. "No. Never."

Diona! What should she do?

She spun in her chair toward the window, and gazed out at the majestic rise and fall of the horizon, the dark gray mountains capped with snow. Before her, across the barren land dotted with sagebrush, she spied the group of three wild mustangs she'd seen during her dream travels.

A wistful envy gripped her. If only she could run like them, she'd travel far, far away, back home to Dorjan. But she was stuck here until the *portal* was ready, and until her *compubot* sensed adequate samples to satisfy the king's orders—a fact she wouldn't be privy to until the sensor alerted her that it was time to go. And with Dorjan's own king among those few healthy remaining males at risk, it only added to her enormous burden. The sensor would also be able to detect waking samples, a deadly mode of semen collection for the vulnerable sperm. Dream-travel was the only safe way for both the spermatozoa and Zoey, for if the king were to receive a transmission that she'd succumbed to unsafe sex, she'd be banned from Dorjan, whether she was their savior or not.

She'd finally concluded that the BunnyRanch would be the perfect place to locate and connect with virile specimens containing strong genetic makeup, whom she could later search for in unconsciousness. Kinky sex, free will of the male's fertile *milt* and untamed fantasies were the norm here at the Ranch, which very much served her purposes. She'd assumed it would be a guarantee to come here to the bordello. In and out in no time, then, once she'd collected the proper amount and the *portal* had reappeared, she'd be back home within several more galactic phases.

But she'd made the mistake of meeting *him*. Never before had she been so torn between loyalty and personal gratification. She yearned to be with him, day and night, in both consciousness and slumber.

Zoey studied one mustang as it galloped off and around a bend of scraggly trees. Yes, she wanted to run, but she longed to take him with her.

Slowly, her hands rose and she cupped them over her tingling breasts. Her eyes fluttered shut, remembering the feel of his hot tongue as it flickered over her nipples. Legs quaking at the bolt of excitement that struck her deep in her gut, it resurrected the inferno he'd started. Oh, how she wished she could run to him, to climb upon him before a fire and ride him like a *stallisor*, out across the meadows, to fly high with him to the mountaintops, to her Dorjanian home.

Her hands fell away. She sighed. No, it couldn't be. He could not survive in her world. The atmosphere on Dorjan could be deadly to humans. There must be Dorjanian blood in one's makeup to survive its low-oxygen air. Conversely, she could never survive on Earth—Dorjan was the only home she could ever accept. Then there was the fact that her mission would give others life. Her planet's very existence depended on her successful sowing of genetic power. So it was futile. This Earthman, while a pleasant diversion and a perfect specimen, would not be a part of her future.

Diona, but it was going to be difficult to stay away from the hunk!

Zoey fixed her gaze on the puffy gray clouds that churned across the canvas of the sky. She craved him, she admitted shamefully. She needed his touch like vegetation needed the coming rain. She'd seen the thick bulge in his pants when he'd emerged from the vehicle, and, with bated breath, she'd watched as he'd stroked it, watched, mesmerized as he'd locked eyes with hers.

Slowly, she slipped one hand into her pants and found the moist, throbbing bud. Flickering her fingertip over it, she gasped as images of their lovemaking, of her dreams, flooded her senses. It released a sudden gush of wetness between her thighs. She pushed her finger down between the swollen folds of her pussy and found the damp cavern where his silk-covered cock had entered her just last night.

Her eyes fluttered shut as fire scorched her to the thickened marrow of her bones. A bouquet of wildflowers sat nearby on a file cabinet, and, with controlled strength, she concentrated on the sweet aroma, inhaled its fragrance and brought herself to a place far, far away. Dizziness engulfed her, and she welcomed the sensation almost as much as the impending orgasm.

"Ah, *mulera…*" she purred. "Come to me! Take me!" And she sank her finger deep into her vagina. But it wasn't enough. She couldn't quite mimic the motion of her lover. Hastily, groggily, she withdrew her hand and unfastened her trousers. Her breath came in ragged, quick spurts of lust. Raising her hips, she slid the garment from her legs and tossed it aside. Naked from the waist down, she allowed her bottom to settle into the curved, rough wool of the computer seat.

Propping her heeled shoes upon the windowsill, she beckoned her imagined lover to the treasure between her thighs. One of her hands sliced upward beneath her blouse and found a taut, aching nipple. The other returned to her clit. She groaned aloud, finding it hard…like his cock had been. She pinched and pulled on her nipple, and recalled the feel of his wet tongue there as it fluttered, sucked and bit with unbridled passion. Her head fell back against the chair, and she raised her hips to meet her finger as it sank deep into her dampness, and she imagined it was his thick rod. Pumping her hips, using the windowsill for leverage, she fucked herself and added first two, then three fingers. She could imagine it as if it were her dream, as if it were his long dick that penetrated her.

Come to me, Rolf. Please, come to me now!

Ravenous, she quickly undid the blouse and released her breasts from the bra beneath. Stroking the fullness of her sensitive flesh, she pictured Rolf in her mind poised above her, entering her passage.

Yes…he was inside her—wasn't he? The fire reached a frenzy. She could now hear his heavy breathing in her ear, smell the musky scent of him mingled with the fragrant flowers, feel the warmth of his body and the thickness of his penis as it speared her over and over.

Time seemed to stand still.

"How can this be?" he asked.

Her eyes fluttered open at the deep timbre of his voice, so soft and loving. And he was there, above her. Somehow, she'd ended up on the floor between her desk and the window. Gold rays of late afternoon sun sliced in, slanted over him and bathed him in a languid glow. By the soft lighting in the office, his eyes appeared as gray as this planet's sky on a winter's day. They sparkled with a mixture of wonderment and passion.

Zoey gasped. Her gaze moved around the room, up to the ceiling, back to the handsome planes of his tanned face. "I…I don't know," she whispered.

He shifted, raising her legs so that they hooked over the inner bends of his elbows. "I don't know either," he said with a shake of his head. "But I've got to have you again. *Now*!"

As if in slow motion, a bead of sweat fell from his jaw. It landed on her left nipple, and she could swear she heard it splash, like a sea creature diving into the depths of the Dorjan Sea. She gripped her breast, and, with her eyes locked on his, she lifted its fullness to meet her mouth. She licked the droplet from her own nipple at the precise moment that he stabbed her to the very depths of her womanhood.

"Oh!" She groaned, and sucked voraciously. He bent his head and took the other hard bud into his mouth, and fire backwashed through her soul.

"I'm burning for you, Angel," he panted. With his hands planted on the floor at her sides, he reared up and raised his head. A deliberate growl erupted from his throat. She could see the bruises on his neck from her own ravenous appetite last night. The sight of them made her long to be marked by him as well.

He was like a *wofler*, a wild, predatory species from the Stalton Forest of her world. Like that powerful creature, he resembled a voracious wolf-man who ate and ravished her, driving her to such an unfathomable level of lust, that she could become an animal herself.

"Yes—*fuego*!" she screamed, and the fire engulfed them in a slow-burning blue flame. She reached out to grip him as the orgasm barreled over her…but he was already gone.

She opened her eyes and stared up at the white ceiling tile. She was alone. The only sound was that of her ragged breathing, and the hum of the computer's motor.

How had that happened? It was a fluke, she was certain. Occasionally, the physics of dream-travel could go awry, and, if the initiator's power is strong enough, it can reverse the travel path, causing the receiver to become the traveler. And, in this case, she'd called to him without thinking, aware he'd be among people of the BunnyRanch where she'd be unable to accost him. Apparently, he'd dozed somewhere—which was unusual given the provocative setting of the bordello—otherwise, he wouldn't have been able to come to her.

Zoey suddenly jerked as her *compubot* transmitted updated material to her via the *datochip*

Stores currently ninety-three point eight percent complete. Repeat. Ninety-three point eight percent complete.

A fraction of a light-year closer to Dorjan, she thought, but immediately dismissed the data to return to the grave matter at hand.

She inhaled a deep breath and scanned the room.

Yes, she was alone. But she hadn't been only seconds ago.

Which meant she was now in *way* too deep. To be in a brothel with many Earthlings' *gametes* to choose from, but to only desire to seek out one particular male, was not good for Dorjan. Nor was it good for her.

And what's more, it was the first time her subject had ever traveled to *her*!

Chapter Three

"He's here already?" Madam Ivana Chavez said on a moan as she rolled in bed and turned her back to Gypsy.

"Oh, yes," Gypsy said dreamily. "All six-foot-two of him. And those bedroom eyes!" She shivered. "Like twin flames of blue fire."

"Gypsy," Ivana groaned. She'd be the first to appreciate a fine specimen, but when the stomach flu roiled headlong through your system, the main thing on your mind would be the trashcan. "Please, honey. Spare me. As for Mr. Mahoney, *now* what am I going to do? All the girls I had chosen for him are all tied up on an extended outdate weekend party until tomorrow morning—when he was *supposed* to have arrived." She turned onto her back and flung her wrist across her brow. Her ample breasts jiggled under her thin negligee.

"Probably *literally* tied up," Gypsy mumbled under her breath. Raising her voice an octave, she added, "Oh, by the way. There are no other girls available, either. They're all either with gentlemen callers, or participating in the outdate party. So he didn't even get a lineup presentation when he arrived."

"Oh, Lord," Ivana moaned. "He's filthy rich and not one girl to greet him?"

"Well," she sang as her sapphire eyes twinkled. "I greeted him. And I suppose, since you're in a bind, I could maybe fill in..."

"Honey," she sighed. "You're my daughter. Yes, I've practically raised you in this cathouse and allowed you to see things that most young girls don't see until they're well on their way to thirty, but—"

"Mother, for crying out loud!" Gypsy's auburn brows drew together. "I'm twenty-two years old."

Yes, Ivana knew precisely how old her daughter was. And true, at twenty-two, "Gypsy" was seven years older than Ivana herself had been when she'd given birth to her restless daughter. But that didn't change the fact that a mother still had the right to protect her daughter…as much as one could in a bordello.

"I know good and well how old you are," she snarled as another wave of nausea overtook her. Pushing the fiery red locks away from her face, she hung her head over the edge of the bed and heaved into the wastebasket.

Gypsy moved to her mother's side. When the wave had passed, she continued. "He's demanding to see Zoey."

"Zoey?" she croaked. "How does he know Zoey?"

"He doesn't," she replied with a roll of her eyes as she handed Ivana a clean wet rag. "He saw her in the window when he arrived. And now he insists on having her."

"How do you know it was Zoey he saw?" She wiped her brow and settled back upon her silky pillows.

"Because, he said it was the second or third window down—both being the accounting office. Besides, who else *is* there in this abandoned mausoleum today but me, you and the strange"—she forced a mocking tone to her voice— "arrive-suddenly-and-heroically-out-of-the-blue-when-the-Ranch-is-in-secret-unknown-to-the-public-financial-trouble Zoey? Now, no one dares to go in the queen's suite when Zoey's working her royal magic on your screwed up accounting books. I told you long ago that you should have canned that asinine, dweeble accountant Boris what's-his-name, anyway. If you would have listened to me back then, Zoey wouldn't even be here causing all this look-at-my-big-fucking-boobs-instead-of-the-hired-girls' trouble, and you wouldn't have lost millions to that scum."

"Gypsy…" The tone was one meant to warn a girl of ten. Gypsy promptly ignored it.

"Zoey is stuffy and territorial, and you know it. She thinks her ass doesn't jiggle when she walks. So why waste her on *him*? He's too hot for a prim bitch like her."

"*Gypsy!*" Ivana sighed and closed her eyes against the growing jealousy and contempt her daughter felt. Zoey had been a godsend of an accountant that'd walked in off the street weeks ago, just when Ivana was about to succumb to insanity. "Zoey is—except for you, of course—all the hope I have left of keeping this establishment from the government's greedy hands."

Gypsy crossed her arms over her midriff and let out a forced breath. "Of *course*."

Ivana couldn't take this anymore. Between the recurring nausea and her rebellious, hardheaded daughter, she was about to lose her ever-loving mind! "Goddamn it, go fetch Zoey for me."

"Why?" Gypsy deftly removed the trash bag and placed a fresh one inside the can, then she sponged her mother's brow none too gently. "You're really going to give him boring, tightass Zoey?"

"She is not a tightass." Madam closed her eyes as a blessed wave of calm entered her belly. "I think she's just been deprived of the fun of immorality all her life. Now go and get her before I pass out."

"My ass, if she's not a tightass," Gypsy muttered as she slipped from the room.

* * * * *

"No!" Zoey's eyes flared with panic. "I'm not going to entertain one of your clients. I'm your accountant—and a temporary one, at that."

"Zoey. Calm down." Madam placed the cool rag over her eyes. "You've only been filling in for two weeks and—"

"Three weeks, and that's beside the point. When you discovered Boris Fletcher embezzling from you, I agreed to come in temporarily, straighten your books out, and ready the office for a *new* accountant—but I did not agree to become one of your lady's of the evening!"

"Really, Zoey," she said as she flicked a hand in the air, her parched lips pursed. "Don't be so dramatic. I'm just asking you to spend some time with him, keep him company until tomorrow morning when Katya and Zena and Sascha and PJ and all the rest are freed up."

"But-but...*I'm* not free." Zoey shoved her thick hair away from her face. *Flek*, all she needed was for this woman to insist she become one of the girls, which, without the safety of dream-travel, would endanger every last incubating spermatozoa she'd collected. "I hardly think that huge mess Boris left behind can be fixed in"—she snapped her fingers—"an instant. Ivana, I'm not sure I have the time to do as you ask."

Truthfully, she had the powers to do just that, but she wasn't about to dissolve her own excuse for being here.

Ivana groaned and clutched her stomach. "Please, Zoey, I..." she begged as she snatched the trashcan and shoved her head into it.

"Ivana..." Zoey clucked as she came to the bed and held Ivana's hair back from her face. "Why are you having such a hard time getting over this flu bug?"

"Please, please," she pleaded, waving her away. "Will you just go spend some time with him so I can concentrate on getting better? At least greet him, have a drink or two with him?"

Zoey studied Ivana's deep brown eyes. They were lovely, even in sickness. Her eyes traveled over the woman's body, and mentally, she compared it to her own. Where Ivana was all voluptuous and painted up with flamboyant Spanish style, Zoey was tall and lean and built for Dorjanian combat and space travel. Ivana was ten *manoyears* her senior, but it did not show in the softness of her skin or the excellent upkeep of her body.

In Zoey's rapid research, she had learned that the BunnyRanch had been Ivana's self-made legacy after she'd scrimped and saved and purchased it from a wealthy Carson City businessman, and it would be Gypsy's birthright in the end. But for now, Zoey was expected to help Ivana bring it back afloat financially. She would never compromise her uppermost Dorjan goal, but she knew she could do as Ivana asked her, thereby relieving some of the major stress the woman was obviously under, and still fulfill her main mission. It was just a matter of self-control when in contact with the man. She could do that, couldn't she?

She laughed to herself. *Of course you can!*

But still, there were little seedlings of doubt. Fear at facing him in the non-dream-travel state of consciousness nagged at her.

"I know nothing about the man," she said as she rose and paced the ornate suite. "Nothing."

Nothing except the feel of him inside me, the taste of his kiss, the scent of his hard body as he empowers me with his lust.

"You know very well that in this business, they don't *want* you to know anything about them," Ivana insisted.

There was a long silence. Then Ivana added with a whiny tone, "Please…?"

"Oh, all right," Zoey finally said on a heavy breath. She collapsed in a wing-backed chair near the patio door. "I'll go and meet with him, have a drink or two. But just this once."

Ivana sighed. "Good. Well, just so you know, I've specifically chosen certain girls for him based on the criteria he supplied. But, as I said, he's early and they're not yet available. So give him all you can to tide him over."

"If you think I'm going to sleep with him, you've got another thing coming."

Ivana efficiently scanned Zoey's body. "No, you don't have to sleep with him—unless you choose to."

"I'm not sleeping with him! Absolutely not!" *At least not during waking hours.*

"Okay, okay," Ivana chuckled weakly as she held up a jeweled hand. "But you must dress accordingly."

"Accordingly? And what would your meaning of that be?" As if she didn't know.

"Sexily, seductively..."

"Oh, no."

"You can't go dressed in that stuffy business suit, for heaven's sake! I have a reputation to uphold here." Ivana propped herself up on a shaky hand. She swung her shapely legs over the edge of the bed and unsteadily crossed to a huge walk-in closet next to her own equally large one. It was furnished with varied flimsy and seductive clothes in diverse sizes and colors, which she stocked for the girls. She pushed through them until she found the one she'd obviously had in her mind's eye.

"Here. This one will do." She held up a black barely-there getup with a matching red and black push-up bra and thong.

Zoey scrunched her face and carefully lifted one lacy strap with a finger. "Noo...way."

"If you wear this, Zoey," she said, exhausted, "I'll pay you one thousand dollars."

She gasped and stood for a moment, agog with shock. "*One thousand dollars*!" Zoey backed into an enormous rack of stiletto shoes. "Are you crazy?" Oh, how this intrigued her! If only she could. Money wasn't truly an issue, for she could never get the currency exchanged on Dorjan. But the thought of this whole turn of events was making her soaking wet! To become one of Ivana's girls in broad daylight, to totally ravish the man and get paid for it...it was a Dorjan woman's dream come true to have a male counterpart at her beck and call, to drool over every step she took.

And yet, there was the issue of the delicate *gametes*...

"No, I'm not crazy. But I'm sick and I need to get some sleep." She pushed the satin-covered hanger into Zoey's hand and made her way back to the bed. "Apparently, you don't realize how wealthy this man is. He's paying me a dozen times that, just to get a look at my lineup."

Zoey followed close on Ivana's heels.

"The things you could do with a grand!" Ivana coaxed as she drew the sheet over her perspiring body. "You could use some new clothes and shoes, honey—some sexy ones—and maybe even a nice dildo or two. You could get a new TV or dine out in style. Or you might even—"

"Let me get this straight," Zoey cut in as she sat on the bed next to Ivana's supine form. "All's I have to do is wear this sleazy costume, socialize with this Rolf Mahoney tonight, and you give me one thousand dollars? Did I get that right?" She was starting to see the common sense in it. If her return portal never arrived, or if she somehow got marooned here on Earth indefinitely, it would be wise to stash away some money for her own future.

Ivana slid her a sly look before she covered her face with a pillow. "Yes, that's the *minimum* you have to do," she said in muffled tones.

Zoey smiled and fell back on the bed in a fit of laughter. Her stomach swirled with the excitement of what she was about to do. "Well..."

"So you'll do it?" Ivana asked as she peeked out from under her pillow with a hopeful expression.

She chuckled huskily. "I guess I'd have to be really uptight not to."

* * * * *

Rolf shook his head and came awake with a start. There was just the sound of the fire crackling, along with the tinkle of glasses in the next room as the bartender stacked mugs with precision. What in the hell had just happened to him?

Had it been another dream with the seductive witch? Only this time, it hadn't been in the cottage where he temporarily resided. It had been, he was almost certain, in some room here at the BunnyRanch.

He shook the sleep from his head and stretched. Pressing his fingertips to his temples, he closed his eyes and struggled to recall her face. It was foggy, but he could remember with crystal-clear clarity the feel of her hot body beneath him, the sound of her slightly accented sultry voice as she purred in his ear, the aroma of flowers and sex.

He'd gone and lost his freaking mind. That was all there was to it. With trembling hands, he reached into an inside pocket of his suit jacket. But, of course, his cigarettes were gone. Like an idiot, he'd quit six months ago. But he was damn sure going to start back up again when he found a quick shop that sold the strongest ones available on the market!

He glanced at his watch again, as he'd repeatedly been doing before his catnap. He estimated that he must have dozed for at least thirty minutes, long enough for someone to attend to him. Where the hell were they? Alone in the parlor, he finished off the remnants of the melted ice from his martini, then rose to go study the interesting wall decor. In the far-off distance, he could hear an occasional door close, a throaty song of laughter, the chef tinkering in the gourmet kitchen down the hall. There was the lingering scent of Gypsy's perfume mixed with the unmistakable aroma of glazed ham. Nearby, a fire crackled in the hearth keeping him warm and toasty. But, despite the inviting comfort of his surroundings, if someone didn't come soon, he was damn right going to demand his hefty deposit back!

He heard the echoed clip of heels on tile in the distance. With a set to his jaw, he didn't turn from his scrutiny of the stunning photo of a blonde centerfold displayed on the wall. Gathering his calm, Rolf didn't say a word when the *clump-clump* sound of muted heels moving onto carpeting approached him from behind.

"Hello, and welcome to the BunnyRanch."

The voice was like a swish of silk over his penis. It sent a swift surge of blood to his loins. And it was strangely familiar. Whirling, he faced the source of the husky, accented voice.

Score one for Madam Ivana—it was the woman in the window!

"Well, well, well..." She was so near to him, he could detect the tempting fragrance of her. He sniffed it a second time, this time deeper. His brows furrowed. Where had he smelled that scent before? In Los Angeles? On some overly eager actress attempting to claw her way up him to the top?

He shrugged, swept her with a suddenly hot stare, and concluded that it didn't really matter. She was fabulous with or without the perfume! Well worth the wait. He looked into the expertly painted, grape-colored eyes—or were they aqua?

"Hello to you, too."

Her gaze widened and snapped like a lively bolt of lightning. "Mr. Mahoney?"

"Yes, first name's Rolf." He lifted a hand to twine a pale curl around his finger. Soft like silk, strong and thick like a sea captain's rope, he concluded, and perfect for gripping while in the throes of ecstasy. "Please, call me Rolf."

"Rolf, then." She pressed her fingertips to her full lips, and stared at him as if awe-struck. "Excuse me one moment. I'll replenish your drink." She stepped away and the tendril fell back among all the other glorious ones lying upon her ample breasts. He watched the jiggle of the luscious little rear as she sashayed across the room and requested a martini from the bartender. How she knew it was his drink of the day, he didn't know, but he supposed it was the way of a brothel to cater to, and know instinctively, a man's every desire.

And, wow! How he desired this one. Her slim, bronzed hands moved in animated tune with her words as she spoke softly to the tall man behind the bar. Rolf took in the stunning face when she turned briefly to indicate who the drink was for, and he imagined it up on the big screen. It was the kind of face that women envied, and that men longed to call their own.

It was the kind of face that drew crowds and made box office ticket sales soar to record highs.

As he moved stealthily closer, he studied her like a scientist would his lab subject. Silver-blonde hair glimmered with golden highlights as it cascaded in an unruly, thick mass over her shoulders. It came to rest at the small of her back, and Rolf fought an urge to go to her and stab his hands into the spun silk of it. The facial bone structure was refined with high cheekbones, a small nose, a regally delicate jaw and lips that bloomed like scarlet roses. His gaze followed the smooth column of her neck down to the off-the-shoulder, slip-of-a-dress she wore, and he itched to slide it the rest of the way down her toned arms. Firm, full, caramel-toned breasts were shoved upward to form a cleavage the likes of which he'd never seen before. When she stepped away from the bar and glided toward him, he felt his hands clench at a sudden need to trace the inward curve of her waist down over the outward swell of her hips. The dress was short enough to be classified as a mini-dress, and he greedily took in the lean length of the tawny legs it allowed him.

"I'm Zoey. I've been designated as your temporary hostess. I apologize for the delay in your perusal of a lineup, Mr., er…Rolf," she corrected. "But Madam Ivana is a bit under the weather, and you've arrived one day earlier than your planned stay." She pressed the drink into his hand, casually moved away from him, and left a scorching fire where her fingers had brushed his. He watched as she chose the puffy, cushioned bench before the fire, and sat primly to present him with an arrogant yet feminine profile that any photographer would scramble to catch on film.

Zoey. The name had a strange affect on him, like some sort of godly experience. And it nagged at his memory… Where had he heard that name before? Had he met her before today, before glimpsing her in the BunnyRanch window upon arrival? Rolf shook his head. No. He would have remembered the sultry beauty, the fragrance of her, the grab-your-balls-and-stroke-your-cock husky voice.

"Apology accepted and another offered…Zoey." He sat across from her on the sofa near the fire, and studied the way she eloquently crossed her legs—but not before he'd gotten a glimpse of the crimson and black strip of lace between her thighs. His balls simply melted. "But I am a rather impatient man. I do have deadlines to meet."

She folded her hands in her lap and tapped a red-tipped nail against her knuckle. "Don't we all."

"Mine are money-related."

He watched the unique lavender shade of her eyes ignite to flames of…what? Irritation? Resentment? But when they just as quickly softened to soak him with a kindness that he somehow sensed wasn't genuine, he knew he'd found his girl. Haunted eyes were what he'd wanted, eyes that hid pain and secrets, eyes that changed color and every now and then, revealed glimpses of an esoteric past.

"Money," she scoffed. "Isn't that why we're all here?" Apparently, it didn't require a response, for she went on. "What do you do for a living, Rolf?"

Son of a bitch, he loved the sound of his slightly accented name on her lips! "I'm a producer."

She arched one finely waxed golden brow. "Really? Well…" She rose and went to fetch herself a bottled water. Returning, she regarded him as she twisted off the cap. "We get all kinds, don't we?"

He didn't know what in the hell she'd meant by that, but at the moment, he didn't care if she tossed every filthy curse word in the book at him.

His search was over.

The glee of it slammed into him. He had a camera in his bag. He could snap a few still pictures and upload them in an E-mail to his casting director. Yes, that's what he'd do.

With a satisfied smile for having come a day early, he replied, "I like to sample what I'm paying for."

Zoey considered him over the raised bottle as she sipped. "Tomorrow will come soon enough." She went to a side table and removed a pamphlet from the rack. Clutching it to her, she crossed the room and offered the literature to him.

He felt a swashbuckling surge of hormones when she lowered herself graciously onto the divan next to him. Rolf glanced down at the brochure in his hand, then back at her. Her enticing scent wafted airily about him, and her warmth encouraged the thaw of his heart. Though he didn't blame his sex in the least for rising to attention, he wondered why flashes of his dreams suddenly came to him. Was he that possessed by them, that they could override the allure of this vixen?

"Compliments of Madam Ivana, you may choose your fantasies for your week-long stay from the menu provided. You know the old adage, all work and no play…" She reached over and leafed through the black and neon-pink booklet, as if he were incapable of turning the pages himself. "There's the *Lingerie Show, Dirty Dancing, Mutual Masturbation, Bunny Style* or the *Salt and Pepper Party*. The kinkier ones are listed further on down. If you prefer one of the others," she flipped to another section indicating the list continued, "you'll have to wait until our group of Bunnies return from their excursion, since many of the offered parties require…more than one person."

He chuckled low in his throat. Did she think he was here to actually bang someone? He'd have to be an ice-blooded fairy to have not allowed the thought to enter his mind, but business did come first—at least during waking hours. He peered down into the cleavage she made no move to hide. His eyes wandered over the long legs that were stretched out next to his. She turned then and looked deep into his eyes, and he saw that flash of something again…pain, vulnerability, loneliness or anger?

Or could it be desire?

Hell, he was never one to mix business with pleasure. Not once in his five years as a producer had he slept with any of his on-screen actresses. The gorgeous stagehands, the hot young interns, and yes, maybe even his female directors *after* the movie had wrapped up, but never the actresses—well, at least not the ones that were cast in *his* movies. If one frolic caused a change in the quality of the acting, he'd be the first to remove himself from the project. The actress had a duty to dig deep down inside herself, to reflect the correct image to the audience. And he'd never compromise that commitment expected of his cast. It was a personal policy that he'd never violated.

He watched as she flicked her tongue out and moistened her lips, heard the soft exhale of breath.

Never violated, that is…until now.

"I'll take the *Dirty Dancing* party."

* * * * *

Zoey inhaled sharply and shot to her feet.

"And I'll take it in my bungalow, please. It's been a long morning." He gazed up at her and flashed her a weary yet steamy smile.

Desire and temptation swirled in her belly. She swallowed a lump of excitement in her throat. "Oh, but I meant starting tomorrow. I've been instructed to entertain you with a bit of conversation and drinks until—"

"I'd like to have those drinks in the comfort of my suite. With you."

For the love of Dorjan! Why had she agreed to this dangerous meeting?

"But…but what about the lineup? Don't you want to wait and get a good look at all the gorgeous women Madam Ivana has planned for you to see?"

"Right now," he said, almost with a growl as he rose to tower over her, "you're the gorgeous one that strikes my fancy."

"But—"

"Zoey, was it?"

Her eyes widened at the abrupt manner he'd suddenly taken. She nodded.

"It was a long flight with a longer layover last night, then I didn't sleep worth a damn, and to top it off, Madam Ivana has reneged on her agreement to provide me with a lineup to choose from—at least for now. So I'm not exactly in a negotiating mood right at the moment."

"She hasn't reneged. The lineup will be here tomorrow, as promised, Mr. Mahoney."

"It's Rolf, remember? And I don't give a flying fuck if they'll be here in an hour, or a week. I paid a very large sum of money to be catered to as I see fit, and I intend to get what I *already* paid for."

Her gaze swept him from the thick dark hair to the pale blue eyes, narrowed just now in snide arrogance. Despite his less than appealing attitude, desire coiled through her gut. The strong and well-proportioned bone structure, along with the small little scar that ran along the side of his nose, lent him a rakish look. With his massive height and wide shoulders, standing before him simply awed her. Her hand itched to brush the boyish lock of hair from his brow. And she realized with a twisted sense of control, that she knew things about him—like the fact that he would sire many Dorjanians—he would never know about himself.

King Luran, what have you gotten me into? She shuffled her feet and stared into the smoky depths of his eyes.

He cocked one dark brow and said, "So, shall we?" Then he sidestepped her and strode up the hall toward the rear door that led to the cluster of bungalows.

As she trailed along behind him, down the long corridor lined with Bunnies' quarters, she tried to fling the azure glow of his eyes from her mind. His suit-clad, masculine body filled the space of the passageway before her. A distinct, manly scent engulfed her in a cloud of desire. As he clutched his briefcase, he walked ahead of her without even checking to see if she followed.

What a conceited, cocky Earthling, she thought, and a thrill traveled through her system like a rush of Dorjan sun-heat during summer radiation showers.

If there had been any trace of doubt up to this point, it was now completely gone. Her *compubot* had positively identified him as a match for some of the *milt* stored currently within her *nidus.* Oh, yes, it *was* him—the man she'd made love to in her out-of-body dreams. She hadn't needed him to reveal his name for her to confirm that fact.

Before her stalked the great specimen who would father Dorjanian offspring far into the future.

She followed him up a sloped floor to an end exit door. He pushed on the bar and brilliant light flooded over him, outlining his massive form with a great glow. With each step she took, with each *manosecond* that passed as she forced her feet to carry her on his path, her heart fluttered dangerously fast within her chest wall. Anticipation held her spellbound, while fear of ruining her mission played havoc on the nerves in her abdomen.

It had been so very shocking to finally come face-to-face with him during alert, daytime hours, when no lovemaking at all took place. She'd nearly staggered backward when she'd walked into the parlor and laid eyes on him as he stood there in his deep navy blue suit, his dark, blue-black hair just brushing the back of his collar. When he'd turned to look at her, it had taken all the self-control she could muster to suppress the gasp that had lodged in her throat.

He was simply beautiful in day-waking, real life! How in the universe was she going to resist him? How could she possibly wait until bedtime to jump him? And how would she stave him off until tomorrow morning when the lineup would be available?

She'd used every ounce of composure to ignore the familiar male scent of him. Zoey hadn't been able to escape the blazing cerulean eyes set in his handsome honey-toned face. And then there had been the jarring jolt of electricity that seemed to pass through her when they'd touched hands. How would she fight the devastating assaults of this charismatic, egotistical man?

But there was not time to research her own line of questioning. He stepped out onto the patio where the hot tub frothed and swirled vacantly in the high-noon sun. She followed and caught the mixed aroma of his cologne entwined on the breeze with the sharp odor of chlorine.

Diona! What was she to do? Her stomach fluttered with nerves as she pondered her question. When they arrive at his suite, should she just say, "Let me explain something very important here. I'm the woman who's been making love to you in your dreams. And, by the way, our encounters will result in making you a father on my planet less than a light-year away. Congratulations! You're going to be a daddy to hundreds, maybe thousands of Dorjanians! But, remember…we can only mate during dreams, or your chances of being that daddy will virtually disappear."

No. She drew in a cleansing breath as they passed through an area lined with lounge chairs. That was ridiculous. He'd think her entirely mad!

She glanced up and saw the posted sign that read *No tops allowed. Bottoms optional but frowned upon.* With a rush of excitement, she forced back the memories of her naked body against his. As the cool spring winds whipped up, he escorted her to a gate behind the building where three quaint bungalows lined the property, the mountainous horizon tucked behind them. She was right on his heels now as he followed the walkway to the center cabin, so near, she could feel the energy of his massive body as it moved agilely before her.

Holy mother of Venus, he was so very hot! she thought, and trailed him up the deck that led to the front door of the bungalow. She recalled the feel of his touch in the dreams, his firm yet gentle ministrations upon her body, that thick length inside her… *No, shake it off,* mina. *You need more…but can never have it from him. Don't let him touch you, Zoey! Think of the poor little* gametes. *Wait until it's safe, until sleep.*

Remember…two different people, two different worlds, she thought.

Quickly drawing the key from his pants pocket, he unlocked the door and showed her into the small kitchen. Hurriedly, Rolf tossed the key onto the island. "This is a very nice, cozy place you've put me up in. I really appreciate it," he said, and set his briefcase on the glass table near the breakfast bar.

"I can give you a tour of the ranch and Carson City if you'd like." There was a hopeful tone to her voice—a hopeful, *pathetic* tone.

He glanced into the comfortably furnished living room. "What about that *Dirty Dancing* party I asked for?"

"I…well…" She shifted her stance and nearly fell off her spiked heels. Did he really expect her to dance for him? You *imputee*! she screamed at herself. Of course he did. He's in a bordello, for stars' sake!

With all the grace of a panther, he stalked toward her. She stumbled backward until the island was between them.

"What's wrong, Zoey?" His eyes twinkled with mischief as if he thought her evasiveness was all a part of the seduction he thought he'd purchased. "You going to play the dancing *virgin* instead?"

She couldn't breath. Her heart pounded against her windpipe and choked her. He stealthily rounded the counter and came to stand inches from her, so close she had to tip her head back to look up into his handsome face.

"Well?" His stare caressed her forehead, her nose, her eyes, and then his gaze devoured her lips. The hot penetration of his eyes dipped lower, down over her tight throat to her cleavage. She groaned inwardly and remained mute and catatonic. Why had she listened to Ivana? Why had she worn this revealing dress?

He trailed a finger up her bare arm. The fire ignited immediately, just like in the dreams, and at that moment, he chose to fix his gaze on her heavy-lidded eyes. She suppressed an involuntary pant as the finger went up and over her shoulder, across her collarbone, down deep into the valley between her breasts. His eyes never left hers, though she fought to break the spell, tried desperately to ignore the wetness that already soaked her G-string. Nerve endings she didn't know existed, cried out for satisfaction.

"You're absolutely stunning," he murmured as his free hand slipped around her waist and drew her against the hard length of his body. Before she could ascertain just what he had planned, his mouth slammed into hers with a fevered hunger. Her knees buckled and he hauled her up tighter against him. And she finally discovered what could happen if they came together during daylight hours, outside the safe dimension of dreams.

Chapter Four

Rolf felt the strange yet familiar tingling as soon as he'd touched her. The jolt had gone through him as they'd made contact, and that zinging sensation returned much like the zaps he'd experienced in his dreams. Dizziness now washed over him, a lightheadedness that hit him like a potent drug. What the hell was wrong with him, anyway, that he suddenly couldn't seem to tame his appetite? It seemed blatantly obvious that he'd be unable to resist this woman, just as he'd been unable to endure the enticing seduction of the siren that haunted his dreams.

Well, he was in a bordello, after all. He could only attribute his sudden inability to control his libido with that particular fact. What else could it be?

When his lips met Zoey's, he was lost, and he could swear he heard a distant concerto of harps, as if angels strummed their approval. A proverbial fire that he'd found only in his wet dreams, combusted in his system and backfired into his cock. She tasted like honey, and the wild scent of her mesmerized him as it filled his nostrils. He couldn't hold her tight enough against him. It was as if his body had been starved for the touch of this one woman all his life. Her full, firm breasts were pressed into his chest, and his hands were now filled with the curves of her ass.

He had to have her. Not just a mind-blowing screw, but a possession seemed to be what his soul craved and demanded. A connection of…something, he wasn't quite sure. But instinctually, he knew it was imperative that he claim her and that she claim him.

Just for one night.

He muffled her soft moan with his mouth. But it wasn't enough for him. Breaking free of the electrified kiss, he set her down and snatched up her hand. He led her through the small elegant dining room into the living room furnished with cream, overstuffed sofas. There was a large white bearskin rug on the floor before the blazing gas fireplace, and he made a beeline for the welcoming bed. Someone had prepared for his arrival. Someone had set the mood so that he didn't stand a chance with this beguiling witch.

"No…I…" she stammered as he pulled her into his arms.

"I like the coy routine, but I want to see the dance you promised me," he demanded, and claimed the velvety, delicious spot in the crook of her neck. God, he could just simply eat her alive!

"I…" She whooshed out a strained breath as her head went back swan-like. "I have work to do."

"Damn right, you've got work to do." He trailed a finger over the curve of her cleavage and freed one breast from the tight confines of the satiny fabric. "Expensive work"—he groaned at the sight of the dark-tipped areola already erect on the swell of her breast—"that's going to be worth every fucking cent I paid."

"No, you don't…" She lifted her hands, placed them against his chest, and branded him even as she pushed lightly against him. But he didn't give her the opportunity to continue with her weak protest. Like a ravaging wolf, he ducked his head and sucked the taut nipple voraciously between his teeth.

*****

Zoey fought the hot rush of excitement that flooded her panties. The exhilarating, heady sensations were there, just as they were in her dreams. It was not a simple sexual arousal, as she had occasionally felt with other Dorjanian men, or the many Earthling men she'd collected from in the past weeks. It was like a conjoining of souls, an enticing, irresistible, almost orgasmic connection that could not easily be broken.

And, oh, how she wanted this, longed to make love to him outside the fantasy world she'd become accustomed to. But it was forbidden, outright dangerous for the *gametes* to transfer to her chemical makeup in anything but the safety of dream-travel. Her *nidus* just could not receive cells for incubation without it.

But she was doomed if he kept up this sweet assault.

His tongue flicked back and forth over her *tetron*, immobilizing her with cosmic pleasure. Groaning helplessly, she allowed her hands to slide up to stab her trembling fingers into the thick hair at the back of his head. She studied his every move, entranced as he dragged the other side of her dress and bra down, and bared the other vulnerable nipple for his heated gaze.

"Holy, sweet God…" he mumbled, just before he captured the newly exposed jewel. With one hand, he lifted the mound and brought it closer to his greedy mouth. The other went around to haul her up and grind her crotch into his until her feet dangled above the bearskin rug. His hard rod abraded erotically against her throbbing sex, and she moaned her pleasure at the sudden ploy.

How could she fight this tempting assault with the man of her dreams? She desperately wanted it, but it was far too dangerous for the wellbeing of his seed. In addition, she couldn't risk contaminating the whole store she already carried within her *nidus*. That would negate the purpose of the whole trip—and she would be banished from Dorjan for flagrant defiance of the law.

Suddenly, she wondered what he would do if she were to explain her rationale for not mating with him during waking hours. How would she explain the logistics of the implantation of his cells into her incubation chamber? How would she ever make him understand?

It isn't possible, Zoey. Continue to make love to him, but only within the safety of your dreams. He mustn't find out where you're really from. He can't learn that you're an alien, and above all else, that you carry his biological material for the reinstatement of a population in another solar system…

You must stop this nonsense now!

But before she could muster up the strength to escape from the onslaught of his desire, he bent and dragged her legs up on either side of his hips so that she straddled him. He then knelt on the rug and his hands raced up and under her dress, up over the backs of her thighs. Those hot hand traveled across the roundness of her rear, up until her dress bunched into her armpits and her lacy undergarments were all that protected her from him. The entire disarray of it only added to the wetness that drenched her panties. She inhaled his wild, clean scent combating the enticing sensations he bombarded her with.

His eyes flared as he beheld the sight of her nearly naked body. Then they went limpid with a sexual fever.

"No…Rolf," she objected, just before his mouth covered hers.

The warmth of the fireplace didn't help matters. It only made her long to fall upon the rug and submit to him, to feel the sensations he was expert at eliciting in her. Except for the lack of dream protection, everything seemed right…the brand of his tongue speared into her mouth, swiped her lips and mated with her own. His hard body demanded to possess her. Oh, yes. Perfection was within her reach. And despite her mind's silent screams of protest, she slid her hands into his suit jacket. Seeming to possess a mind of their own, they trailed over the sinewy chest, around to explore the tensed muscles of his back. He breathed raggedly now and he clutched her to him so that her *tetrons* tingled with the pressure.

She made one last frail effort to escape and shoved her hands weakly against him.

"You want this, I know you do." But he didn't wait for her rebuttal. Instead, he gathered her in his arms. The blaze of the fire, of his gaze and his touch, melted the last of her resolve. As if the heat were too unbearable for him, he divested of his suit coat. The sculpted expanse of his chest through the white dress shirt rendered her speechless. Before she could react, he had her back pressed into the rug. He drew her wrists above her head and clasped them in one strong hand. One-handed, he yanked his tie over his head and wound it swiftly around her wrists.

"Don't…what are you…?" She moaned as he bent his head and sucked a nipple into his mouth. Helplessly, she whimpered, for the sensation of being held prisoner by the weight of his body, the strength of his grip and the tie at her wrists, was simultaneously erogenous and unsettling. An aching ball of need tumbled from his wet tongue at her breast and settled into her engorged clit. "Rolf." She drew in a ragged breath. "Rolf!" she finally shouted it.

His head came up and she looked into the crazed eyes of a man she knew was too far gone. Jet-black hair all askew, he looked as if he'd just rolled out of bed. Beads of perspiration dribbled down his temples. The muscles of his upper body tensed through the fabric of his shirt as he held her in place. Ashamed, she silently admitted that she wanted nothing more than for him to take her savagely—to in effect, make the decision for her.

Holy mother of Mars, she hardly knew this man! And the thought of it brought a sense of power and freedom to her. She could partake of what he offered her, allow him to pleasure her then put an abrupt stop to it before things progressed to the ejaculation stage. Or, she could show him oral bliss and he could give her a lusty release…all without actual penetration.

"You're the most delectable, beautiful thing I've seen in forever," he declared, looking down at her with glazed eyes. "Give it up, honey. Don't fight it. We both want it, and you know it."

"No, I—you don't understand."

"I understand that you're a tease," he growled as his free hand skimmed over her ribs. Expertly, he found his destiny at her juncture where he pushed aside the narrow panty strip. Gently but firmly, he sank one finger into her.

She arched her back and cried out. A searing flood of icy-hot lust slammed into her.

"And you've got that special something I've been searching for," he added. He withdrew his finger and joined it with another before he buried them together inside her cunt. It sent her spiraling into an aching flurry of pleasure.

The tears soaked her eyes. The sensuality of the whole thing was more than she could fight. She did want it, there was no doubt about it. She wanted it as much, if not more, than any of the call girls at the Ranch wanted their clients' money. *Crulo,* she admitted silently, she'd wanted him the instant he'd turned around in the parlor and snared her with that smoldering gaze! No, the very moment she'd located him in dream-travel and saw him lying on the bed, exhausted and oh-so handsome in slumber.

But she just couldn't risk it without dream-travel protection for the *gametes*. This man would never be satisfied with oral sex alone.

And neither would she.

"Let me loose," she ordered as she wiggled and yanked against the tie.

He chuckled. "Promise to put out?"

She held his stare and nodded.

Rolf unwound the silk tie and tossed it aside.

Zoey flexed her wrists and sliced her hands up his shirt, over and across the firm muscles. Just one touch, one last caress before ending this sweet torture…

His skin was smooth and warm against her palms. The corded muscles of his chest fit nicely in her hands. She pinched the tight nipples and delighted in the intake of breath it elicited from between his clenched teeth.

"Oh, yes, you do know what you're doing, don't you Zoey?" he drawled, and captured her mouth in a ferocious kiss. But the kiss grew frantic and hurried even as she tasted the delicious flavor of him in her own mouth. She stiffened, unsure of her control as lust coiled wickedly in her womb. His stiff *ketka* hovered dangerously close to her damp *pless.*

Zoey, don't do it, don't do it!

Her quiet cries doused the flames. If she went on for one second longer, she'd be a goner in more ways than one.

"No!" she panted and tore her mouth from his.

As if he sensed she was about to bolt from him, he tightened his arms around her. "No need to play that coy wanton anymore, Zoey. My money's riding on this, so let go, babe. Just let go," he added huskily.

She shook her head frantically. Her Dorjanian self-defense training kicked into gear. With a strength she didn't know she possessed, she shoved him away. She lurched up, darted through the kitchen and yanked her clothing back into place. With a gulp, she burst out into the cool April afternoon air and raced down the sidewalk. Her hand trembled as she pushed open the gate and fled into the courtyard. She panted for each breath as she passed the hot tub, and fleetingly wished it were filled with ice water so that she could dive in and cool her sweltering ardor.

* * * * *

Rolf looked down into the empty circle of his arms. His chest rose and fell with each breath he heaved in and out of his lungs. Trembling, he fisted his hands and groaned in frustration. Christ, he was on fire! And oh, how his cock ached, he thought as he clutched his crotch. He could just picture his balls swollen and blue from the torment that sexy nymph had just put him through.

He staggered to his feet. Sweat soaked his rumpled clothing. Locating the flipped, he switched off the gas fireplace and curled his hand into the opening of his shirt. Frantic, he yanked it open, sending a shower of buttons across the carpet. Rolf ripped the shirt off, rolled it into a ball, wound up like a pitcher on the mound, and hurled it into the big-screen television.

What in the fucking hell had that been all about? He jabbed a hand through his damp hair.

You *are* at a bordello, aren't you? And, correct yourself if you're wrong, Rolf, he silently taunted himself, but isn't a cathouse supposed to give you whatever fantasy you desire in exchange for money?

And, by golly, he'd sent Madam Ivana enough money to sample every woman in this damn place a hundred times over!

Well, he thought as he went to locate the phone. It was time to pay the elusive madam a visit.

Dialing the main BunnyRanch number, he barked, "This is Rolf Mahoney. I'm on my way over this very minute. I expect to see Madam Ivana in the parlor when I arrive. And you can tell her if she stands me up again, I'm going to demand every fucking cent of my money back. Got it?"

The sweet voice on the other end of the line placated him expertly, and assured him the madam would be informed.

But he was in no mood to have his ass kissed.

He just wanted what he wanted, plain and simple.

Zoey.

With long, purposeful strides, he stormed out of the bungalow and retraced his path back to the main building. Outdoors, there wasn't a hint of human life to be found. The cool quiet of the afternoon assaulted his revved senses like ice to fire. Arousal now on hold, he allowed his anger to fester in his gut. Hell, he had every right to be pissed!

And Madam Ivana wasn't going to tell him otherwise.

He entered the rear door and made his way down the long corridor, past the kitchen, offices and cocktail lounge, until he reached the parlor.

Of course, there was no one there except a brunette in a see-through white teddy and six-inch heels. She lounged lazily on one of the sofas before the fire. Somehow, he knew by the way her eyes devoured him, that she hadn't a clue he was about to have an aneurysm.

"Hi, handsome," she purred, and rose seductively, never taking her smoky gaze from him. Though she was breathtakingly gorgeous, he gave her a wary look. She wasn't the madam—and she obviously wasn't Zoey. Placing a hand above her head on the gold strippers' pole, she leaned her bare back into it. Slowly, she slid down the brass length, her knees spread wide as she went. He watched, helpless, as her pretty little sex lips were bared for him. She licked one finger then found her bud, her eyes glued to his. "Wanna party?"

He heard her moan before she made a sensuous play of slithering back to a standing position. Turning so that he could get a view of her tight little ass, she gripped the pole, threw her head back to allow her hair to cascade down her back, and ground her clitoris into the shiny brass, gyrating and rubbing.

"This pole could be you, mister," she said throatily. "Whatd'ya say? Party with me?"

There was no denying she possessed clear talent at seduction, and would, no doubt, be an expert at pleasure and sexual satisfaction.

But again, she wasn't Zoey.

"Um, can I take a rain check?" he asked gently, and made every effort to ogle her. "I'm waiting for the madam. A meeting," he explained.

"You don't know what you're missing," she said playfully, and bared one round breast for him to sample.

"Oh, believe me, I do. Business," he said with a gentle smile. "Let me take care of business first."

She shrugged, as if she suddenly didn't care one way or the other. "Suit yourself." Then she slinked over to the fireplace and plucked up a magazine on the side table.

Rolf turned and crossed to the bar. He needed a stiff drink, one that would cool both his ardor and his anger.

How long did it take to go and fetch one goddamn woman?

"Madam Ivana will see you now," Gypsy said in a clipped tone as she entered the room. He noted the cool air about her, the way her pretty blue eyes chilled him to the bone. Apparently, she wasn't going to let him forget that he'd scorned her. "Please, follow me," she added saucily.

With an exaggerated sway to her hips, she led him down the opposite corridor from which he'd taken Zoey not an hour ago. It was long and elegant with deep red carpeting and soft lighting along the walls. At the far end, Gypsy entered a set of heavy oak double doors.

"Have a seat, Mr. Mahoney. Ivana will be with you shortly." She indicated one of two finely upholstered, wing-backed chairs set before a massive cherry wood desk. He obeyed and chose the one closest to him. Peering over his shoulder, he watched as Gypsy quietly exited the room, shutting the door with a resounding click.

He studied his surroundings and wondered how he'd come to this point in his life where he'd been reduced to complaining about not getting any pussy. He'd always gotten pussy whenever he chose to have it!

Until now.

He shifted in his seat and scanned the explicit, gold-framed paintings upon the maroon and cream walls. Depicting various acts of a sexual nature, they were disturbingly enticing, especially for a man already sporting blue balls. Rolf let out a long sigh. Was it their intent to torture and tease him, or was he just getting testy and impatient in his old age?

He sniffed the cool air. The office smelled of a woman's seductive perfume and had been outfitted with the finest furnishings. He snorted to himself. No doubt, bought with his hefty monetary contribution.

He considered an interesting sculpture set upon a pedestal near the heavily draped window. It was a hand-molded depiction of a threesome—or was it a foursome? He squinted and tried to follow the flow of arms, legs, torsos. It was a mirage, that's what it was. Hell, this whole damn fiasco had turned out to be some sort of fucking, demented, torturous mirage!

In fact, he was beginning to wonder if he wasn't in the throes of some sort of mixed-up dream.

* * * * *

The phone suddenly buzzed behind her.

She startled, then whirled back around and plucked up the handset. "Accounting. Zoey speaking."

"What in the hell happened?" Ivana's demanding tone immediately put Zoey on the defensive.

She released the breath she'd been holding. So, Ivana had already heard. "Your precious tycoon forced himself on me, that's what."

"Forced?" she countered.

"Well…he was extremely amorous, let's put it that way."

She heard Ivana groan. "Zoey. Do you know what you may have cost me? He's flaming mad and demanding his money back!" She could have sworn she heard Ivana shiver. "Now he's waiting in my office to see me so he can chew me out."

"And I'm flaming furious, too!" She spoke through clamped teeth. "That man! He thinks I'm one of your girls!"

Ivana's soft, husky laugh filled her ear. "And what a terrible thing that would be."

"Yes, a tragedy." A tragedy for the future savior of Dorjan to demean the honored carrier of his precious seed, she added silently.

Ivana blew out a heavy breath. "Look, Zoey. I'm sorry I didn't inform him that you were simply the accountant, but I was desperate. Besides, it wouldn't hurt you to get a little love and affection from a man. And from what I hear, he's quite a striking man, at that."

"I told you, I won't sleep with him." *Unless we're dreaming and he treats me with the utmost respect deserving a Dorjan* gamete incubot.

"Okay, okay. I'm not suggesting you sleep with the man. Just have dinner with him, show him around. Cool him off and entertain him until tomorrow. And he'll not assume he can touch you if I tell him you're my account—"

"No!"

"But—"

"Don't you dare tell him!" Why it bothered her for him to learn she was an accountant instead of a lady of the evening, she didn't know. One was respectable, while the other seemed just plain sexy and mysterious. She supposed she liked sexy better—and that had her feeling utterly confused, for the last thing she wanted was to be viewed as a prostitute.

"What's going on, Zoey? You're not making a damn bit of sense," Ivana said suspiciously.

What *isn't* going on, she wondered. "You wouldn't understand."

"I'll understand, honey. I deal with dozens of girls. Are you ill? Are you coming down with my flu? Should I call the house doctor?"

"No...no."

"Does he have halitosis or reek of body odor?"

Zoey had to laugh. "No, Ivana. He doesn't have bad breath or smelly perspiration." But he sure perspired, she thought as a sudden flash of his hard, glistening body filled her mind.

"Then why not do your favorite boss a humongous favor and keep him mollified until tomorrow? Huh?"

She suppressed a grin. "You're my only boss, Ivana." *Except for King Luran.*

"Oh, well, then your time won't be divided." At Zoey's silence, she went on. "What is it, *chica*?"

"I'm not sleeping well, that's all."

"Is that all? Well, I have a pill or two you can borrow. You'll be good as new come morning."

She spun her chair around and propped her elbow upon a spreadsheet. "No. That's quite all right. But thank you."

"Well, if you change your mind..."

"No, I won't change my mind. Now, I have some work to do." She reached for her coffee mug, took a sip of cold sludge and grimaced.

"You...you didn't say whether you'd have dinner with him or not." It was a distressed tone that Zoey couldn't ignore.

"Look," she groaned with dread. "If you promise not to tell him who I am, I'll take him to dinner tonight. Let him go on thinking I'm one of your ladies. It'll hold his attention a lot more than a boring accountant will." *That'll get me through until tonight when I can go to him in sleep. Then, by tomorrow, he'll have a full lineup to occupy him.*

And the thought did strange, painful, twisty things to her gut.

A deep, husky chuckle filled Zoey's ear. "Sure you don't want to try a shot at a normal, honest relationship? He's rich and hot..."

"No, Ivana. I just can't get involved with him."

Ivana blew a long breath into the phone. "You're an odd duck, darling. You've gotta be completely out of this world to pass on that sugar daddy."

*****

She showered and chose a more conservative dress than the one she'd worn earlier that day. Though it still clung to her and revealed every curve and plane of her body, the shimmering midnight-blue garment made her feel softer, ultra feminine and definitely classy. No harlot here, she thought with relief.

Her cleavage was just apparent over the V of the bodice, yet it still hid much more than her earlier costume had. She clamped a fist over her stomach. It fluttered with nerves as she reached for a pair of white-stud earrings and a modest teardrop necklace. She donned them as she slipped into her high heels.

Zoey gripped her small clutch purse as she turned this way and that before the cheval mirror in her BunnyRanch suite. She tugged the snug dress down so that it covered more of her upper thighs. Her long hair had been swept up into a clip, and a cascade of overflowing curls trailed down her back. Studying her face, she was satisfied with the moderate amount of makeup she'd painted on—a touch of blood-red lipstick, some faint blush, a little mascara and eyeliner. It was nowhere near the amount a call girl would wear, she mused, silently appeasing her doubts.

"Well, Zoey," she spoke to herself. "Here goes..." She went to the door and scanned her quarters one last time then she let herself out and bolted the door behind her.

She took her time walking up the hallway, through the bar area and parlor toward the rear exit. The bartender stood behind the bar polishing a glass, a maid feather-dusted framed art upon the wall, and one lone blonde lady of the evening sat in a corner reading a paperback novel in her lingerie and stiletto heels.

What about her? Zoey wondered. Why couldn't *she* entertain Rolf Mahoney? She was certainly available. But even as she thought to go in search of Ivana, the guest announcement buzzer sounded and a handsome man in a business suit was allowed entrance. He made a beeline for the girl. She smiled coquettishly and tossed the novel aside, obviously spying an abundance of credit cards in his wallet with her X-ray vision.

Inhaling deeply, Zoey turned, continued up the corridor and let herself out onto the rear patio.

Goose bumps shimmered in mocking waves over her flesh. But it wasn't the cool, high-desert mountain air that had triggered the reaction. His bungalow loomed threateningly before her.

Chapter Five

Rolf had calmed down only after Madam Ivana had finally made a showing in her office to inform him that the elusive Zoey would escort him to dinner. He snorted as he stepped from the shower and toweled down the lean length of his body. She'd most likely informed this Zoey that there were big bucks involved. Green was always a woman's favorite color, he thought wryly—and especially if they doled out sexual favors for a living.

He shook his head in disbelief. How was it that he was in a brothel and hadn't gotten laid yet—with the exception of in his dreams? True, he hadn't come here for sex, but still, it somehow rankled him. Had he lost his touch, even with a woman who should be eager and willing to get his testosterone pumping?

He thought of the dozens of women he'd had over the last seventeen years or so since his first sample of female delights. None of them were prostitutes, per se, but each and every one of them gave it up in exchange for dinner, the theater or a weekend getaway to Hawaii. And there'd been a few grand slipped here and there for the ones in need of rent money. So, to Rolf, most women were the same, whether they worked in or out of a cathouse. And there wasn't a damn thing wrong with that, he concluded with a grin. They were to be pampered, spoiled and tasted, and Rolf was willing and able to do just that.

It wasn't like breaking his no-mixing-business-with-pleasure rule placed him in any other category, nor did it categorize Zoey in any particular class. Whether they had hot sex or not, it was still a transaction in which he'd wine and dine her in exchange for her female charms…which hopefully included curing his blue balls.

Rolf dressed in a dark suit, starched white dress shirt and an interesting multicolored tie. He took some gel to his hair and slicked it back from his face, then slapped some aftershave on his bronzed cheeks. Staring at himself in the mirror, he loathed the eyes that reminded him he was a mutt. He rather liked all the dark traits of his father, the chiseled cheekbones and tawny complexion he'd inherited. But the blue eyes were a rather spooky touch to the picture—and a constant reminder of the mother he'd never known.

Which was what brought him here in the first place.

The movie.

There was a soft rap on the kitchen door. He raked a hand through his hair and checked that his tie was straight. Then he moved through the house until he was at the door. And through the window he saw the unmistakable outline of her as he tugged open the door.

"Well..." he drawled with a low whistle. "Good evening, gorgeous."

His heart tumbled from his chest. She was stunning...dazzling. He took a quick sweep of her as she stood on the deck. The cool night air rustled her glorious hair while the yellow full moon glowed fat above her. She appeared serene, aloof, almost otherworldly. Her dress shimmered the color of deep midnight, and despite covering extra flesh, it somehow stirred his sex even more so than the other one had. A flash of something familiar—what was it?—nagged at him. The perfume? He could detect its soft floral scent from here, and it seemed to grab his cock and stroke with expert, sensual precision. His eyes fell to her breasts. They revealed just the right amount of cleavage to keep a man fantasizing about burying his face down in its valley.

"Hi," she murmured huskily. Her gaze fled then returned. She resettled the shawl about her shoulders and drew it around and over her chest. "The limousine is ready...that is, unless you prefer me to drive. Madam has a car we could use."

Mentally, he weighed his possibilities. Hmm…Zoey, on one hand, driving and in control of everything. Or, on the other hand, ride in the limo together with time, privacy and the asset of control on his side. "The limo will do fine." He stepped out onto the deck and locked the door behind him. Turning, he offered her his arm.

She looked down at it with wide, disbelieving eyes, blue-violet irises that rose and captured his with a hesitant gaze. "Are you serious?"

"Dead."

She slowly tucked her hand in the crook of his elbow.

Quietly, he led her through the back of the BunnyRanch and out the front door. Handing her into the limo, he climbed in beside her and inhaled the fragrance of her once again. "You smell delicious," he whispered. Leaning toward her, he planted a feathery kiss at the smooth flesh below her ear.

Zoey shifted and moved several inches away from him. "Thank you. Now that we're settled…" She lifted her nose a notch and presented him with her regal profile. "I'd like to apologize for today, but at the same time, warn you I insist there not be a repeat of it."

He chuckled flatly. "I came here for one reason, and one reason only, lovely Zoey." He taunted her and trailed a finger over the slim hand she'd set upon her thigh. "Obviously, you haven't any idea what my motives are. Therefore, I'll honor your wishes."

"I think I can take a wild guess," she replied glibly.

He watched with delight as she blinked and shot a penetrating look at him. And the emotion and confusion he saw buried there in her haunted eyes only reinforced his decision that she was the perfect one for the part.

Rolf tore his gaze from hers and stared out the tinted window as the limo moved through Carson City. Which meant he needed to stand firm and return to his original rule of not mixing business with pleasure. But how would he get through a night with her at his side and not, at the very least, touch her silky skin or claim those plump lips? It was one big damned dilemma by his way of thinking.

* * * * *

Zoey shivered. The mere touch of his hand to hers had sent a wave of fire coursing through her veins. *Mama Luna, how will I get through this night without giving in to his charms?* She had but to look at him and her heart thudded painfully against her breastbone. Not to mention the fact that she was in a constant state of arousal just knowing what magic those hands were capable of.

What did he mean, he'd honor my wishes? He'd keep his hands off me? The thought both relieved and disappointed her. She craved to be in his arms yet the danger of it was too threatening to Dorjan's future.

But there were always dreams following dinner and dancing.

And the excitement, the anticipation of being able to go to him at will tonight in slumber, sent a wave of exhilaration through her she had no right feeling.

* * * * *

He almost bent to lift her into his arms but thought better of it. They'd dined quietly on filet mignon and swordfish. The seven-course meal had evolved into "just one dance", but after several dances, she remained in his arms on the dance floor as the orchestra played a romantic melody. Her cheek and the palm of one hand were pressed against his heart, the other hand laced snuggly with one of his. Limp and relaxed in his embrace, he could feel every arc and swell of her body as it moved against his. Tense with sexual frustration, he tightened his arm about her for fear she'd melt at his feet. He could smell the fresh clean scent of her hair as its silky softness caressed his jaw. Where he'd mustered up the power to resist her, he didn't know.

The music stopped but Zoey continued to move with him. He heard her sigh.

"I think we've closed down the place," he murmured in her ear. Releasing her hand, he reached around and gathered her closer. "Should we be going?"

"Huh? What?" She lifted her head and blinked as the overhead lights came on, flooding the room with a florescent-blue glow.

His gut did a flip as he looked down into her limpid, dazed expression. God, he could wake up to those sleepy plum eyes every day, he thought with a groan. If only she wasn't a hooker with money and greed in her heart. If only he didn't have that blasted rule about sleeping with the cast members—because she *was* going to become one of his actresses.

"They're closing the restaurant. Would you like to find some other place to resume our little party?"

"Oh…" She stiffened and smoothed the front of her short little dress. "I…I suppose we should be going on home, don't you think?"

He grinned wolfishly at her. "Well, this wasn't exactly the kind of 'dirty dance' I'd had in mind, but if you're ready to call it a night…."

Her lips twitched. "No, it wasn't dirty. It was lovely. Thank you." Her lashes fluttered, she looked away, and he could have sworn he saw a flash of white stars in her eyes along with a coquettish flush to her honey-toned skin.

Stars in her eyes... Something nagged at him. But he couldn't quite bring it to the forefront.

He shrugged it off. "Here," he said gently. He pulled out her chair and gestured for her to sit. "Wait here and I'll go fetch your wrap."

With amusement, he watched as she hesitated before finally lowering herself into the chair. When he returned, she rose with her purse in hand and turned to allow him to drape the shawl over her shoulders.

He slung an arm around her and guided her from the room. "Had a little bit too much to drink, didn't you, gorgeous?" he murmured and drew her closer to his side as he pushed open the door.

"Yes-no," she stammered. She stepped through the vestibule, out into the crisp clear night. "Well, maybe a little. The champagne was exceptionally smooth and delicious."

Jesus, she was hot when her accent thickened with the effects of alcohol! A renewed flame of desire ignited his cock. As he followed along beside her, he watched her shut her eyes and breathe in the fresh evening air.

She took a few wobbly steps with her eyes still closed, and he smiled fondly as she stumbled. He steered her firmly but gently toward the limo. The driver was already out and posted at the open door.

"Obviously, it was to your liking. I believe you had more than two-thirds of the bottle all to yourself."

"That's not true!" she said outraged as she climbed none too graciously into the limo. He watched with delight as she plopped down on the seat and teetered precariously on the edge before she gained control and situated herself upright.

"No," he growled as he climbed in and gathered her to him. "I'm not fibbing. The bottle was empty, Angel. And I had just one glass."

She braced her hands against his chest. Her eyes flared with fear. "You promised…you'd…you'd not…" She stuttered breathily, almost as if she longed for him to defy her.

In his mind's eye, he drew a square around her face. Yes. He could picture it upon the big screen, all vulnerable and yet full of determination. Her emotions swam in those unique and strange eyes, and they often contradicted her actions. The ambivalence was what would attract the viewers—along with her stunning beauty, of course.

"I don't know what's going on here, doll. Most call girls are eager to get in a man's pants…as long as there's a wallet in the pocket. But you?" he said, and pressed a hand against her small cheek. "You're an intriguing puzzle. I like that." And he couldn't resist drawing her stunned, pouty mouth to his.

* * * * *

In her besotted, alcohol-induced state of mind, Zoey reasoned with herself. Why turn him away? It was just a harmless kiss. And whew! What a kiss it was! His hand slid from her cheek to the mass of curls at the back of her head, firmly holding her mouth against his. His lips were like a soft refreshing Dorjan rain against hers, but with one thrust of his tongue into the cavern of her mouth, she could have sworn she heard the combustion of an explosion. Under her hands, through the soft cotton of his dress shirt, she could feel the power of his flexed muscles. Maddeningly, his alluring scent was wrapped around her like a *zigong* fur, and he tasted of decadent *corfu* desserts.

He dragged one of her hands down over his rippled abdomen to the bulge in his pants. With his hand over hers, he forced her to cup him. "See what you do to me?" He said it almost accusingly against her mouth, and she opened her eyes to look into narrowed slits of the sea. His shaft swelled as hard and thick as she remembered it in her dreams. She groaned as the throbbing between her legs increased in tempo and rumbled through her system like an ongoing earthquake.

"And I'd wager to say…" He removed his hand from hers to begin a scorching trail along her thigh. It snaked up under the hem of her dress until she felt the zap of ecstasy when he expertly found her crux. "Ah…yes, you're just as hard as I am."

It brought her off the seat. She cried out at the same moment her panties dampened with a traitorous vengeance. "No…I…" she panted and yanked her hand from the menacing length of his sex in order to grip his hand and pull it from her. "Please," she begged and heard the pathetic whine to her voice. "Please, give me more time."

More time to get this limo moving so I can go home and pray for dream-travel to you!

She watched with a mixture of relief and dread as his jaw tensed. He snatched his hand from her and turned so that he sat erect and facing forward. "Time is money." He insinuated she was a call girl and she gasped with indignation. "Granted, I have enough money, but if you drag this out, that money won't be yours or the madam's."

Ivana would throttle her if she returned with an irate customer. And if Rolf Mahoney didn't mind his manners, they would return with an irate *call girl,* as well! But she had to hold him off. Timing was delicate in this precarious situation she'd found herself in. If the girls Ivana had chosen for his lineup arrived early enough tomorrow morning, they'd flock around him, and he'd forget she even existed.

She shifted uncomfortably on the leather seat. Why did the image of him surrounded by a bevy of stunning centerfolds and porn stars cause her heart to feel as if it'd slumped into her gut? With a mental reminder of her important duty, she shook the envy from her mind.

It was the only solution.

"Tomorrow." It tumbled from her mouth before she could stop it. "Give me until tomorrow," she pleaded, well aware of the risk she took. What if the girls didn't arrive on time? What if their trip was extended?

He inclined his head and stared at her for a long moment, as if he debated her honesty and dependability. "Tomorrow." He nodded slowly and trailed a finger over her bottom lip. "Meet me at my bungalow at five p.m.?"

All she could do was nod. Helpless, she soaked the deep, menacing song of his voice into her *audiotrap*. It stroked her just as his finger had, and she shivered, knowing that if she wasn't able to reach him in sleep tonight, he would succumb to another woman's charms. It was the law of averages. His *ketka* had gone up and down too many times to withstand yet another tease.

They arrived at the BunnyRanch and climbed from the limo in silence. Entering through the parlor, he didn't spare one glance for the two girls who lounged seductively, waiting for the next guest. Instead, he turned and winked at her just before he made his way up the long hall. Zoey nodded her goodnights as she passed through to her quarters.

Letting herself in, she crossed to the sofa and propped her heeled feet on the coffee table. Sighing inwardly, she clamped her lip between her teeth. How to sort through this dilemma with the fogginess of alcohol swimming in her head?

She was just so very tired! Tired physically, exhausted mentally, drained emotionally.

She missed the colorful terrain of Dorjan, the beautiful triple-moonrises and stunning sunsets. With her eyes closed, she concentrated and recalled the soothing tempo of the waves as they crashed on the beach below her home. There was the call of the *mergulls* and the sweet scent of the Dorjan Sea. Then there were the people—people who depended solely on her to keep their world thriving.

Somehow, the thought of home turned her thoughts back to him. She still burned from his touch. Raising a hand, she inhaled the lingering scent of the masculine cologne that had rubbed off onto her fingers during that explosive kiss. The spicy flavor of his demanding lips on hers, the look of rabid hunger in his eyes haunted her soul. The feel of his sinewy body against her as they'd danced was etched in her mind with vivid, permanent clarity.

Zoey wanted him again, needed him desperately to soothe the smoldering ache that seemed to never ebb. Maybe she could go to him, satisfy her desires…and his. So that he wouldn't feel the need to have her as the harlot he thought she was, she could dream-travel to him and appease his lusty appetite. Then maybe, just maybe, he'd leave the BunnyRanch as a satisfied client, and she'd fulfill her mission.

And go home without him.

The thought tore at her heart. Realization slammed into her.

She wanted him for her Dorjanian mate!

She chuckled. No. It couldn't be. He would die in transit, and if not, the harsh atmosphere of her planet would do him in. Dorjanian lungs were equipped to withstand the imbalance of chemicals in their world, but Earth humans' lungs were not so resilient.

It was a silly revelation—that she was sure of. She simply needed a good, long, satisfying orgasm. Another carnal meeting with him in dreamland would certainly mollify her needs, afford her another store of his viable sperm, and scratch that itch he'd started.

Sleep, Zoey, and pray for the dreams to come.

She staggered up and weaved her way to the bed. With a gusty sigh, she disrobed, collapsed, and buried herself naked under the quilts. Rest. She just needed a little shut-eye—that, and his thick cock between her legs.

Sleep came swiftly. She accepted the transition from the black of unconsciousness to the fuzzy harmony of dreams. The jolt of her soul rising from her sleeping form always brought her to the dream state of awareness. For a brief time, Zoey traveled down a glowing passageway, and thoughts of him, the sexy images, the smells and sounds and flavors of him, all cradled her as she traveled to him. She could go anywhere, she knew, but there was only one place she chose to go.

So her innermost desires beckoned to her, seduced her to him.

She journeyed there in the sweet arms of slumber, and began her move through walls and space. With a trace of bewilderment, she detected the sharp scent of chlorine as she approached her target. Crisp night air whipped around her and fluttered her hair. When she came out on the other side, she looked down upon him where he lounged in the hot tub on the rear terrace of the BunnyRanch. His head was propped on the rim of the tub, his eyes shut. Lines of stress creased the outer corners as he dozed fitfully. She clenched her hands into fists and longed to soothe him with a touch, a kiss. His dark hair was slicked back, his strong arms thrown over the edge of the pool, and she thought she'd never seen him look more handsome. Bathed in bluish moonlight, he was a breathtaking, awesome sight.

The glowing golden cord that connected her to her dream subject seemed to tug on her, to draw her nearer to her goal. She moved closer and lowered herself into the hot bubbly swirls. When she was within arm's length of him, the cord dissipated into the night air.

She closed her eyes and sighed. The contrast between the cool atmosphere and the heat of the water was delicious, naughty. Steam wafted off the surface of the pool and surrounded him as he continued to catnap.

Zoey moved in on her focal point, rejoicing in the fire that immediately ignited between her legs. *Soon he'll bring you into the heavenly firestorm of his lovemaking. You'll appease your own carnal urges and satisfy him enough so that he feels sated…and leaves without delay.*

Under the water, she set her hand on his knee. She closed her eyes tightly and moved into his mind, into the realm of his sleeping thoughts…and it pleased her to see that he dreamed of her.

His eyes popped open in the illusory world of the dream, and he gasped. "What the…?" He straightened and blinked in confusion. "Who…where did you come from?"

"Shh." She floated closer and pressed her lips against his stunned mouth. "Relax. It's a fantasy, a moonlight mirage. Just enjoy."

"You again." He said it with an accusatory, yet relieved tone. "Who are you, and why are you always haunting my dreams?"

She ran both hands up his thighs, the muscles tense against her palms. Staring deep into his limpid gaze, she allowed her naked body to float behind her like a mermaid of the seas. "I'm your fantasy fulfilled. I've come to relieve you of your sexual tensions."

"Oh, yes, you're one of them. One of Madam Ivana's girls." He relaxed a small measure.

Let him think she had been sent by Ivana to accommodate him. "Yes, Rolf, I'm one of them." She flicked her tongue out and traced his lips. "Now, what would your desire be? Traditional? Sixty-nine? Doggy-style? Standing, sitting—"

He rooted for her mouth. She knew he saw her as a fuzzy form. But he found his target quickly, devouring her tongue as his arms reached for her slick, naked body. He wrenched her against him with a sudden jolt, causing her to drown in their hot, coupled lust. She spread her legs and accommodated him while he sat on the underwater bench, and she moaned in anticipation, as if parched by too many *manoyears* of sexual drought. Fueling her ardor further, she rejoiced as the petals of her sex pressed against the rising naked flesh of his penis. The walls of her passage tightened in anticipation. His hands moved in a frenzy over her back, shoulders, buttocks, thighs. With the hunger of a Dorjan beast, he ravenously engulfed her mouth. He delved in, out, around, sucked her tongue between his teeth then allowed her to reciprocate the move. His kiss tasted of champagne and dessert—sheer decadence!

Her breasts tingled feverishly as he held her desperately to him, and the nipples dragged against his own. His shaft, thick and hard as granite, found her throbbing cunt. He moved his hips so that the front length of him slid up and down in a teasing, grinding dance against her feminine mons. There was no entry, yet he'd already brought her to the brink of Eden. He catapulted her headlong into the star-filled velvet sky.

She clung to him. And with the discipline she'd learned in her *astrolage* training, she tried to force drab thoughts from her mind. Thoughts of the day her *nidus* would detect one hundred percent fullness and prepare for the return journey to Dorjan.

Zoey prayed it wouldn't be tonight.

*****

Just when he was sure she was about to reach her climax, Rolf shoved her away from him.

"What…?" She panted and reached for him. Her arms flailed and splashed. "What are you doing?" she whispered hoarsely.

"Come here," he demanded, and dragged her through the water. He turned her so that her back was to him. "I need to feel all of you when you come."

The switch in positions enflamed him further, like nothing he'd ever experienced before. Her bare bottom pressed against his rod as he pulled her snugly onto his lap. His hands shimmied upward until he filled both of them with her firm breasts. Between his index fingers and thumbs, he rolled the dark beads and brought them to precious life. He heard her moan, nearly died when she relaxed and threw her head back onto his shoulder.

He knew it was a dream, knew he was still at the BunnyRanch. The last thing he could remember was taking a cold shower as soon as he'd arrived back at his bungalow. After watching a bit of sports on satellite TV, he'd decided to go for a soak in the hot tub. It was a quiet, cool night and moonbeams slanted across the high-desert terrain. All he'd wanted was to relax, to forget the wanton tease who'd been his escort of late. Now, here he was with his fantasy lover once again. It was bizarre, he knew, even in his dream-induced state of mind. But he needed her like fruit upon a tree needed sunlight to grow rich with nutrients.

He was so goddamn horny he'd explode if he didn't get release soon!

Abandoning one luscious mound, he trailed his palm over her flat belly. With one finger, he located her mons and gently parted the petals as he moved ever lower. She gasped and writhed upon his lap. The jerky movements further aroused him when her round buttocks danced against his cock. From behind her, he greedily suckled her silky neck. He slid his tongue into her ear at the very moment his finger sank into her stickiness.

"Oh..." She cried it out and reached her arms behind her to clasp at the back of his neck.

"Between you and that chick—hmm, what was her name?" he asked hotly in her ear. "You've both left me like a dog in heat. I need release, Angel. And I need it now."

He didn't give her time to protest or agree. He gripped her hips and lifted her in the water. In one violent, smooth motion, he sheathed himself in her satiny wetness. The ecstasy of it was like a drug addict's fix finally hitting the blood stream. He growled aloud his pleasure, his voice carrying out across the cool desert night.

She whimpered, fluttered her arms, and splashed the water about them.

He chuckled softly and gathered her tightly against him. "Hold still, little filly. You can relax. I've got the reins."

At her husky sigh, he began a slow rhythm using her body to stroke him, to draw out that release he so badly needed. She was light in his grasp, and the sensation of her heat alternated with the warmth of the water. He pumped her up and down on his long length, and it was one of the most erotic things he'd ever experienced. From behind, her glorious mass of hair, gold-streaked and silver in the moonlight, swirled around them in the water. Her shoulders were delicately shaped, her back smooth and slim, shimmering in the desert-mountain night.

As the fever rose, moonbeams showered upon them and spun the steam of the tub in a whirling cocoon. The call of a lone raven echoed across the terrain, lost to the lovers as they drove higher toward ecstasy.

He was close, oh, so close. Out of desperation, he clamped one arm around her waist and pushed his free hand down until he found the swollen knob of her clitoris. She sucked in a breath and moaned as he strummed it like a harp. With his arm hooked around her, he moved her in time to their rising desire. Rolf thrust deeply, and by way of his finger, he heightened her need and expertly brought her to the edges of orgasm.

Suddenly, she stopped and withdrew from him. In comparison to her hot pussy, the water felt shockingly cool on his dick. "What are you doing, Angel? Please, please don't leave me unfulfilled like she did."

"No, Rolf, no." She turned and faced him, climbing upon his lap so that she straddled him under the water again. She pushed her hand beneath the surface of the pool and found his cock. It throbbed and ached within the curve of her small hand. Guiding it to her, she slid slowly down on his shaft…and he nearly came in that one bold, aggressive moment of hers. "I've got to be able to put my arms around you, to press my chest into yours, to bury you deep into my soul."

"Oh, God…" He groaned and closed his eyes. Behind the fog, he could make out every beautiful curve of her face, and he knew she was his, if only in his dreams. "I'm about to come…" He moaned it regretfully, somehow aware that when they each reached their peak, she would disappear.

"Come to me again tomorrow night," he said with a rushed tone as he strained to stave off the orgasm. "After my date with…with…what's-her-name."

"I'll try." She panted as she planted her knees on the seat at his hips and lifted herself for leverage.

It was no use. He leaned his head back on the edge of the hot tub and stared up at the pinpoint stars scattered like diamonds over black velvet. It was inevitable. The pleasure claimed him. Rolf heard her sharp intake of breath, felt her go still, then cry out his name. He filled her with his hot lava just at the precise moment that her inner folds pulsated around him, drawing out his lust.

In the next instant, his eyes burst open and he was alone in the tub.

"Son of a bitch!" He growled with frustration and slammed his fist down on the rim of the pool.

* * * * *

It had been so incredible. And it had been ruined by her *compubot.* Zoey lay in her bed, wet and naked. She tried to forget the echoed message that had reached her during reverse-travel.

Subject's nidus *at ninety-four point nine percent capacity. Mission nearing completion. Repeat. Mission ninety-four point nine percent complete.*

Dread swirled in her gut. Each encounter drove her further from him, back toward Dorjan, and yet there was an unusual connection that seemed to draw them together.

Zoey, you have a duty to your planet, to your people. Do not fail them!

She stared at the ceiling as she struggled to get her breathing back under control. There was no use dwelling on it. When she was relatively sure she wouldn't die from lack of oxygen, she swung her legs over the bed and swaggered to the bathroom.

Her skin was alive and still tingled with the feel of his touch. She could smell chlorine, could still taste him in her mouth. Shivering, she pushed through the door and flipped on the light. Stars, she felt like *crulo*! She was cold and wet, her head pounded and she needed a drink of water desperately. He'd drained every ounce of energy from her, sapped her as arid as the desert.

She swiped a towel from the rack and briskly dried herself off. Leaning at the waist, she wrapped it around her head, flipping it up as she stood. She stared at her reflection in the mirror. Her tawny skin was heightened with a pink glow, her lips bruised and swollen, as were her nipples. In her eyes, she could still see the edges of passion satisfied, but never completely sated. *Diona!* He was an amazing lover! She had to have him again. How she desperately needed to quench her thirst for his touch—but only in dreams. She must maintain the safety of dream-contact with him.

She groaned. "Solaria, my head aches. No more alcohol for you, Zoey." She swung open the medicine cabinet, drew out a bottle of aspirin, and shook a couple in her palm. Twisting on the faucet, she threw back her head and tossed the pills into her mouth, then bent to suck a swallow of water from the tap.

She stood and stared into the reflection of her amethyst eyes. And an idea suddenly came to her. Her mouth curved with the mere thought of it. Rolf had asked her to meet him at his bungalow at five p.m. tomorrow night. He'd also asked "Angel" to dream-travel to him again tomorrow night after his date with "what's-her-name". She rubbed her palms together and felt the rise of anticipation.

Oh, yes! She had a plan that would put the arrogant Rolf Mahoney in his place—at the mercy of her greedy, horny hands! But first, she needed to make a special trip to the store.

It was time to stock up on some select magic potions.

Chapter Six

"Finally!" The following morning, Rolf set the phone in its cradle and snatched up his portfolio. Madam Ivana had called to inform him that the lineup had arrived. Though he was relatively certain Zoey would be his first choice, he was no idiot. A wise businessman always made certain all of his options were thoroughly researched.

He flew from the cottage and made his way to the back door of the BunnyRanch. As soon as he stepped into the softly lit corridor, he detected the change. Boisterous song, laughter and conversation drifted up the hallway. Many of the girls' suite doors stood ajar, each decorated in their own style, some frilly and feminine, some hardcore with leather and dark themes. A cloud of seductive perfumes hung in the air. He chuckled to himself and imagined that, if a man were to engage one of the girls, he'd be hard pressed to successfully remove the evidence from his skin and clothing before he returned home to his significant other.

He'd almost reached the parlor when a door to his right flew open.

"Oh, well…good morning, Zoey."

The stunned look on her face was enough to make him want to throw her down and take her right here in the hallway. As if she'd been caught doing something naughty, she fidgeted and stammered.

"I…oh…" She reached behind her and fumbled to shut the door. Stiff and prim, she pressed her back against its closed surface.

He moved his gaze questioningly down over the conservative business suit. While the red blouse under the suit jacket revealed very little, he could still detect the swell of her breasts. His body responded with a swift bout of hardness. Slowly, he perused the snug, above-the-knee skirt, the low pumps and sheer, regular pantyhose.

"Playing the shy secretary with some high-paying customer today, Zoey?" At his own words, his jaw clamped and a strange envy sliced through his gut.

"I…yes," she said with what he thought was a trace of confusion.

Her eyes, a conglomerate of violet and blue today, were wide and stunned. As he studied the swollen pupils, he caught a flash of white in the center, like a twinkling star in the night sky. But it was gone before he could determine if he'd only imagined it. Shoving the disturbing, somewhat familiar sight from his mind, he inhaled the spicy scent of her, a mixture of her natural female aroma and a unique perfume she'd applied.

She'd left her long tresses down, and he couldn't resist lifting one soft wave from her breast to twine it around his finger. As he twisted it, he studied her plump red lips, now open and suddenly drawing in ragged breaths. He coiled and wrapped the strand until his finger reached her ear and he drew her closer to him.

"Get on into the parlor," he said in her ear. There was but an inch of space between their bodies. The heat from her slim form reached out and stroked his cock. Energy crackled around them. He gripped the portfolio in his other hand to keep from tossing it to the floor and slamming her against his arousal. "The lineup is here. I want you to be a part of it."

"What?" The word had tumbled from her mouth in a croak.

"I said—"

"I know what you said," she cut in. She lifted a hand and drew the lock of hair from around his index finger. "What I mean is, *why?*"

He slid his hand, which tingled to high hell, into his trousers pocket. "I'm sure you already know why I'm here,

Zoey. To hopefully choose one of you to play the part in my movie."

"I *know* that! But why me?"

"Well, you *are* one of the girls, aren't you?"

She started to say something, then shut her mouth with a click of her teeth.

"The parlor, Zoey. In two minutes flat, I want to see you lined up with the rest of them."

He couldn't resist and pressed his hand to her cheek. It was smooth and silky soft against his palm.

Her eyelids fluttered down, and she swayed subtly, so much so that he wasn't sure if he'd detected it correctly.

"I…okay," she said huskily.

"Okay," he shot back. "See you there." He turned on his heel and sauntered down the hallway.

*****

"See you there," Zoey whispered as she watched his massive form move down the corridor and into the parlor.

She was the accountant! Why couldn't she bring herself to just tell him the truth? Because, her baser side needed him to think she was one of the seductive, highly sexual beings of the BunnyRanch. Leaning back against the door, she closed her eyes and drew in a deep breath. His earthy scent still lingered around her. She'd detected his aroma just before she'd turned to find him standing there right outside her office door.

And one whiff, one quick glance at him, and her heart had rumbled like thunder and sent a thrum of hot, aching blood to her loins. Willing the fire to squelch itself, she quickly assessed her situation. She couldn't continue to see him during daylight hours. Safety for the *gametes* left her with only the dream option—unless her theory last night worked. She'd drunk enough alcohol to alert her *compubot*. Data had been transmitted to her and proven that the spermatozoa environment within her chamber had nearly reached a level that could be safe for their survival during transport from the male body to hers without the protective atmosphere of dream-travel. Which, she assumed meant that if she could maintain enough alcohol in her system during waking hours, she just might be able to make love with him outside of dreams without compromising the security of his potent *milt*.

But for now the problem was that he expected her in the lineup. Why, that was ridiculous! She had no desire to be an actress in his movie. In addition, she had a duty to return to Dorjan so their species could carry on generation after generation. To be chosen would mean she would have to stay behind and abort her duties.

Which would mean that she could have him whenever she wanted him.

Images of his naked body filled her mind. Squeezing her eyelids tighter, she plopped her head back against the door. *Mama Luna,* this was the most difficult mission King Luran had ever sent her on!

"Zoey?"

The voice jolted her from her thoughts. She opened her eyes and looked into dancing brown ones. "Ivana."

Ivana was dressed in a wispy, two-piece pantsuit that looked more like nightwear than business attire. She gripped Zoey's elbow. "Come on. What are you waiting for?"

"What—wait!" Ivana was much stronger than she looked. She tugged until Zoey was dragged along beside her.

"The lineup," Ivana said as they neared the parlor. "You're gonna miss it."

"But, Ivana, I don't want to be a part of it. I'm your accountant, for stars' sake!"

"*Sí,* and I'm paying you to make me a lot of money. But believe me," she said with a sidelong look, "you can make a *lot* more money being an actress than an accountant."

Zoey stumbled along behind her and tried to wrench her arm from Ivana's vise-grip. "But…but I don't–" She cut herself off. "Aren't you supposed to be sick?"

Ivana sent her a look of pure relief. "I'm much better today. Besides, no illness is going to keep me from missing this."

They entered the parlor where at least two-dozen ladies of the evening lined up in various stages of dress. Ivana hauled Zoey along until they reached the end of the line. She deposited her there and went to sit on a butterscotch sofa next to Rolf. He nodded at Ivana and spoke a few words of approval to her as he studied his casting choices. His gaze slid up the line until it reached the end. Until those icy orbs sent Zoey's body into a shiver of reluctant delight. The look of sheer lust in his eyes caused her belly to coil with desire. Obviously, he was pleased that she'd made a showing. And obviously, he only had eyes for her—at the moment.

"Well, Mr. Mahoney," Ivana said, looking pleased and replete, "what would you like? A dance from each, a twirl around the stripper pole, a blowjob?"

He chuckled and crossed his ankle over the opposite knee. In the blue ski sweater and jeans, he looked positively delicious. Zoey fought to keep her gaze from him, but it was no use. He was a dangerous glue that her eyes were helplessly drawn to, despite the threat of that glue permanently setting.

"I'm sure each and every one of them can dance and strip and give some great oral. But what I need is to examine each one, study their eyes, their personalities…and hold them in my arms for size and fit."

"Ah," Ivana said on a nod and a throaty laugh. "Get a *feel* for them, huh? Well, I assure you there's other more sure-fire ways to get *that*."

He nodded, but didn't take the bait. All business, he shuffled through a thick stack of papers stapled together at one corner. His eyes scanned the documents, flipping and studying the pages. He raised his head and said, "Katya."

A curvy brunette attired in a black leather vest and matching G-string stepped forward on her spiked heels. She didn't say a word. But she didn't have to. Her sultry, dominatrix gaze—which she had trained on Rolf—said it all.

He set the papers aside and rose. Zoey held her breath as he took five long, slow strides and stopped mere inches from Katya. She was nearly as tall as he was. Her dark hair was an unruly mass of curls and waves that cascaded over her shoulders and back. From her place at the end of the line, Zoey could see the enormous outline of Katya's breasts, and the naked curve of the girl's firm buttocks. Her legs were long and lean, and Zoey got a flash image of them wrapped around Rolf's hips. The thought shocked her. But more than that was her body's contradictory reaction. A reluctant fire curled in her loins and spiraled out to tease her every cell.

Rolf stroked his freshly shaved jaw and crossed the other arm over his chest. "Hmm," he mumbled as his eyes scanned Katya's body. He twirled one finger in the air and she spun on her heels and gave him a full view of every inch of her frame.

"Come here," he ordered, crooking a finger at her.

Mesmerized, Zoey watched as Katya slunk into his arms. She melted around him like the practiced wanton that she was. Her arms snaked up and around his neck. With the wild look of a feline, she captured his eyes with her green gaze and rubbed her plentiful breasts against him. His hands slid lower to cup her rear. Zoey's heart raced at the gesture. She couldn't catch her breath. Why did this display of blatant affection turn her on so much? Where was the full-blown jealousy she thought she would feel?

Before she could decide on a halfway reasonable explanation, Rolf's gaze found Zoey's as he pressed Katya against his long length. He held her captive with a hot stare while he stroked the fullness of each of Katya's ass cheeks. Zoey's breath caught. For the Dorjanian life of her, she could not keep her eyelids from going limp with desire.

Abruptly, he released Katya—and Zoey—and returned to his paperwork. Katya stumbled back into line while Rolf threw over his shoulder, "PJ next."

PJ was an animal in disguise. With her dark-blonde hair in pigtails and the short schoolgirl skirt, she appeared every bit the innocent virgin—that is, until the details were noted. Her bronzed belly with the pierced navel was set enticingly below the knot of the snug, low-cut white blouse she wore. Her breasts, while small, were pushed up to her throat like juicy, ripe peaches. And her mouth, full and pouty, only added to the innocent allure. With wide cool-blue eyes, there was something about her that Zoey was sure would appeal to Rolf, whether for his movie or his own personal use.

And the thought of it both worried and thrilled her.

After she spun around for his inspection, PJ flew into his open arms. Her petite little body didn't stay there long. It slithered downward so that her mouth was level with his crotch. Rolf merely stood there and looked down at her. PJ took that as consent and wrapped her arms around his hips. Her mouth nudged and prodded the bulge of his jeans. One hand came around to cup the swell of his sac while the other massaged his ass cheek.

Again, Rolf's gaze moved to Zoey. She watched as the blue of his eyes turned to a stormy gray. PJ continued her assault on him, attempting to win his heart and his cock over so that she could become that rich and famous actress.

He groaned and gently set her from him. She sighed and returned to her place in line.

"Zena?" he called out and scanned the lineup for the next contestant to step forward.

"Woo-hoo!" Zena leaped forward. She was a ball of fire from her long flaming-red hair down to the see-through, barely-there, hot-pink negligee and black, four-inch stiletto heels. Bubbly and energetic, she wore Zoey out just watching her.

Rolf grinned at the girl's enthusiasm. "Too much coffee this morning?" he asked good-naturedly.

"Honey," she purred and raked coral claws down his chest. "*No* one needs coffee to keep them awake when you're around!"

He chuckled and reached for her. She squealed and pressed a palm to her mouth, her chocolate eyes warm with delight. Rolf lifted her hand and spun her around like a ballerina as he examined every inch of her voluptuous curves. But he didn't tarry long. As if anxious to get on to the next, he pulled Zena into his arms and gave her the embrace test. And still, just the sight of him touching another woman so openly, stirred Zoey's blood.

What was happening to her? she wondered with a trace of panic as her panties flooded with a sticky wetness. The jealousy she thought would be there with him in the company of all these gorgeous women, was present only in miniscule amounts.

But there was no time for Zoey to ponder the topic. He moved on to the next Bunny.

"Sascha."

A woman of medium height stepped slowly forward. Rolf moved to her, and his gaze scrutinized every inch of her cocoa-colored skin. Her hair fell over her shoulders in a long, thick and kinky fluff. Combined with the graceful, sensual movements, the compact, curvy body exuded confidence and class. Within the circle of her finely boned face were the darkest eyes Zoey had ever seen. A small, wide nose and full scarlet lips completed the picture of an exotically beautiful face.

Rolf paused and held up his hands in a square. He squinted and looked at Sascha through the space between his hands. Then he gestured until she swiveled on her high heels and pirouetted before him as she gyrated her hips in a seductive dance. He hooked a finger in the V of her halter-top and pulled her into his arms.

Again, his eyes found Zoey's, and she watched helplessly as he raised a hand and cupped one of Sascha's breasts. Sascha purred in cat-like approval, the guttural sound of genuine satisfaction carrying seductively to her ears. Zoey couldn't breathe. Her eyes were fastened to Rolf's hand where Sascha's ample bosom overflowed. Zoey shifted her stance and wished she had fresh panties to don.

But Rolf continued the voyeur torture and released Sascha to move on to the next, and then the next…

By the time he reached Zoey, she panted with unbridled carnality.

"Zoey." He said it as if he were meeting her for the first time. Standing before her, his eyes were pools of foggy lust. She could detect his musky scent above all the perfumes in the room. Heat from his body permeated her perspiring skin.

And she knew they all watched.

"Mr. Mahoney…" she said with a nod, hoping to appear as formal as possible. But it was no use. Her voice came out in a whisper of pathetic desire.

"Take off the jacket," he ordered.

She blinked, and a warm heat flooded her womb. Slowly, without taking her eyes from his, she complied. The suit jacket fell to the floor behind her. She heard a collective shift of feet from the lineup.

"Very nice," he said thickly. "Now, unbutton the blouse."

She could only stand there without moving so much as a muscle. Her hands would not obey, no matter how much she instructed them to do so.

Rolf stepped close and leaned down so that his mouth was against her ear. A burst of stars shimmied down her spine. She could feel his warm breath in her ear as he said in a raspy tone meant only for her, "Do you want me to do it for you?"

Zoey swallowed a dry knot of panic. "No."

His hands came up and gripped her upper arms over the silky fabric of her shirt. "Then do as I say." Again, he said it for her ears only.

"Here? In front of everyone?"

"Zoey," Ivana chimed in from across the room. "Cooperate for Mr. Mahoney's sake, and your own. He's paying big money for this inspection."

"But I don't—" Her words were cut short when one of his hands slid around to her back and drew her closer. With her heels on, his arousal was positioned over the space between her vee and her navel. Her own sex was now swollen and pressed against his jeans. Gradually, he unfastened every button with his free hand. Cool air rushed up to caress her bare skin when he slid the blouse from her shoulders.

"Ah, beautiful," he growled. "Just beautiful."

He stepped back to get a better view. She hadn't realized that he'd been holding her up. With a stutter-step, she caught herself and stood proud. There were a couple dozen or so eyes on her bare breasts—why had she decided against a bra today? But there was one pair of eyes in particular that had the power to bring her to her knees. Zoey hissed in a breath when each nipple puckered at the smoldering gaze he swept her with. A renewed rush of wet-hot desire flooded her senses.

With careful steps, he arced around her and prowled as he considered her half-naked form. Zoey kept her chin high, her eyes fixed across the room, but she could sense his nearness behind her. One hand went up, and he dragged a finger from her nape down to the top of her skirt. She shivered and stiffened when he unfastened the hook, drawing down the zipper.

With one practiced tug, the skirt slid over her hips in a whoosh. Gasps rang out from the line of Bunnies. Zoey didn't flinch this time. She just stood there, stared straight ahead and tried to get her breathing under control.

And hoped her panties would hold all the stickiness that oozed from her slit.

The thong she wore did little to cover her rear end, which she knew he inspected by the way his hands roamed her body. He shifted at that moment, and suddenly, he was pressed against her backside. The full length of his manhood wedged between the cheeks of her ass as the rough denim fabric abraded against her sensitive flesh. His hands slithered around to cup her breasts, and she muffled an involuntary moan when he flickered his thumbs over them simultaneously.

"You like this, don't you, Zoey?" he asked raggedly in her ear. He trembled, and it was at that moment that she realized this had nothing to do with his movie. "You like to watch and be watched."

Dorjanians weren't always monogamous by any stretch of the imagination, but she had to admit, voyeurism was not something highly practiced in her world. Therefore, the question had never been presented to her before. But she couldn't deny it. There was something quite naughty about it, so naughty it made her wish she were one of the girls.

"Answer me, Zoey," he hissed.

"Yes," she said with a whimper. "It's....it's very...arousing."

He chuckled wickedly and tightened his hold on her. One hand moved lower across her bare belly and found the top of her pantyhose...then her panties. Her legs trembled and she sagged against him for support. He ground his cock into her buttocks at the same moment his hand invaded her thong. It moved sensually slow, caressed in circular motions, returned to her abdomen then dipped back into her undergarment. Over and over he repeated the teasing dance, each time, delving deeper still. Finally, he reached the destination Zoey had anticipated.

"Ah, yes, you're as hard as I am." His finger slid down over her clit and between her damp folds.

Zoey cried out and bit her lip for control. At that moment, she glanced to her left. Several pairs of women petted and kissed each other as practiced hands roamed eager bodies. Had she and Rolf aroused them all to this point? The concept of it further enhanced her desire. She panted and struggled for air as he plunged one finger into her passage.

"Rolf..." she said on a breathy sigh. "I...I—"

He tore the digit from her. Gripping her tightly, he dragged her back and fell onto a nearby sofa so that she sat upon his lap with her back to him. She could feel his body quake as he located her hard bud again, and strummed it with expertise. His other hand clutched her right breast and composed the same sweet torture on her nipple. She couldn't stand it anymore. She was going to blow right here in front of all these people if he didn't stop soon!

Oh, but she didn't want him to stop! No. The naughtiness of it felt almost as potent as his skilled touch. His mouth was now on her neck. He nipped and sucked as he drew ragged breaths in and out of his lungs.

"Zoey..." he panted. "Please...I've got to have you. Say you'll give it up to me, babe."

She could no longer fight it. "Five o'clock tonight..." she whished it out on a sigh "...as planned."

"And you'll make love to me?" He whispered in her ear, and the gentle, private manner of it brought her to a whole new level.

She angled her head and half-turned, lifting her face so that she could look into the passion-filled glaze of his eyes. One arm rose to hook behind his neck. Astounded and outrageously aroused, she caught an errant glimpse of their twined bodies in the mirrored wall. "Yes, I'll make love to you. Tonight."

At her admission, he picked up the pace. The steady pressure of his finger turned to an unbridled, rapid rhythm of expert masturbation. Zoey braced herself. The orgasm was near, so near she could taste it. Then it slammed into her with such force, she cried out. Her voice echoed in the cozy, fire-lit parlor. The swells of passion engulfed her. Rolf's heat was behind her, all around her, his erection grinding into her ass.

Without thought for her actions, she pivoted in his embrace and threw her arms around him. He cradled her, his breathing tattered and hot.

Reserves remain at ninety-four point nine percent. Repeat. Ninety-four point nine percent.

Oh, shut up! Just shut the flek *up!*

"Tonight, Zoey," he said and he held her captive against his cock. "Don't disappoint me."

Zoey took a deep breath. Her eyes scanned the room. There were various stages of intimacy in progress around them. Many of the girls had either slithered to the floor where they'd stood, or found a spot on one of the sofas to finish off what Rolf had started.

"I…I guess—"

Before she could complete her response, there was a lone round of applause.

"Bravo!" Ivana stood right in front of them, a leering gleam in her eyes. "Are you sure you wouldn't like to switch from accountant to call girl, Zoey?"

Chapter Seven

"Accountant?" Rolf said with a disbelieving tone. "She's your *accountant*?"

"Well, yes." Ivana tossed a dismissive hand in the air. "I guess I forgot to mention that."

"Forgot to mention it?" Rolf stood abruptly, almost unseating Zoey to the floor. She scrambled to her feet. Flying across the short space, she plucked up her blouse and skirt and hastily donned them.

"It's not important. What counts is the connection you two made. So, you've found your gem for the movie, right?"

Zoey's head came up with a snap.

Rolf sent himself a swift mental kick to the ass. *Yes, I found her, but I've also gotten involved with her—a no-no in the past, but not, apparently, for the future.*

"Yes," he replied. Coming to his feet, he readjusted his pants. "Zoey's the one."

There was a concession of sighs and grumbles from around the room.

"Excellent!" Ivana said gleefully.

"*No*, I'm not."

That from Zoey. Rolf swung his gaze to her. She had already put herself back together, but there was still a flush to her cheeks and that just-tossed look to her glorious mane of hair. He slid a look over her conservative dress. And he'd thought it to be a coy costume! With an inward chuckle, he stroked his jaw as he studied her further, rubbing the still-wet tip of his finger below his nose. Her sex-scent filled his nostrils and he could still feel her body's warmth against his chest. She was alluring, beautiful—absolutely breathtaking.

And she was an accountant!

"What do you mean, Zoey? Of course it's wonderful. You've been chosen to play a part in Mr. Mahoney's movie. It's every girl's dream to become a movie star," she said, and gestured to indicate the evidence of all the envious ladies in the parlor.

"It's not *my* dream," Zoey said, combing her hands through her hair. "I have other…responsibilities in this galax—um, in this world."

There was an abrupt scamper. Suddenly, Rolf was surrounded by dozens of Bunnies. They groped, whined and begged for his attention.

"Me, me! I'll take her place!"

A half a dozen hands spanned his chest, another few clutched his ass, massaging and rubbing.

"No, not *her*. Me, Mr. Mahoney! Me!"

One hand cupped his sex. Still half hard, he gritted his teeth and attempted to step away, but the sofa was behind him.

"That's ridiculous," Sascha chimed in. "He obviously liked me the best during his examination!"

PJ flung a pigtail over her shoulder. "Um, excuse me, but I'm the one who got him hard first."

"Ha! That's a frickin' lie!" Zena retorted. "*I* did!"

Rolf stumbled back and fell onto the divan. One little sable-haired beauty dropped into his lap and wound her arms around him. "I've taken some acting classes and done some off-Broadway plays," she purred and slowly trailed a fingertip across his lower lip. "I'm *real* good at fooling people."

I bet you are.

Katya rolled her eyes. "You're all freakin' crazy. *I'm* the one he couldn't take his eyes off—well, at least in the beginning," she added, and slanted a glare at Zoey. She inhaled and lifted her ample breasts a level higher. "Besides, I'm the most photogenic of all of you bitches."

"Bitches? Why you—"

"Now, girls!" Ivana cut in just as the one called Autumn made a beeline for Katya's lovely throat. "That will be enough. To your rooms! *Now*!"

There was a collective groan throughout the parlor.

"Now, or you get a cut in this week's pay."

That shut them up like a whack to the ass. With various glares and sighs and even the sticking out of tongues, the room was slowly vacated.

"So, Zoey it is," Ivana asserted happily. Said so, Rolf was sure, because Zoey had been the one he'd placed the highest finder's fee on.

Rolf drew in a sharp breath. The room was filled with a conglomerate of various perfumes. A fire roared in the fireplace across the room. He was glad to see the room now calm and serene. Now he just needed…Zoey.

"Zoey?" He spun around and scanned the parlor. Peering into the lounge, he saw that is was empty, with the exception of one very pleased looking bartender. "Zoey, where the hell are you?"

Ivana sighed. "Looks like she's gone back to her precious books. I'll go and see what I can do about this."

"Ivana?"

She halted in mid-step. Slowly, she turned around to face him. He saw the dread in her eyes. She knew what he was about to say.

"If she doesn't agree, the final fee gets cut considerably."

She closed her eyes in frustration and nodded. Turning, she threw over her shoulder as she sailed from the room, "She'll agree if it's the last thing she ever does."

* * * * *

An actress! He wanted *her* for the part! Why, that was ridiculous! And all this time, she'd hoped he was genuinely interested in her as a person, as a lover—not because of his damn movie!

Well, Zoey thought, rifling through a crate of lingerie Ivana had asked her to "store" in her quarters. She would show him a side of herself he'd never forget! After she was through with him, he'd only be able to view her as a lover. Oh, yes. She'd be long gone to Dorjan while he pined over her, wishing to the cosmic heavens that he hadn't insisted on such foolery.

Her hand closed around the red leather garment. It had been buried at the bottom of the box, but instinct told her it wouldn't be forgotten once she donned it. Excitement coursed through her as she held it up and inspected it. The one-piece, strapless garment displayed various strategically placed zippers. Though it resembled a corset on its upper portion, it also had a strip that ran between the long leather legs. Of course, there was a zipper there, as well, and a flood of cream soaked her panties at the thought of him sliding it open to expose her pussy to his ministrations.

She startled as a knock sounded at the door.

"Who is it?"

"It's Ivana, honey. Can I come in?"

Ah, the money-hungry bitch comes sniffing around with her tail between her legs, Zoey thought. "Come right on in."

Ivana stepped gingerly inside and closed the door softly behind her. Her eyes were wide and dark like two morsels of moist chocolate. Clearly, she knew she treaded on dangerous ground, and would use some of her own acting skills to get what she wanted.

"Going somewhere?" she asked, leaning against the door.

"Oh, yes, but not just yet. First, I have a mission to complete. And something tells me tonight is the night…"

"Really?" Her tone rang hopeful, and she took two steps closer.

"Really." Zoey tossed the garment upon a nearby chair. "The man's wooed and seduced since he first laid eyes on me, and all the while, you and he planned every deceitful move. You, so you could earn your filthy money. Rolf, so he could snatch me up as an *actress*. Hmph!" she snorted and flung open the door to the small bathroom. "Let's see how well old Zoey can act, huh?"

"Zoey, sweetie—"

"Look, Ivana," she said as she stripped off her suit jacket. "I don't have time for games. If you only knew what sorts of responsibilities were on my shoulders, you'd never have put me in this position. But don't you worry. I'll handle it from here. Because, frankly," she said through gritted teeth as she slid the skirt over her hips, "I don't give a flying *flek* anymore if you get your books straightened out or not."

"*Flek?*"

"Yes. *Flek*. On Dorjan, it's equivalent to your 'fuck'."

"Dorjan? Honey, what are you babbling about?"

"Babbling?" She had to laugh. "Look, Ivana..." She leaned inside the shower and adjusted the knobs. Steam rose and permeated her chilled skin. "You'll get your money," she said, anxious to rid herself of this woman. "Believe me, you will. I may not end up on the big screen, but this will work out, I'm certain of it."

Ivana sighed. She collapsed on Zoey's bed in the far corner. "The man is determined to have *you* as his actress. It's the only way he'll finish paying."

Zoey tossed a towel over a peg near the shower stall. "No, it isn't. Trust me. Now, I'm going to make you a list of girls. I want you to send them to the Orgy Room at five-thirty p.m. this evening. That's five-thirty, not five-fifteen or five twenty-five. Five-*thirty*. Got it?"

"I...got it."

"And tell each and every one of them that this is an audition for the movie role. Do you hear me, Ivana?"

Ivana rolled her eyes and crossed her arms under her ample breasts. "You're not making any damn sense."

"Believe me, Ivana," she said, stepping out of the thong. "I will make you your *cents*—and lots of it. *If* you do as I say."

The madam's eyes flared with anticipation. "Well, I can't imagine what you have in mind, but, if you really mean what you say, I'll trust you and have them there at five-thirty sharp. Just don't blow this deal for me, Zoey. Just don't."

"Did I blow your books for you?"

Ivana shrugged. "I sure hope not."

"No, I didn't. In a short few weeks, I've reorganized your accounting mess, zeroed in on some legal evidence against your former accountant and saved you millions. Now, if that isn't trust, what else could be?"

"You did?"

She started to step into the shower, stopped and turned. "Yes, I did. But I won't surrender the final documents until this incident with Rolf is over. Understand?"

Ivana's eyes widened with apprehension. She clamped her teeth together and nodded.

"Good." She clicked the glass door shut behind her and tested the water with her hand. "Now, in addition, I'm going to send along a list of things I want readied for me in the Orgy Room. See that they're all there by that time."

Zoey watched Ivana through the glass. Ivana gave her a slow nod that wavered rather than complied.

But Zoey didn't care. It was time. Time to complete the filling of her *nidus*, time to locate her *portalship* and return to Dorjan. And time to prove to Rolf Mahoney that the last thing he'll want her for is an actress!

"Now," Zoey added with a cold smile as she ducked under the spray of steaming water, "if you'll excuse me, I have a very important date to ready for, as well as a planet to save."

"Are you on drugs?" Ivana blurted out.

Zoey had to laugh at that. She squirted a dollop of floral shampoo into her palm. "No, but I'll admit, that idea did cross my mind for a brief moment."

Ivana let out a forced breath. Through the clear shower door, Zoey watched as she rose, moved out into the main room, and crossed to the desk. Plucking up a pen and pad, she returned to the bathroom and sat upon the closed toilet seat. "Go ahead. Finish your shower. I'll make a list as you call out all the girls' names and items you'll need for the Orgy Room."

Zoey scrubbed her scalp vigorously. She inhaled with bliss as the hot water pounded over her clammy flesh. "Better have a lot of paper."

*****

Rolf took another long swallow of his beer. He stared at the TV screen, but he didn't see the sports highlights. He saw *her*.

Damn, he had it bad! His system sped in overdrive. He'd waited all afternoon long like an impatient schoolboy on Christmas Eve. Someone, he'd been informed, would be phoning him soon to instruct him on his secret destination. All that had been divulged to him was that he would have a special meeting with Zoey and that he would not be displeased.

Well, that was an understatement. If Zoey was involved, pleasure would surely follow. Their date of five o'clock fast approached, but if Zoey didn't put out this time, he prayed his dreams would again produce the sex-angel who'd haunted him since his arrival two nights ago.

He had to have release. After that highly arousing, voyeuristic masturbation incident in the parlor with Zoey, he needed to blow big-time. Her sensuality and abandon, despite the threat of onlookers, had done something to him, something that he couldn't quite define. And even though she'd flat-out refused the phenomenal offer he presented to her, he was confident he could persuade her to be his next box office hit.

It was just a matter of time.

When the phone buzzed, he clunked the beer bottle onto the side table and leapt from the sofa. Already, he was hard with anticipation of the coming night. But the phone only added to his arousal. It would be someone to inform him where to go, what to do. Each ring further inflamed him, moved him closer to her.

He crossed to the cordless and plucked it from the base. "Hello?"

"Rolf?" His insides quivered. The voice was familiar, husky, promising.

"Well, hello, beautiful." Rolf perched on the arm of the couch and crossed one ankle over the other. His pulse danced in his throat. "Are we still on for tonight?"

"Yes..." Zoey said, her tone cryptic and soft as butter. "Are you ready?"

Am I ready? Rolf chuckled. "Yes, ready when you are."

"Good." There was the odd conglomeration of various noises in the background, hums, sloshes, creaks. Not the usual clamor expected in an accountant's office, he mused. "Come on over to the lounge. The bartender will instruct you from there."

He supposed he could use a good martini to bolster the beer, anyway. "Be right there."

In response, there was a click on the other end of the line. Rolf held the phone out from his ear and stared at it. With a shrug, he set it back in its cradle and snatched up his jacket.

He didn't waste time. When he reached the main complex and pulled open the door, the boisterous sounds and genuine laughter pleasantly assaulted him. He liked the BunnyRanch, he suddenly decided. Despite its clandestine nature, it was a warm, friendly, fun place to hang out. There were no gray areas in either the business or the gratification aspects of its nature. The equation was simple—that is, if the patron wasn't looking for an actress. You pay X amount of dollars, you get Y. No questions asked, no threat of being arrested, no inhibitions or judgmental attitudes. Rates were fair, the women were hot, and the madam was willing to work with you on whatever endeavors you chose.

The corridor was long, but Rolf covered its length in no time. He was anxious to get this project off the ground.

And, of course, he was eager to see Zoey.

He moved down the red-carpeted hallway. Every suite door was closed. Either the girls were otherwise engaged at the moment, or they were a part of the lively activity that grew louder with each step he took.

Within a single minute, he reached the lounge.

"Mr. Mahoney!" Ivana was behind the bar assisting the bartender. He got a glimpse into the parlor and saw that it was filled to capacity with gentlemen callers in various stages of negotiation. A lineup just now concluded, and several customers were being led away by negligee-clad ladies on spiked heels. Being led back to those closed doors for some privacy…

Yes, Rolf thought with a wolfish grin. The BunnyRanch sported a heroic, perfected profession—customer satisfaction with high volume sales.

"Ivana." He tipped his head and planted his elbows on the bar overhang. "Good to see you tonight."

She gave the shaker one last jolt and poured the martini into a stemmed glass. "And you, too. Now, here you go—and it's on the house, of course. After you've finished that, I'll escort you to your destination."

"Well," he replied suavely, then tipped his head back and drained the cocktail in one swallow. "I can't very well argue that intriguing offer, now can I?"

"But, of course not." She eyed him, obviously pleased that he'd enjoyed her martini so thoroughly. "Well, number two coming right up," Ivana purred, and promptly poured the remainder of the mixed drink into another glass. She slid it across the hardwood surface.

Rolf reached for it and set his boot on the brass bar at his feet. "Zoey called me. I suppose you're the bartender she alluded to."

"Yes, sir," she said with a wink as she rounded the bar. "Now, you just hold your guns, there," she added, and sliced a look at the bulge in his pants, "and follow me."

"Guns on hold..." he replied glibly and trailed Madam Ivana's curvaceous form as she led him down the opposite corridor.

They reached Ivana's office and turned toward a double door positioned at a right angle from it. Black iron sconces glowed on either side of the elegant, wooden portal. Already, he could detect various scents wafting from the room, enticing perfume, amaretto, spices and...chocolate? His interest was peaked, as was his cock. It was obvious his money would finally be put to good use.

"Right this way, Mr. Mahoney," Ivana said as she swept open the door.

She stepped into the room and widened his view. He shuffled forward. And his jaw dropped to his chest. The room was like a gymnasium full of odd contraptions with dozens of enormous cushions strewn across the floor. Nearby sat a kitchenette and bar area, and Rolf caught a glimpse of some sort of dark liquid bubbling on the stovetop burner. Off to one side, there was a board tipped upward, and for all intents and purposes, it appeared to be a seesaw. Just down from it was a sunken, bright-red vinyl, round ring, he supposed for engaging in messy sexual play. A corner had been angled off with a panel of prison bars, and various chains hung from its inner walls. Then, of all things, a roped cage, much like those in outdoor restaurant playgrounds, stood in the corner full of tiny balloons. He could only imagine what *that* would be used for!

"Holy hell, what is this place?" It reminded him of the set of a porn movie!

Ivana smiled warmly, clearly pleased at his fascination. "It's the Orgy Room where many multi-partner activities take place—among other things. It's been Zoey's wish to treat you to the ultimate night of pleasure."

"Zoey planned all this?" Desire stabbed him sweetly in the gut. His balls drew up to painful attention.

"Yes, I did." She'd apparently hidden behind the door. It was then that she emerged and sidled up beside him. He swallowed as his gaze moved over her. Her long, pale hair had been swept up into a high ponytail on top her head, leaving her slim shoulders bare and ripe for his touch. The bodice of the red bodysuit clung to her, thrusting her breasts up so that her deep cleavage made him salivate like a dog. There were golden zippers over each nipple, but soon he discovered those weren't the only zippers. They were everywhere, down the sides of her slim waist, across her navel, just above her pubic area, and, yes, he thought with animal satisfaction, there was one from clit to…where? Her asshole? He couldn't quite discern where the trail ended, but he was no dummy.

The thought of revealing tiny areas of her skin at random, then that final jewel, made him go rock-hard. An aching throb rushed through his gut and choked the head of his cock. He didn't even notice as Ivana slipped from the room, but he did see the zippers on Zoey's backside as she turned to close the door. Several ran in slashes across her spine and down the backs of her legs. Those on each cheek of her ass seemed to wink at him enticingly, but it was the one right down the middle that held him spellbound. *Holy fuck, she looked totally edible in that get-up!*

"Oh, Zoey…" he groaned, and clutched at his erection through his jeans. "Oh, Zoey."

"Rolf," she said with a nod. And that was when his eyes finally found her face. His pulse skipped a beat. In all of his years as a Hollywood producer, he'd never seen a more perfectly painted face. Her golden brows were arched seductively, her eyes outlined with fuck-me flawlessness, and her irises glistened with various colors—he was sure due to the odd, sensual lighting in the room. Crimson color splashed her cheeks matching the plump, ripe cherry lips. Licking his own lips, his mouth watered, and he knew she'd taste better than fruit, better than sex itself.

"Wow. Shit." He raked a hand through his hair. "I'm fucking speechless."

She giggled softly and reached for his hand. He caught a whiff of her naughty perfume. It seemed to tap him on the dick and yank with sensual expertise. "Come with me. It's time to get started."

Where had he heard that giggly melody before? His head began to spin pleasantly, but he shook it in an attempt to clear the fog and recall.

It was no use. With all the blood in his veins now pooled in his cock, and the nice buzz he had going on, what did it matter if he'd heard it before? He still had his martini in the other hand, and as she led him across the room, he tipped his head back and drained it.

"Take your clothes off," she ordered as she stopped next to the sunken ring. "Quickly."

"Well." He drew the sweater over his head. "Apparently, you like to get right down to business."

Her eyes touched him with the flame of a fire. He watched as her gaze slid over his chest, and with each blink, he could swear she stroked him. There was no sense in wasting time, so he went right to it. Kicking off his boots, he unbuckled his belt, unfastened his pants…and down they came. Cool air caressed his sizzled skin, and, like a compass, his shaft bounced up against his abdomen as he straightened.

"Now," she almost whispered it. "Climb into the ring and lie down."

"Uh…" She moved away and crossed to the kitchen area while he struggled to find his voice. "Only if you join me."

She returned with a stainless steel pan. Steam curled from its surface. He bent and sniffed at the dark-brown liquid. "Chocolate?"

"Homemade fudge," she amended with a nod. "Now get into the ring."

He obeyed but raised his brows mockingly at her. "Sex and fudge? Hmm, don't usually have a sweet tooth—but I can feel one coming on."

She followed him into the ring and suppressed a grin all the while. He unquestioningly sat his bare ass down on the red vinyl and hissed as the cold surface touched his skin. Slowly, he lay down so that he looked up at her.

Standing with her feet apart, she tipped the pan and dribbled the thick liquid onto his belly. He flinched then sighed when the heat, just on the verge of scalding him, cooled enough to be bearable.

"Look, honey, not that it's a bad idea, because everyone loves fudge, but can I ask what the fuck you're doing?"

"Getting you ready to eat." Zoey moved the pan so that the candy dribbled over his nipples. He sucked in a breath, and a slow warmth curled into his groin. One by one, each nipple hardened.

"To eat?" he croaked.

"Yes." She aimed lower until the liquid trickled over the edge of the pan and onto his balls. Then she stepped over him. He could see all the zippers of her ass. As she continued to drip the sweet, sticky mess over his shaft, up until the head was completely covered with fudge, he reached up and slid down the center zipper. He heard her sharp intake of breath.

Tugging on the red leather, he brought her to her knees so that she straddled him with her ass in his face. He pushed her so that she bent forward on all fours, forced to set the pan aside. Raising his head far enough so that he could study her beautiful holes, he spread her cheeks wide. Her erotic scent wafted down to entice him. His mouth watered and he drew in a long, audible sigh of ecstasy.

And that was when he saw it. Right there on the tender flesh between the anus and the vagina, glowed a strange tattoo. The black and red design made him think of Chinese markings, or some sort of exotic symbol. An odd sensation slammed into him. Had he seen the tattoo before? Something nagged at him, yet his foggy mind refused to allow anything but the luscious ass to register.

Filing the discovery away for future reference, he gave in to the powerful urges that assailed him. Rolf reached down and swiped some fudge from his chest. As if to cleanse her, he smeared it up and down the garment opening, and ground it over the odd mark.

Zoey cried out. Her stifled, soulful moans went on and on, escalating with each stroke he took of her.

Rolf twitched and endured an extraordinary zap within his loins. And he knew a sudden need to plunge himself inside this woman that far surpassed any sexual experience in his entire life.

Chapter Eight

Zoey was shocked that he'd so expertly manipulated her *sencore*. Rarely had she undergone the rapture of this special sex-trick. Generally, for a Dorjanian, it took a connoisseur's touch and much experience to correctly influence a lover's satisfaction level with the *sencore*. Now, as he unexpectedly had the tables turned on her, she was trapped in an endless cycle of beloved orgasms, and she knew that she must have him soon.

He continued to pleasure her, and she rode the waves as she ravenously sucked all the fudge from his cock. He groaned and writhed beneath her expert fellation. She could detect the scent of his manhood mixed with that of the candy. Hunger overtook her as his sexual flavor burst in her mouth, and her tongue trailed the veiny hardness of his cock.

"You're an evil witch," he insisted with a groan. But she ignored him and continued to sample her dessert. She used her tongue like a rod of fire, slurping and sucking, and the fudge turned to lava as it dribbled down his hips.

But he chose to intensify the level of madness. His tongue flickered over the *sencore*, as if he thought it to be a clitoris, as if he knew it was *the* spot for ultimate gratification.

Zoey warred with the temptation to allow it to go on endlessly. What great, delicious ecstasy it was! But her training won out. Always following the orgasms of the *sencore*, a Dorjanian must mate. Complete satiation by way of coupling or full penetration in some manner, was the only way to stop the cycle so that further mating could occur later. Mere manipulation of the *sencore* alone served to feed an endless sequence of insatiable lust. All too aware of this risk, Zoey hurriedly licked his penis clean. Without further delay, she crawled forward with her back to him, sat upon her knees and took him in.

The answer to her suspicions would soon be relayed to her.

In the meantime, her head went back and she growled feline-like. She cupped her breasts and gripped them with desperate fervor. Another jolt of bliss washed through her system.

Donor and recipient transmission environments safe to nidal *route. Repeat. Transmission environment safe.*

She smiled with confirmed relief and joy. Just as she thought! The *compubot's* message confirmed her suspicions. But she didn't have time to rejoice in the statistical message. Rolf neared his release.

"Son of a bitch!" he howled. His body went taut. Every single muscle tightened into hardened cords. Stilling her movements to allow him time to gather his control, she stroked his tense thighs. His hands came up to grip her hips. It didn't take him long—he was ready to proceed. With the strength of a wild *wofler* in the Stalton Forest of Dorjan, he pumped her up and down on his rod.

A guttural cry filled the room. Rolf spilled his seed safely into her. The alcohol they'd both consumed fed their bloodstreams and served to preserve the little *gametes* en route on their journey to the *nidus*. Which was why she'd requested that beer be delivered to his cottage, and why she'd demanded that Ivana see to it that he'd had a couple of martinis before being sent to her.

And it was also why she had prepared herself and consumed a full bottle of wine within the last couple of hours.

Zoey collapsed so that her back lay against his chest. She executed a quick mental scan. Her internal *incubot* did not signal fullness. Therefore, it was necessary to proceed as planned.

Data transmission. Subject ninety-five point six percent complete. Warning, subject ninety-five point six percent complete. Portalship *in repair,* portalship *in repair.*

But her risk had been worth taking. She shivered at the thought if King Luran ever discovered her chancy behavior. Thank the comets above that her selfish plan had worked. Otherwise, her *datochip* would be stripped from her, and would, thereby, leave her as an insane and nonproductive Dorjanian citizen—stranded forever on Earth. Not to worry, though, she thought with an inward sigh. Stores were safely higher than the last calculation.

And alcohol had become her one saving grace!

A knock sounded upon the door.

Rolf gathered her close and sighed, his softening manhood still within her wetness. He groaned in protest. "Tell whoever it is to go away."

You're not done with your Dorjanian contribution yet, Rolf.

"Come in," Zoey called out.

The soft swish of a door opening and closing preceded a shuffle of heels across the tile floor. "Hm, fudge," one voice said. "Too fattening."

Zoey knew it to be PJ.

Sascha came into view. "Yeah, it'll go straight to my thighs."

"Who gives a shit," Zena said on a snort. "Men'll pay to fuck us whether we're blubber or babe."

Katya stepped down into the ring and slithered on all fours to the fudge-splattered center. "Yeah, but this babe is going to get the acting part if she has to suck Mr. Mahoney off all night long."

* * * * *

Rolf's eyes popped open. Katya was going to blow him? No, it was the last thing he needed—the last thing he wanted.

Especially now, he thought as he inhaled Zoey's wild scent. The leather of her costume glided pleasantly over the sticky goo on his chest. In his mouth, he savored the lingering taste of fudge mixed with her tantalizing flavor. Why he'd zeroed in on the area between her pussy and asshole, he hadn't a clue. He'd never been fascinated by that particular section of a woman's anatomy before now. But it had tingled against his tongue and drove him to levels he'd never been to before.

It made him want only her.

Forever.

He jerked at the thought and Zoey rolled off him. Katya eyed the candy plastered to his chest.

He ignored Katya and allowed the red warning lights to flash in his head. Forever. He hadn't even realized the word was part of his vocabulary. What was it about Zoey? In a couple of short days, he'd gone from an independent, gun-shy playboy, to a pussy-whipped, one-woman wimp.

"What's the matter, Mahoney?" Katya purred. She trailed a nail over his belly and licked the chocolate from her finger. "You're not a one-shot wonder, are you?"

His ego reared up and bit him in the balls. "Hell, no."

She swiped some more from him and forced her finger into his mouth. "Then what are you waiting for?" He suckled the fudge from her fingertip in order to avoid being choked and stabbed by a painted, fake claw. "You have half a dozen ladies here waiting to pleasure you."

At Katya's words, Zoey's gaze met his. There was something there. Was it a flash of jealousy, or did passion still prevail? Her eyes glistened in a kaleidoscope of colors, so very unusual and unique…and so familiar.

"Stand up," she ordered, and rose to tower over him in her fudge-spattered, red get-up.

Though his head spun pleasantly from the alcohol he'd consumed, he dragged himself up and stood in the ring before all the hungry eyes. Gazes caressed him, devoured him—and his penis tingled, engorging with renewed blood.

"PJ," Zoey said. "Get the two boxes of cellophane. The rest of you, lick him clean."

PJ nodded and went to retrieve the boxes.

"Cellophane?" Rolf mumbled. Mobbed, he stood stunned as several tongues slurped over his abdomen and chest. Moans and heavy breathing echoed around him. He clamped his teeth together when a mouth closed over one of his nipples. Rolf looked down to see his sex swallowed up by Zena's wide mouth and his sac sucked off by the sable-haired little hot chick who'd dropped into his lap after the lineup earlier today. Lust washed over him. He struggled to regain control, to remain unaffected.

But it was useless. He'd had too much to drink. The alcohol intensified his pleasure and drew it out to tempting levels of bliss.

"That's enough. Don't let him come," Zoey warned as PJ returned with the boxes. Groans were heard, but they all obeyed and stepped away. PJ yanked out the clear wrap, slapped the free end upon his chest and circled him. She wound the plastic around his shoulders and his arms so that they were pinioned at his sides.

"What the fuck…?"

"Don't worry, they're going to do the same thing to me," Zoey assured him, and he saw pure desire in her eyes as she looked down to see his cock jutting from an opening they'd left between the strips of cellophane. Slowly, she unzipped her leather costume and pushed it down her body. It was the image of unadulterated perfection. From the abundant breasts peaked with light-brown areolas, to the narrow waist and flared hips, she was an absolute stunner. Her labia bloomed smooth and pink, the juices glistening upon the flesh of the clean-shaven lips set in the hairless vee of her mound. And her legs! Jesus, he hadn't been a legman before now, but he'd never seen such long, lean perfection in his entire life!

Zena snatched up the other box and pressed the loose end to Zoey's back. Around and round she circled Zoey. She bound her breasts and secured her arms, covering her stomach and back. But Zena didn't leave those gorgeous legs for his continued perusal. Instead, she wound the plastic around them.

Forcing them together, she left a hole only for her crotch. One last strip was torn from the tube and wound around her head so that her mouth was completely covered. Finally, they lowered her onto her back so that she lay upon the floor of the ring.

As PJ continued to circle him, she wrapped him in much the same mummy fashion, with one exception. His legs were wrapped individually rather than together as Zoey's had been.

And he was starting to get the picture.

No upper body contact, no touching, just plain old animal mating, organ-to-organ, thrust-to-thrust, hard to wet. And obviously, due to Zoey's plastic gag, no kissing.

The beast awakened within him. His penis rose higher and hardened to granite. Carefully, he fell to his knees. They stuck to the plastic of the ring floor, and he knew it would afford him the friction he would need to drive himself into her without the aid of his arms.

"No, no," Katya said with a tsk. "Hold it right there."

Rolf paused in his pursuit of his helpless prey. Glancing up, he watched in horror as Katya splattered massage oil across the surface of the ring.

"What the hell are you doing? Now I won't be able to—"

"Precisely," she cut in wickedly.

She rolled Zoey back and forth and coated her like a piece of meat for the frying pan. More oil sloshed under her form and Katya slid Zoey across the surface toward Rolf. He looked down at the glistening, stunning mess she made. Her eyes were limpid pools of colorful passion while her breath came in heavy spurts from her nose. Through the cellophane, he could see the blur of dark nipples atop rounded mounds. Below those perfect mountains, the valley of her navel rested within the flat plane of her belly. And lower still shone the opening that drew his gaze like a bee to its hive. He was ready to sting her there, but, given their states of restraint, he knew the task would be a difficult, awkward one.

And the challenge of it fueled his libido and made him rock-hard. Already, the head of his dick moistened with his own pre-cum. Excitement coursed through his veins in a mad rush. He couldn't wait to sink his cock into that luscious slit of hers!

"Well, what are you waiting for?" PJ and the group of call girls perched on the raised edges of the ring like spectators at a rodeo. "Go get her!"

Laughter filled the room, but Rolf found no humor in the situation. It oozed carnality in its most elemental, absolute form. He lowered himself onto the greased floor, surprised when he fell onto his back and slid a bit too far from Zoey. But he would get there, one way or another. He rolled onto his stomach, and the oil now covered the entire circumference of his body. A groan escaped him when his stiff rod was coated and slid silky-soft over the plastic. With each bend of his knees, inchworm-like, he slithered and propelled himself closer to his goal, which further intensified the erotic sensations. His balls ached for release. He couldn't wait to plunge himself into her hole. Rolf wanted nothing more than to claim her once again, to sate himself between her legs.

Finally, he reached her side. She watched him closely, her eyes now full of desperate need. Carefully, he maneuvered himself so that he could thrust his body against her and send her sliding over to the opposite edge. When he had her secured against the ring's elevated rim so that she wouldn't slide away from him, he wiggled up onto her hip to enable him to reach her cunt with his mouth. In its framed cellophane window, her moist pussy shimmered decadently. The lips glistened with pearly white sap. A spicy scent drifted up to entice him. Mouth watering, he bent his head and buried his face in the open hole, reveling in the muffled moans that erupted from her bound lips.

* * * * *

Holy Luna! Zoey was already about to combust. The muzzled and restricted sensation coupled with the vulnerability of her bared nude body and *pless* nearly equaled euphoria.

Against the gag of the wrap, she moaned and growled deep in her throat. The icy fire of his talented tongue dipped into the basin made by the cellophane's hole. A heavy warmth spread through her core and settled deep in the marrow of her bones. With her legs wound tightly together, the tip of his tongue could barely reach her passage. The urge to spread her legs and rear up gripped her with mind-boggling intensity. Wetness pooled in the folds of her sex.

"Here," she heard Katya say. "Make yourself a cocktail."

Collective giggles rang out.

Rolf lifted his head. The bliss ebbed and disappointment nagged at her womb. Engorged almost painfully, she desperately needed him to continue. Glancing down toward her hips, she watched as Katya tipped the bottle of Amaretto liqueur and held it poised over her exposed flesh. *Oh, yes, more alcohol to ensure the safe transmission of* milt. It was a secure tool to allow her to thoroughly enjoy herself without guilt or worry. She poured the container until the dark-gold liquid dribbled from the narrow mouth of the bottle. Zoey held her breath, certain the fluid would sizzle as soon as it came into contact with her *pless*.

One by one, thick, cold drops splashed onto her clit. A thrill slammed through to her soul. Katya filled her juncture with the alcoholic drink, and Zoey was certain Rolf's response would delight her. And it did. She whimpered against her closed mouth as he ducked his head and slurped up the liquor from the cup of her vee. The alcohol had a cooling yet fiery feel to it. Coupled with the swipes of his tongue, it was as if a campfire sat upon her crotch and sparked and sputtered into a roaring flame.

But it seemed Rolf could take no more. Gulping down the last drop, he wiggled and moved so that he lay parallel to her.

"Zoey, work with me, babe," he panted as he rolled and pushed against her body. "Try to prop your back against the side wall of the ring."

Still somewhat slippery, she made muted attempts at squirming. With his strength and determination, and her efforts, they finally achieved the position he sought. Now facing him, Zoey saw a raw passion in the depths of his eyes. Like stormy clouds, they promised excitement and power yet to come. There was just enough space between them where she could glance down and see the fully erect, slick mass of his manhood. It sent a renewed wave of desire through her.

Her gaze moved back to his eyes, and she tried to speak. Her words emerged muffled and frantic, but she could tell that he immediately understood her plea. His eyes glowed with sympathy-laced passion.

"I'm going to stick it in now..." His deep voice cracked with breathy emotion. He aligned the head of his cock with her lips. Her clit engorged and throbbed against him. But he didn't stick it in right away as she'd hoped. Rolf closed his eyes and pressed a long, gentle kiss upon her forehead. "I'm going to make love to you, Zoey."

Every orbit of every planet in every galaxy of the universe ceased their motion. He drew back and stared deep into her eyes. Tenderness shimmered in the depths of his gaze. Swirls of heat slammed into her. Warm as the waters of the Dorjan Sea, his deep and alluring stare bewitched her with beauty and dangerous things alike buried in the depths of them. And they soothed her and left behind a delicious tingle everywhere those cerulean orbs touched her.

Her heart swelled and her pulse shifted from erratic to nonexistent.

But not for long.

He probed between her legs and buried himself in one sharp stroke. Her back slammed against the edge of the ring. Zoey gasped closemouthed. Never in her entire Dorjanian life had she been taken with her legs clamped together. The bombardment of sensations overwhelmed her to insanity. The pressure against her clit was almost unbearable yet so utterly blissful. She yearned to wrap her arms and legs around him, and being denied the instinctual movements further aroused her.

Rolf had the luxury of a full, openmouthed growl. Then he dipped his head and rooted at her cheek. With his teeth, he located the edge of the wrap that had been wound around her head and over her mouth. Holding his cock still within her, he dragged the binding down and exposed Zoey's lips. She sucked in a ragged breath at the precise moment his mouth came down on hers like a *portalship* during a crash landing. He took her mouth and the tight Y between her legs with a simultaneous, reckless abandon. Plummeting and withdrawing, he drove into her with the ferocity of the wild, legendary Dorjanian *zimute.*

Time and time again, he plunged into her mercilessly, his arms bound, his cock free. Against her mouth, he whispered, "They're watching us, Zoey. Does that turn you on?"

She nodded and could only reply with a whimper. Though she'd totally forgotten about their audience, the concept of it did give her a charge. Tuning in her *audiotrap,* she listened to the random moans and "yes, yes!" screams that echoed throughout the Orgy Room. Their little show had obviously aroused the Bunnies of the Ranch. The thought of it pleased Zoey and further intensified her own excitement.

He panted and kissed her tenderly. "It is a turn-on, I agree," he said as he stroked himself inside her wetness. "But I want to be alone with you next time. Will you grant me that?"

His plea twisted her heart into knots and resulted in an unfamiliar ache deep in her chest. "Yes, Rolf," she murmured against his mouth. "After this night, I will come to you, and we will make love alone."

As if her promise had been all he'd needed to push him over the edge, he moaned, "Oh…here I come!"

Zoey was there, too, and at the exact same moment, her clit spasmed against the oil-slicked surface of his *ketka.* Stars shattered behind her eyes and shot their fire through her raging system. Asteroids of pleasure slammed into her core. With her legs so tightly pressed together, she was able to squeeze and hold onto the bliss of it for eons. Then, as sweetly as the phenomenon had occurred, it ebbed.

But it no longer tantalized her to have her arms and legs restricted from reaching out to him. "PJ, Katya, anybody. Release us at once."

As Zoey waited for the women to disentangle themselves, a zap went through her. It traveled from her *compubot* to her brain receptor. A gasp escaped her.

"Zoey..." Rolf kissed her mouth with a gentleness that would normally have taken her breath away. "What's wrong?"

What was wrong, indeed. The transmitter's message echoed loud and clear in her mind.

Attention, attention, compubot *ninety-seven point seven percent complete. Initiate plans for flight preparation. Repeat. Initiate flight preparations.*

Chapter Nine

Two days ago, that important transmission would have been welcomed.

Zoey stared into Rolf's worried gaze. Saturn and Venton, how could she leave this man behind! But she had no choice. An entire species depended upon her safe return with adequate *gamete* stores. It wasn't as if she could change her plans at the last minute and pass the task on to someone else.

As the sole *astrolage* left on Earth, Zoey had an obligation. And, except for his potent *genetoid* material, it did not include this man.

The thought both frightened and saddened her. Her eyes stung with unshed tears. Oh, to never see him again! Sudden panic seemed to snarl its vicious fangs at her.

"Katya, hurry! Get us out of this mess!"

"I'm coming, I'm coming." Katya made her way carefully across the slippery ring. She knelt beside first Zoey, then Rolf, and released the binds with careful upward cuts of the scissors.

"Thank you," Zoey said. She sat up and rubbed her raw skin. Cool air assaulted her moist flesh and her nipples tightened. Already she wanted him again. With a sidelong glance, she watched as he shed the plastic and stretched, his graceful body rippled with powerful muscles. "Now, leave us, please."

PJ chimed in. "You want to be alone in the Orgy Room?"

She didn't look at them. Her eyes were trained on Rolf, and his surprised gaze infused her with another wave of desire. "Yes, now hurry. Go!"

None of them argued. With a mad rush, they gathered their garments and shuffled from the room, pulling the door shut behind them.

"Well," Rolf said, his dark hair mussed in a rakish style, "if it weren't for the fact that they were getting paid big-time for their services, I think every one of them would have gotten their feelings hurt."

She didn't so much as smile. "I want to be alone with you." She took a step toward him.

He backed up cautiously until he could step one foot out of the slippery ring.

She followed his path and continued to track him as she stepped onto the tiled floor. "I want to be able to wrap my arms around you, to hold you close." His eyes flared with desire. But still, he moved further from her and appeared to enjoy his sudden new status of hunted.

The more he moved away, the closer she got.

"I want every constellation in the universe to hear my cries of ecstasy when you fill me with your stiff cock. I need to wrap my arms and legs around you and be seduced with raw masculinity and male prowess."

His eyes flashed with glowing lust. She watched as his *ketka* engorged with his excitement. "God damn, you sure know how to turn a man on!"

"Before I have to go, I want you," she said, and backed him into the pit of tiny balloons, "to make *love* to me like you do in your dreams."

The backs of his calves pressed against the outer wall of the pool of balloons right below the slotted net opening. Zoey could smell a mixture of the cellophane aroma that still clung to his skin, along with the oil and his own human scent. Inhaling deeply, she etched every fragrance of him, every cell of his body into her brain's *datochip*. She watched, mesmerized, as confusion flickered through the gray of his eyes like a powerful Dorjanian hurricane.

"What did you say?" he croaked.

"I said, I want you to make love to me like you do in your dreams." She raised a hand and pressed her palm to his bare chest. Like silk over granite, it beckoned her to touch, to caress. And she did.

"My—my dreams?" He caught her hand in his and stilled her movement. Her eyes rose from the glorious hardened pebbles of his nipples, to those orbs of bewilderment.

"Yes, Rolf, your dreams." She dipped down, took one *tetron* between her teeth and bit gently until she elicited a throaty response from him.

"Stop it," he said on a gasp. "I can't think when you do that."

"You don't need to think." Her hand slid down over his tight abs and found his jutting *ketka*. Enormous with renewed lust, she could barely span her fingers around its circumference. Gripping it firmly, she stroked its long length, and fluttered her eyes upward until she could snare him once again with an unwavering stare.

He hissed in a breath. "Jesus, Zoey, can you—" His hand covered hers and ceased her fondling. The tides of his eyes moved over her face with indecision. "What do you mean, my dreams?"

She pulled her hand from him and wrapped her arms around his neck. Looking deep into his eyes, she replied, "I've been visiting you in your dreams since the first night you arrived. I tied you up, I ravished you, I took your seed…and I loved you to utter distraction."

* * * * *

The shock of her words barely had time to sink in before her eyes formed into those of the siren of his dreams. Shimmering like a scattered mass of various gems, the multicolored irises bewitched him. The longer she held his gaze, the easier it was for him to see. Then the stars appeared, one large one in each eye, and the black pupils faded. Twinkling white quasars held him spellbound. It was carnal power in its most primitive form.

And it frightened the fucking hell out of him!

"What, are you some kind of freak or something?" He heard the panic in his own voice, but there was no stopping it. His pulse pounded with both desire and alarm. The heavy hard-on he now sported wouldn't take no for an answer. Yet his intellect told him the amaretto he'd sucked from the cup formed by her luscious cunt and closed legs, must have been laced with some form of lunacy.

She didn't appear to take offense at his accusing tone. "No, not a freak," she replied with a sultry tone. She pressed her lips to his and snaked her tongue out. "Just a…foreigner." And with that, he zoned in on the strange accent. He'd gotten used to it, but now he heard it loud and clear. Aha, so she was from another country. Then how did that explain the dream nonsense?

But he didn't have time to ponder that thought. The scent of the plastic wrap faded as her sex-perfume soared up to grab his libido by the balls. Though she hadn't directly drunk any of the amaretto, its sweet and spicy flavor, mixed with her own musky taste, swam in her mouth, and he knew she had gotten it from his kisses. The thought of it further inflamed him, and he slid his arms around her tiny waist. Pressing her abdomen against his throbbing cock, he dove into the kiss and savored every drop of her.

She threw herself at him with a growl. Together, they tumbled into the pit of small balloons. The squawk of latex against latex resounded in the room. As they settled into the bouncy softness, the music of her moans filled his ears. On top of him, she kissed him voraciously. Her small tongue darted and probed, chased and retreated. A sweet ache of something unfamiliar perplexed him and settled in the region around his heart.

"Rolf..." she panted and rained kisses over his mouth, his cheeks, his neck. "Promise me you'll never forget me."

Given their short acquaintance, it would normally be an odd request. But he understood, somehow, that an urgency prevailed here, something real and bigger than his world.

"Oh, Zoey," he groaned. "Oh, honey, I promise. I promise."

Tiny, glimmering, unshed tears pooled in her eyes. His hands shot up and cupped her face. Behind him, he could feel the firm-yet-supple smoothness of the balloons against his backside. They sunk lower surrounded by the bubbles. It was as if they floated on a cloud of air. With a sudden voracious need, he drew her down and slammed her mouth against his. Fire torched him from the soft command of her lips against his, down his entire front side where he pressed her lithe form into his body. He had her trapped in his arms, so she had no choice but to wrap her arms around his torso. One hand skimmed down and cupped her firm ass and left a brand of handprints upon her naked flesh.

His tongue plundered hers, darted around, in, out. If he didn't have the support at his back, he would surely collapse, for his legs trembled with weakness, his hands with awe. She flooded into him, her taste, the alluring scent, the warmth of her hard little body against his. Then she rose up and moved her hips in a daring dance as she stroked her slit over his cock. Her pussy embodied the ultimate slickness and heat, pure, elemental animal. He filled his palms with the globes of her breasts and watched heavy-lidded as she threw back her head and moaned out her pleasure. Tweaking the nipples simultaneously, Rolf pulled and rolled the hard pearls between his fingers. But she didn't seem to be able to tolerate it. With awkward yet purposeful movements against the bumpy bed of balloons, she aligned her wetness over him and plunged herself downward.

"Oh!" He heard himself groan it out as if in pain. The shift of weight drove them deeper into the rubbery bed. And it drove him deeper into her passage. Tight and hot, sticky and silky smooth—every possible pleasant sensation bombarded him at once. He wanted to drown with her, to be buried completely in their mutual needs.

Suddenly, he had an urge to feel her close. Reaching up, he hooked his hand behind her neck and yanked her down so that her breasts covered his. Together they sank into the cavernous, latex pit. A cocoon of clouds enveloped them in a protective shield.

But he realized he could never get enough of her, never get close enough, and a panic blended with sadness and impending, inevitable loss filled his heart.

* * * * *

"I want you," he panted. "I want you more than I've ever wanted any woman." He combed his fingers through the loose tendrils of hair at the base of her skull, damp wisps that had fallen loose from her ponytail. In one smooth move, he had her mouth on his devouring it with the expert tool of his hunger. His other hand busily kneaded one breast. At the brush of the erect nipple against the callused surface of his palm, blazes of desire shot through her system. And she felt herself go helplessly wet around his cock.

She opened her eyes, broke free of the kiss and grappled for control. Zoey wanted to delay the extraction of his seed and what could possibly follow—one hundred percent *nidal* capacity and her subsequent departure. And yet, she could not resist him. The cylindrical rock of his *ketka* abraded over her internal erogenous spot and made it virtually impossible to delay the inevitable coming orgasm. The scent of the rubber, the faint trace of chocolate, and his natural aroma filled her nostrils and fueled the assault. The flavor of her juices and that of the sweet amaretto and fudge continued to flow through his mouth into hers. It was all a potent combination that proved too much for her to fight.

And his eyes…oh, those eyes! Twin torch flames, they scorched her restraint and melded it into an undeniable, desperate carnal need. She jerked her gaze away, fearful that the look in his eyes would shove her over the edge. Uncertain if this would be the final extraction, she dreaded the moment of his ejaculation.

He lifted her chin until she was forced to look into the heated turquoise eyes.

"I've never met a woman like you before," he said, his voice raspy.

"Never?" She clamped her lower lip between her teeth. Conversation—anything to delay his release.

"No. You're just what I've been looking for all my life." He drew her mouth to his again and Zoey knew she had to have relief. Yet, to seek the completion of her pleasure would mean his, as well. Which would mean that this could possibly be their last encounter. If he filled her with enough of his *milt*...no, she didn't want to think of what would happen!

"No, wait..." She attempted to squirm out of his hold, only to cause them to sink deeper into the pit as she lay sprawled over the top of him. "I can't—we can't—oh..." His hand snaked behind her and located the one spot she'd prayed he would not think to use against her. Her *sencore.* The fire of one hand raced down the cheek of her rear while one finger from his other hand massaged and stroked that sensitive spot near her anus.

The orgasms crashed into her. It hurtled her through the cosmos past every star and nebula, through every dust cloud and black hole. She was on an endless journey of mind-shattering euphoria that tumbled on and on. At his mercy, she sobbed and begged him to stop, to not stop, to go slower, to accelerate his ministrations.

"Rolf!" she cried and tears streamed down her face. "Rolf, please..."

Through her narrowed eyes, she looked down to see him hold hard to her *sencore,* and she knew he was trapped in the endless cycle with her, unable to cease giving her such pleasure.

"You..." She panted and jerked with each spasm that racked her. "You must stop."

"Zoey…I—I've never seen such beautiful abandon from anyone. Come again, babe, come again!" With that, he reared up and clutched her to him so that he could reach the *sencore* better.

"No!" Stars, how she wanted it, but the tempting cycle had to be broken. "Come inside me first, please."

His eyes were glazed and icy like two of the moons of Dorjan. "Oh, babe, you're such a hot lover, so horny!" But he complied. Removing his finger from the *sencore* he wrapped his arms around her waist and fell back into the cushion of balloons. It didn't take long. He clutched her body and pistoned her up and down on his rod. By the sudden onslaught of fire, Zoey was certain he stroked her there again. Yet it was his rod alone that brought her such *sencore*-like bliss. The thickness of his cock plunged deep inside her. His strong arms lifted and pounded her down upon him. It went on and on in wave after wave of pre-come pleasure.

Rolf lifted her time and time again. She dug her legs into the rubber and clamped them around his hips. In response to her move, he rammed himself deeper inside her. She didn't think the sensations could get any more delicious, but ecstasy called to her, wetness flooded her inner walls. Gasping for air, she craved release yet fought to delay it.

She'd never felt such an indefinable connection with anyone else before now. There was something…something about him she couldn't define. As he moved her in a dancing rhythm, she planted her hands on his cheeks and leaned down to press her mouth to his. Now she tasted amaretto and martini mixed with a desperate need and her own passion-juices. His tongue met hers with an equal fervor, and they sang the song of lovers, groaning, moaning. He pumped her frantically now, grunting and panting like a savage, as his taut muscles glistened with slick perspiration.

Then the white-hot waves of ecstasy reached out to caress her. It started as a vague tickle deep inside her where the tip of him moved up and down over that special spot. As if someone had injected her with a hallucinogen, fire and ice, pain and pleasure suffused through her whole body from her crotch all the way out to the tips of her fingers and toes. Immediately following the blissful sensations, a second wave of rapture slammed into her more powerfully than a typhoon.

She screamed out her relief and let out a simultaneous groan of remorse.

His hot, pulsating release erupted inside her. He held his moan on a tight gasp, spilling the precious seed within her *nidus*. The electrical zap of conduction jolted through her veins. It didn't take long for the *compubot* to transmit the information to her *datochip*.

Warning, warning! Nidus *at ninety-nine point four percent volume per* metrospace. *Repeat. Ninety-nine point four percent. Prepare for* portalship *launch following final sample extraction at one hundred percent capacity. Repeat. Prepare for* portalship *launch following final sample extraction.*

*****

She was sprawled belly-up on the balloons. The rise and fall of her breasts as she struggled to catch her breath brought him to life again. He'd almost dozed, but suddenly, his radar geared up for round—what, three?

Damn it, would he ever tire of her?

"Come here," he demanded. Hooking his hands under her arms, he dragged her upward and turned her so that she faced him. "You've still got some chocolate on you."

Gorgeous, he thought as he rubbed her womanhood against his half-hard cock. Deliberately, he guided her further up and over him so that her soft folds were perched over his mouth as she sat on her knees and straddled his head. The pussy lips were pink and swollen from the sweet, loving abuse of his rod, her clit just as engorged as he was. From his angle between her thighs, he could look up at the underside of her breasts, and an electrified surge shot to his loins. Above the perfect twin mounds, he could see her lovely face as she looked down at him with anticipation. She waited for the first flick of his tongue, poised for the coming onslaught against her sensitive flesh.

"Tell me you want me," he commanded as he positioned his tongue so close, he could nearly taste her already. He inhaled deeply, smelling his own sex-juice there within hers. Then he blew on her tender folds and watched as her clit twitched in response.

"I want it." Her breaths came in shallow, quick spurts. Golden brows drew together as if she worried he wouldn't deliver. "Please, now," she begged.

He held her firmly away from him. "No, tell me you want *me*," he reiterated.

"I want *you*," she wheezed impatiently, and slammed herself onto his face.

She tasted of bitter cocoa, sweet nectar, womanly sex, his own semen. He swiped his tongue upward over her lips and found the hardened nub. Gripping her hips, he held her firmly to him, and she turned to stone against his tongue as she trembled on a sharp intake of breath. He gazed up at the length of her flat belly, across the mounds of her breasts, and she threw her head back with the throes of rapture.

As if time would soon run out, he moved her up and away, and pressed her back onto the bumpy surface. "Hmm..." Leaning out of the net slot, he gripped the handle of a nearby cart and rolled it closer. He scanned the various food items and reached for a small stainless steel pitcher. "How about heating things up a bit?"

At the surprised flare of her eyes, he defiantly tipped the container. She hissed when icy-cold, sweet cream dribbled over her breasts, across her quivering belly, and into that luscious spot between her thighs. She writhed and grasped at the balloons, her nipples hardened to sharp buds. The contrast between the white liquid and her honey-toned skin was startling, beautiful, appetizing.

He licked his lips and hunched over her to begin his feast.

She planted her hands on either side of his head and lifted him until she could stare into his glazed eyes.

"Make love to me," she begged. "No more kinky stuff. Just love."

He watched as the pupils of her eyes dilated, and he could swear he saw glimpses of those white stars flickering deep within them.

"Zoey," Rolf breathed. He spanned his grip over her hips and moved up her rib cage. Her words had stirred a tenderness inside him that had struck him as unfamiliar, daunting and thrilling all at once. "Oh, how I *could* just love you."

"Your bed," she said urgently as she gestured toward the door. "Take me to your bed."

Yes, he liked the sound of that!

"Come with me." He rose and reached for her hand. Together, they waded naked through the multicolored balloons to the net opening. He climbed out and lifted her through the slot. In one corner, a door led to an open shower stall. He drew her to it and turned the knobs so that the massaging pulse of the water whooshed out and steam rose upward in a soft misty glow.

Rolf guided her in, stepped in behind her and quickly rinsed the stickiness from his naked body. Next, he soaped up his hands, preparing to cleanse her. When she shifted, the water pulsed over her shoulders and she stiffened.

"Relax. No kinky stuff. Let the hot water ease the tiredness from your muscles, and wash the oil and candy from your skin."

He turned her so that she faced the tile. She pressed one cheek and her palms against the wall.

"Ooh…" she sighed as he scrubbed her from neck to ankles, then spun her around and washed the front of her where tiny remnants of chocolate mixed with cream spattered her front side. Her skin was silk and satin against his palms, soft and yet taut with healthy self-discipline. Streams of bubbly water poured over her puckered nipples and made a sensual path down her belly. Sluicing into her navel, it channeled between her legs. He took a moment to gently cleanse her pussy, drawing a tortured gasp from between her clenched teeth.

She clamped her eyes shut as he moved to her hair and pulled loose the fastener of her ponytail. The glistening mass tumbled over her breasts and he thought of sunbeams slanting across snow-covered mounds. He flipped open the shampoo bottle. Squirting a liberal amount in one palm, he worked the cream to a frothy mass. Then he raked his hands through her hair. He brought the strands to a sudsy lather, and with firm pressure and quick friction, he scrubbed her scalp until she moaned with bliss. With her eyes closed in relaxed ecstasy, he didn't know which tantalized him more, to see her like this, or in the throes of sexual passion.

Finally, he tipped her head under the spray of water, combed his hands through the silken strands, and rinsed every bubble of soap from her hair. As if it were the finale of a magnificent round of lovemaking, her body suddenly sagged against him.

Rolf turned off the water and gathered her close. He reached for a fluffy towel and rubbed every inch of her body down until her skin glowed pink. He wrapped her in the cloth and looked down into the limpid pools of her extraordinary, sultry eyes. There was no feasible explanation for her claims of visiting him in his dreams, or the sudden transformation of her beautiful eyes, but at the moment, he didn't require one. There was an urge to do nothing but protect and care for her—strange, considering he generally formed no attachments to his women friends.

But this one had somehow become more than just a friend, more than a lover.

Lifting her into his arms, he carried her into the Orgy Room and snatched up his pants as he passed by them. He held her close, moving quickly toward the door, his own body still naked and wet. She hooked her left arm around his neck and rested her head against his shoulder. Rolf held her close as he felt for the doorknob and stepped out into the corridor. His heart swelled with a varied range of new, unfamiliar affection, and it surprised him yet somehow, it didn't. How a connection could be forged in such a short time, he didn't know. But he couldn't deny it. It was there and he wouldn't discount it for a minute.

The sounds of laughter, music and sexual propositions drew near. Rolf stared straight ahead as he carried Zoey through the lounge and parlor where a dozen or so guests were being seen to in various stages of welcome. Katya and Zena and the others who'd been summoned to assist in the Orgy Room, were now otherwise engaged and capitalized on the unexpected free time to earn some extra cash.

The drone of activity suddenly stopped. Every eye was on him, but he didn't give a damn. Zoey was all he cared about. True, he was nude and probably presented quite a shocking picture, but she was wrapped safely in the towel, her calves and arms the only skin bared.

"Nice ass and, um…wow, would you look at that cock!" he heard from a woman guest who clung to a man who, in turn, clung to PJ. "Ya know, honey, maybe we should make that threesome a male/female/male instead of a female/male/female?"

He caught Sascha's stare as he made his way by the bar. Her gaze flicked down to his crotch and her pink tongue slithered out to lick her blood-red lips. "Yes. What a shame he ain't sharing it…"

Ivana locked eyes with him. Obviously pleased, she merely nodded with a gleam of victory in her eyes. Rolf snorted inwardly. Victory because he'd offered a very steep fee for Zoey, and it was now apparent—his nakedness and bold claim of his woman were most likely her first clue—that he wanted only this woman.

But he was willing to give Ivana the universe for Zoey. Nothing short of a disaster would keep him from her.

He glanced to the side and caught a glimpse of Gypsy. With her arms folded under her breasts, she shot him a venomous glare. The scorn of a woman, he thought. Truly scary.

"Who's that babe?" one male customer chimed in and nodded toward Zoey. But Rolf kept walking. There was no way in hell he would give her up.

"She's not up for grabs," Ivana replied, shaking her head. "No…definitely not up for grabs. However, we might be able to come to some sort of exchange agreement if you know of an available accountant…"

Rolf looked down into Zoey's upturned face to determine if she'd caught any of the innuendoes. Her eyes were limpid pools of dazed color. It was as if she were in a trance, as if the shower had drugged her into complete submission.

And she looked adorable enough to eat.

He headed across the room to the far corridor. Various perfume and alcoholic scents wafted to his nostrils, but Zoey's fresh-soaped aroma overpowered them all. Anxious to get to the bungalow, he strode hurriedly over the deep-red carpeting. Pushing against the bar across the exit door, they emerged into the desert night. Cold air assaulted his moist skin. The sounds of the Ranch faded as the door clicked shut behind him. And he rushed across the patio to the far gate.

"Rolf?"

"Hmm?"

"Instead of making love," she whispered huskily, "can we just snuggle?"

He sighed heavily. His world rocked and rolled, tilted and spun on its axis. Her words were precisely his sentiments. "You betcha, babe."

She settled against him, her body warm and relaxed against his chilled skin. He had to restrain himself, for the urge to race to his door assailed him with a painful ferocity.

* * * * *

Zoey nearly cried out as he laid her gently upon the mattress. He climbed in and gathered her fiercely to him, then pulled the thick comforter up and tucked it in around them. She turned so that her back was to his chest, and the inferno that ignited inside her breast had nothing to do with sex.

He cradled her in his arms. In her heart, contentment warred with the heavy burden of dread at leaving him. After their next encounter, she would never see him again, that she was sure of based on the percentages. Her *nidus* would, no doubt, be filled to capacity.

Dorjan would survive.

And across the vast distance from her home—here in a world that was not hers—she'd found a man who knew how to bring her to the throes of utmost elation.

He was a man who knew how to still her heart.

"You play the part well, Zoey," he murmured groggily in her ear. "You're worth every cent I allotted out of the budget."

His words didn't surprise her. Since he now knew her to be the accountant, she was aware he said them in jest. But she was also aware he assumed she'd eventually give in and accept the acting role.

"Yes, Ivana's accounting woes are now over."

He chuckled softly and sighed.

As she lay there and listened to his breathing, resentment at a sudden interruption simmered in her system. Her *compubot* began to transmit data to her, disrupting the contentment.

Notice. Portalship *repaired and readied for launch. Following final extraction, report to original site of landing. Repeat. After final extraction, report to* portalship.

She closed her eyes tight against the tears. It wasn't as if she could delay a *manoyear* or so to complete that precious extraction. Though her *nidus* could preserve samples an average of up to two Earth-month's equivalency, Dorjan needed her immediately.

Tonight would have to be the night. Once they were both asleep, once they'd both rested for a bit and the alcohol had metabolized from their systems, it would be vital to go to him in dream-travel.

And she'd be forced to say goodbye.

In a matter of minutes, she heard his even breathing and twined her hand into his where it lay upon her breast. "I love you, Rolf Mahoney," she whispered softly enough that, even if he were awake, he wouldn't have heard her. On a whimper of sadness, the heavy clutches of exhaustion overtook her.

Chapter Ten

"Zoey..."

She stirred, reveling in the warm cocoon that cradled her. She wanted to stay here forever in his arms and forget about Dorjan and King Luran's demands on her.

Shhh, don't talk Rolf. Sleep. Cherish this last night we have together. She sighed and snuggled deeper under the covers.

"Zoey," he said again, and her eyes fluttered open. Something wasn't right.

"Rolf?" Clearly she was in the dream-travel state, she knew that by the sudden lightweight sensation of her spirit. Yet Rolf had awakened *her*.

"I don't know how this happened," he explained as his voice echoed behind her in the realm of dreams. "But I awoke to this out-of-body feeling, like that time I dozed in the BunnyRanch parlor. It was you I went to, I understand it all now."

She glanced over her shoulder to see him propped up on an elbow looking down at her. His soul hovered just out of the boundaries of his body, as did hers. The misty form of him was just as appetizing as his conscious-state body. Her gaze sliced down over the hard body, down to his full arousal. Heat coiled in her gut. Swift need assailed her.

"Rolf...how...?"

"I don't know," he said on a groan, and he pressed his erection against her ass. "But I do know I want you again."

She couldn't delay the final extraction. The *portalship* was, at that very instant, being readied, all prior malfunctions now in working order. Dorjan awaited her arrival with the precious stores of cells. They required her safe return for ongoing life. But more than anything, she needed him inside her, if only to compound the memories she would take with her, to sustain her for the remainder of her existence. To help her through the lonely *manoyears* ahead, she'd already made the decision to put in a request to King Luran for one of Rolf's seed samples.

She'd accepted that she could not have him. But she would have his child.

"Come with me, Rolf, on a journey through dreams," she replied and turned to face him. She offered her hand and he took it without pause.

Together, their spirits rose away from their physical bodies. They moved through walls and space until they floated over the BunnyRanch. The parking lot was full tonight. More clients pulled in as their headlights sliced through the cool desert night. Zoey didn't have to tune into her *audiotrap*. Festive music and laughter drifted up to them, and she knew it would be another profitable evening for Madam Ivana.

Zoey led him over rocky terrain with rolling high hills of sagebrush and bushy foliage. Below them, wild mustangs galloped across the barren land. The scent of fresh night air and wildlife surrounded them. Up they went, farther still until they reached the highest snow-tipped peak of the Sierras. A crisp breeze caressed their bare skin, invigorating as the winds whipped and waned in random succession. The moon glowed fat and yellow tonight, and she could feel its gravitational, orgasmic pull against her internal *compubot*. Pale, gold light slanted across craggy, ice-covered rock and left dark shadows here, shimmering planes there.

It was a mirage, moonlit and breathtaking. And it gave her a sense of tranquility to share it with him.

"Wow!" Rolf drew in a deep breath. His eyes gleamed with boyish excitement.

"I wanted you to see the beauty of what I saw when I arrived here." They hovered at a slanted angle and gazed down over the jagged rise and fall of mountain peaks. Nestled down in the valley, the BunnyRanch stirred with activity. Moonlight peeped intermittently as pale gray clouds crossed its lunar path. Off in the distance, the twinkling lights of Carson City could be seen. But here, at this place high above the hustle and bustle, serenity and the utmost peace dwelled with nature.

He nodded and wrapped his arms around her from behind. "It's sometimes hard to see from a jet, but you're right, it's beautiful."

She didn't bother to correct him that her mode of transportation had been far from a jet. It would do him absolutely no good to be told about her *portalship* or Dorjan or anything else beyond his realm of comprehension. But when she'd passed over this exact spot weeks ago, she recalled how it had touched her so very poignantly. At the time, she'd wished she'd had someone to share it with, someone to enjoy all the majestic power of it.

Her wish had come true.

She covered his arms with hers. Leaning into his broad chest, she sighed, and the landscape shimmered in her vision as she looked at it through sudden tears.

Asteroids alive, I don't want to leave him!

"Remember, you promised to never forget me." She choked it out, and his response was to spin her around to face him.

"Zoey, honey, what's wrong?"

She let the tears fall, if only to clear her vision so that she could look up into the magnificence of his face, illuminated just now by the moon's soft yellow beams as a cloud passed overhead. With a trembling hand, she cupped his jaw, marveling at the roughness of the short shadow of whiskers against her soft, sensitive flesh. He turned his mouth into her hand and kissed her palm, re-igniting the desire that simmered below the surface.

"I'll be leaving..." She said it without taking her eyes from his. There was something twisted in the fact that she hoped to see pain, or, at the very least, disappointment in his eyes. "Tonight."

"Leaving? What do you mean, you're leaving?" His voice rang indignant, and, yes, she detected a measure of pain. In his eyes she saw panic, and the blue of them glowed with something she couldn't quite define.

Relieved at his relatively calm reaction, she sighed. "My job here is just about complete, and—"

"That's ridiculous," he cut in with an edgy laugh. "An accountant's work is never done. Especially now that..." His words trailed off. His eyes suddenly snapped with uncontrolled rage, while his hands bit into her upper arms. He shook her, his face contorted with sudden anger. "You're lying. This has nothing to do with your job. You're not done with your job—you're done with *me*! Aren't you? *Aren't you?*" he growled and pulled her against his chest.

"No!" She'd never seen him like this before. Despite the wild accusation, love swelled in her heart. The heat from his dream-body diffused into her. Warming her blood, it awakened a deep-rooted lust.

"God, I feel like a used harlot!" he snarled.

His arms were suddenly around her, as if to punish her with his ardor. He squeezed her so tightly, she was certain it would send her plummeting back to her physical body. Her breath caught as he buried his face in the crook of her neck. There was no tenderness in it. Desperate passion, wild and ferocious, overtook him. She had no choice but to slide her arms up and wrap them around his neck.

He kissed the flesh where the column of her throat merged with her shoulder. Swirls of pleasure spun in her gut.

"Okay, so you're leaving the BunnyRanch." His voice was muffled against her neck, and his tone was as if he tried to talk himself into accepting it. "No problem. Then you just pack up and come to Malibu with me. I'll find you a job. Hell, you can take the acting—"

"Rolf."

"You can be in my movie—"

"Rolf, I'm not going to Malibu with you, either. I'm not going to be in your movie. I have to go."

His head snapped up. "Where?" The anger was back. His eyes flared with panic.

"Back home. It's…it's a long story."

"I have all night."

"Rolf. You wouldn't understand."

"Try me." His expression clearly challenged her. But she wouldn't back down on this one.

"I'm leaving. I'm sorry, but it's imperative. And that's all I can say." *Pluto and Mercan, why did it hurt so bad to be so strong?*

He sighed and kissed her softly. "Don't leave me," he whispered, his lips warm and coaxing against her mouth. "Please, don't leave me." There was a desperate, almost hate-filled pitch to his voice. It alarmed her, so much so that her pulse thudded in her chest.

"Rolf…" She raked her hands through his thick hair and lifted his head away from her face, holding it between her hands so she could gaze deep into his eyes. And her words wedged in her throat at the sight that she beheld. The entire galaxy, every bit of mass in the whole universe, ceased movement.

Tears. He had tiny diamond-like tears in his eyes that glistened by the light of the moon.

She drew in a painful breath. They both panted with an odd mixture of desire and anguish. The cold wind blew around them, ruffling his hair into a wild, rakish mass. There could be no pain, she determined, like the pain of leaving a loved one—forever.

"Oh, Rolf. *Oh, Rolf!*" she cried.

And they came together in a violent clash. Thunder suddenly rumbled around them. An abrupt torch of fire erupted and surrounded their embraced bodies. Lifted up into another realm, warmth flooded flesh, the scent of a far off sea filled lungs, the cry of a seagull echoed from afar.

Zoey opened her eyes. The moonlight continued to bathe them from above, but a glorious new mirage surrounded them. They now stood in some sort of tropical forest in a dimension even she hadn't ever ventured to. The lunar light pierced through the overhead limbs in glorious spears, yellow, pink and neon green. Their skin glittered with multicolored moon-dust. She could hear the rush of a great sea in the distance and could feel the gravitational pull of three different moons.

Her *compubot* zeroed in on the scents of various classes of plants and flowers and identified them not of Earth and not of Dorjan. There was a pleasant warm mist in the air and it permeated their muscles like a soothing balm. Within seconds, Zoey's already charged libido reached levels of ecstasy she'd never before encountered.

"*What* in the hell…?" Rolf gasped and tried desperately to hang on to her. "Oh…my…*God!*" he shouted, and the timbre of his voice rose and reverberated across distant, unknown lands.

"It's okay," Zoey said with a weak yet reassuring tone. She pressed one hand against his chest and attempted to catch her breath. Euphoria such as she'd never experienced—even surpassing that of *sencore* stimulation—slammed into her. It rushed through her system like a tsunami of the Dorjan Sea. "Ride it. Ride the waves, *mica,* just let go and go with it."

Rolf's eyes suddenly glowed blue, like that of Earth's day-sky. She'd never seen them actually *glow* before, and concern for his safety, even in her blissful state of existence, gripped her. "*Mama Luna,* Rolf… Are you all right?"

He threw his head back, all the while grinding his erection into her stomach. "Oh, yeah! Oh, yeah!"

"I'm sorry…I'm so sorry…if this is too much," she said through clenched teeth as current after current of intense orgasms rolled through her system. She wrapped her arms around him and inhaled his unique, spicy scent, trying frantically to zone in on something to distract her from the overwhelming euphoria.

"*I'm* not sorry!" he bit out as he seemed to ride another wave. Zoey looked down then and noted that he hadn't ejaculated. She was certain he experienced the same level of orgasms she did, yet he didn't appear to expend any seed.

Oh, *diona*! Would it all be for naught? Ninety-nine point four percent *nidal* capacity—she was so close! Well, there was only one way to find out.

"Rolf."

"Oh..." he said on a sigh. His skin glistened with moon-dust and perspiration. Like a rogue, his hair was mussed and wind-tossed. And she thought she'd never seen him look more breathtaking than at this very *manosecond*. "What...? What is it?"

"Make love to me."

"Make love to you? Well," Rolf chuckled. He leaned back against an enormous tree she quickly classified as the largest in the entire universe. "There's not really a need for that, now, is there?"

The tree had various limbs jutting out from its base. Zoey located one that was low and thin enough for her to grip, yet strong enough to hold her weight. She grabbed the limb, drew herself up and clung to it while her body dangled near Rolf's.

"Take me. Take me now! I want you inside me when all this bliss washes through me."

* * * * *

Rolf let the wave pass, then looked up at Zoey where she hung poised in a chin-up position. Her small biceps were flexed, her elbows bent. She held her chin above the scraggly limb while her luscious, glittering body hung with her knees out, as if she sat in an invisible chair. Her legs were apart, and he could see the sap of her pussy gush out with each orgasm that he was sure she experienced.

Licking his lips, he stepped between her legs and draped them over his shoulders.

With a long indrawn breath, he took her scent into his lungs. His eyes closed and he fought the next oncoming wave of ecstasy. He wanted to save it for her, for that one special moment when he drove himself into her wetness, but there was no fighting the inevitable. She whimpered when his mouth closed over her sex-lips. Smooth, silky and hairless, her pussy gave him every reason to devour it. The warmth of her inner walls fused into his tongue as he speared her, and he longed to have it wrapped around his hardness. She convulsed against his face, bucked and cried out. Rolf gripped her hips and swiped his tongue upward, swirling over the hard little bud.

As if he were on an endless cycle of bliss, his body responded yet again. Never in his life had he been able to achieve such unfathomable sexual heights in such massive, successive quantities—and all with little to no manual stimulation. But he was determined that with the next orgasm he would be inside her.

"Zoey." He heard the harshness to his tone, but there was no denying his need. "I have to have you—now."

Her musky scent taunted him, her flavor tempted him to continue his feast. He looked up at her, over the sexy belly, across the amazing breasts to the kaleidoscope eyes. They blazed with white stars of desire. His heart pitched and spun uncontrollably in his chest. And his manhood was about to explode by merely looking at her.

Panic flared in her eyes. "No! No, please. Not yet."

Her legs clamped so tight around his neck his next words came out in a rasp. "No? Why? I know you want it just as much as I do." He disengaged her legs and hooked them around his waist. "Don't deny me, Zoey. Don't ever deny me."

"Rolf..." There was sadness in her tone yet the unbridled passion could not be discounted. "No...please, can we just hold each other?"

He chuckled hollowly. "Oh, I'll hold you, all right. But I need to be inside you. *Now.*" With that, he aligned himself with her hole and shoved his cock deep inside her.

"Ah!" Zoey cried out and clung to the branch. He stroked her body up and down the length of his cock twice more before she panted, "Rolf…I…I'm going to miss you."

He didn't have time to explore the meaning of her words. There was one thing utmost in his mind, and that was to reach the pinnacle once again, this time with her entire warmth wrapped around him. The glitter-dust danced upon the shafts of moonlight, coating their bodies and enveloping them in a warm glow. Rolf held her hips against him as he stood there below the tree limb. The beams of ecstasy reached for him. He took her nipple into his mouth and suckled her sweet flesh, flickering his tongue over the taut pearl.

Once more, he lifted her, forcing her down upon his jutting sex. Zoey screamed and her voracious melody echoed through the strange forest. It was her body's convulsions and the quick spasms of her passage that brought him to his next peak. The beam lanced him, injecting fire and ice and tenderness into his soul. He ripped his mouth from her nipple and buried his face between the fullness of her breasts. Standing there, feet apart and his hands clamped over her ass, he exploded inside her like a bomb.

Within seconds of her soft cries and his own release, she let go of the limb and threw her arms around him. They spun for an eternity in a vortex of sweet, adoring affection. Something was different, quite odd to be exact, and he struggled to define it. But before he had the chance to catch one last breath, he lifted his head and looked into her eyes.

Gems of multicolored tears dotted her cheeks. "Good-bye, Rolf."

Dizziness engulfed him. Her face contorted and her body lifted away from his in a convoluted mist. He was cold, suddenly so very cold.

"Zoey…" His arms were heavy. He could barely lift them, but he fought the weakness and reached for her, grasping only at air.

"Good-bye, my *leetah*!" Her hand went up to cup his cheek. The palm branded his ice-cold skin.

Then she was gone.

"Zoey?" He pivoted around and stumbled over vines and tree roots. The moonbeams flickered out, leaving him in total darkness. "*Zoey!*" he growled. The last thing he recalled was the sound of his own voice echoing through dark space and the feel of his body as it spiraled into nothingness.

Chapter Eleven

Something nagged at him. In his deep state of unconsciousness, he remained aware of an urgency that surpassed his body's demand for rest.

Wake up, Rolf! Wake up!

He groaned and rolled his head from side to side. Gradual alertness seeped into him. Nausea roiled through his gut. Pain lanced his head like a sharp javelin.

Son of a bitch, is there a fucking elephant sitting on my head?

He opened one eye and winced, then promptly closed it. Inhaling deeply, he tried again, this time, both eyes. By the silver light of the moon, the ceiling spun like a top, but if he concentrated just so, he could make it stop for short intervals. He chanced a quick shot at the clock. 4:38 a.m.

"Wow." His voice was raspy and a bit too loud for his own ears. With a lower tone he said to himself, "What d'ya know. I've got a goddamn hangover." And it rankled him, since the last notable one to speak of had been the night of his first Oscar. But that had been years ago. Since then, he knew how to handle and hold his alcohol, and he vowed never to allow himself that kind of self-inflicted bullshit again.

He smacked his lips together and rolled his tongue around in his mouth. It was stale and dry, but the remnants of something…hmm, something delicious, lingered there.

What was it…?

His eyes narrowed. His head snapped to the right to find the bed empty, the pillow dented from her head. A whoosh of blood slammed through his veins.

"Zoey!" Without bracing for the painful throb in his head, he leapt from the bed. "Goddamn it." He snatched a crumpled pair of jeans from the floor. Jabbing his legs into them, he quickly located his sneakers and slid his feet in while zipping the pants. "Zoey, where the hell are you?"

The last thing he could remember was that awesome, euphoric dream with her. Within that one fantasy, he'd had more wet dreams than he'd had during his entire adolescence.

Hell, my whole life has changed in the few days since I met her.

Something drew him out of the bungalow into the biting, cold, desert mountain air. He ignored the chill against his bare chest and the tightening of his nipples. He could be naked in the arctic and he would find her. Nothing would stop him.

Descending the cedar deck, he glanced from side to side. His eyes fell on the BunnyRanch.

It didn't take him long to reach the door. With purposeful strides, he moved down the long corridor, past the bar and into the parlor. He ignored the sweeping glances of the girls and the envious looks of the cavorting customers as his gaze searched the room for her, but she was nowhere to be found.

"Where is she?" he asked, his words directed at Gypsy. She sat on a small divan near the door in a black two-piece, revealing-yet-businesslike pantsuit. Her duty as doorgirl in greeting the patrons and introducing them to the lineup of ladies of the evening seemed to be wearing on her. Slumped in her seat, her glassy gaze was fixed on the ceiling.

She fluttered her gaze down and sent him a smoldering look that continued to speak of a woman scorned. "How should I know? You're the one who carried her through here hours ago like some arrogant, strutting peacock."

His blood simmered with impatience. "Where's the madam, then?"

Gypsy made a play of inspecting her French-manicured nails. She shrugged. "I don't know. Maybe in her office."

He didn't dally. He flew up the hall, taking time only to jiggle the knob on the accounting door. It was locked and darkness seeped from below the door. He pounded on it, and called Zoey's name but got no reply. Within seconds, he was up the hallway. Lifting a fist, he banged on Ivana's door.

"Who is it?" Ivana barked.

"Rolf Mahoney," he snapped back.

There was a long pause, then, "Oh, well, come on in."

He did just that. He shoved open the door, strode into the room and raked a hand through his hair. "Where is she?"

Ivana arched one auburn brow. Her gaze swept his half-naked body. "She? I presume you mean Zoey?"

"Of course I mean Zoey." He wouldn't allow her to play games with him anymore. "And if you don't tell me where she is, the remainder of my fee will be retracted."

Ivana stiffened. She made a sudden show of shuffling papers around on her desk. "I…I really don't have any idea where she is. One of the last times I saw her, you had definitely staked your claim on her."

His mouth hung open. He stared at her in disbelief for one long moment. "*One* of the last times? Ivana, where is she?"

She lifted her shoulders. "How should I know? I assumed she was in your care this whole time."

He planted his hands on her desk and leaned in. With narrowed eyes, he growled, "You *are* the madam of this joint, aren't you?"

She winced and leaned away from him. "Yes, I am. And I'd be delighted to present you with a new lineup of girls to make up for your…um, temporary inconvenience."

"I don't want a new lineup. I found what I was looking for in Zoey." He shoved away from the desk. "Now, where the hell is she?"

She tipped back in her chair. Steepling her hands, she said cryptically, "What's it worth to you, Mr. Mahoney?" She peered at him over her fingertips, her eyes dark-brown pools of hope.

"So, you do know where she's gone to. And you're going to demand further payment for the information."

With mock coyness, Ivana combed her long nails through her thick red hair. "I *am* a businesswoman, you know. You being a businessman yourself, should understand the importance of contracts and sealing deals—one of which, I might add, you didn't follow through with."

"Bullshit!"

"No," she said and propped her spiked heels upon the desk, casually crossing her ankles. "You made a deal with me for one of my *girls*, not my accountant."

He ignored the arrogant gesture. Pacing back, he planted his hands on her desk, closer this time, so that he could barely smell her syrupy perfume, so that he could see the defensive determination in her eyes. "And I amended that contract and paid you a handsome sum for her, did I not?"

She dropped her feet to the floor with a click and rose. Her eyes now spoke of defeat. "All right, Mr. Mahoney. There's no sense in rehashing this. I got what I wanted, you got what you wanted."

"No, not yet I didn't. Now...*where is she?*"

"I told you I don't know." Despite her stubbornness, somehow, he caught the note of honesty in her voice.

"What's your bottom dollar, Madam Ivana? I'm willing to pay you another bundle if you tell me where she's gone. What do you say?"

Ivana sighed. There was a shadow of regret in her expression, in the straight set of her mouth. "I'm sorry, Mr. Mahoney. It's a tempting offer. But she came in about thirty minutes ago and resigned. I truly don't know where she went."

Her words swung at him like a meaty fist. Resigned—with no forwarding address?

Sweat pooled in the space between his waistband and spine. "Well, why in the hell didn't you tell me that in the first place?" he shot over his shoulder as he flew from the room.

Retracing his steps, he sprinted back to the bungalow to retrieve his belongings. He'd just go and find her himself! But dread swirled in his gut along with a hefty dose of fear of losing her.

No. Don't think that way, Rolf, he told himself.

You'll find her.

But something stopped him in mid-step just before he reached the first rung of the deck stairs. A soft yet high-pitched tinkle filled his ears. It was soothing and sexy, and he immediately associated it with Zoey. Raising his head, he spun around until his gaze caught a distant beam of light across a barren field.

What in the hell is that?

The beam shone down like a spotlight on the set of a movie. Surreal, the sight made his heart race with awe. Perspiration trickled down his back and forehead, and his breath caught in his chest.

And that was when he saw her.

"Zoey." He whispered it, his eyes drawn helplessly to her as she receded, as she walked out of his life.

She marched toward the brightness with purpose and a sort of proud determination. Her lithe, womanly form was outlined by the glare of the light beyond her, and his pulse ticked as his gaze touched every familiar curve and plane. She wore a metallic-blue, one-piece jumpsuit that glittered and conformed to her body like a second skin, as did her knee-high, platform boots. He watched her hair flutter over her shoulders and down her back. His body tightened in response as he recalled the feel of those silky strands wound around his hands in the throes of passion. And her arms—ah, those slim arms that were adept at clinging to him—were down at her sides swinging in rhythm with her gait.

She'd never been more beautiful, more alluring. Already, despite the rawness of his overused flesh, his manhood filled with a rush of blood. Flexing his hands into fists, he inhaled sharply to tame the swift rise of desire, but it was no use. He closed his eyes and imagined her unique scent, the feel of her satiny skin against his palm, the tightness of her sex as it gloved him.

He wanted her again—and he would have her after he determined just where she was going.

Without further delay, he took long strides. His shoes crushed tiny sprouts of sagebrush and sent vermin away in a frantic scurry.

She approached the outer boundary of the beam and stopped, but only for a moment. He watched, transfixed, and his steps grew quicker, more urgent. She moved a pace forward so that the light enveloped her. Her hands rose and jagged green streaks zapped her. As if she worshipped a god, her head tipped back, her gaze trained above her.

"Zoey!" he gasped, but she didn't seem to hear him, nor did she appear to be alarmed or injured. It was as if the current energized her, as if she welcomed its power.

What in the hell…? Immediately, he thought of several different blockbuster, sci-fi flicks. Was this a damn movie set? And if so, how was it that he, as a highly involved Hollywood producer, hadn't been informed that such a shoot would be in progress during his scouting trip to Carson City?

Apparently, either someone had kept him out of the loop, or something very bizarre was in the making…

Rolf crept in closer. He could now see that the light was much wider in circumference than it appeared from a distance. Above her, where the streaks originated, hovered a huge round panel of multicolored, twinkling lights…like her kaleidoscope eyes. Strange tunes wafted to his ears, soft and low, high and pleasant. Delicious aromas, sweet and spicy, some odd and unfamiliar, some hers alone, enticed his nostrils as he approached the boundary.

He did a quick scan of the perimeter. There were no cameras, no directors set up in their chairs, no cast and crew watched from the sidelines. It was just Zoey and this eerie glowing thing in the pre-dawn sky.

"My duty to King Luran, great ruler of Dorjan, is complete!" she sang. "This leg of my great mission has met with success. Stores of Earthling *gametes* incubate safely within my *nidus*. I now humbly request transport to—"

"Zoey..." Rolf said, and without thought for its implications, he stepped into the ring of light.

She snapped her head down and zoned her gaze in on him. Her eyes flamed with gems of mystical power. A chilly wind whipped her hair in glorious waves about her body. Never had he seen her more gorgeous and desirable, so strong and powerful looking.

"Rolf!" Her arms were still up. The jagged green bolts continued to zap her.

"Don't go," he said with a warning tone, and he caught the trace of pleading in his voice. "I—I don't even want to know what this is all about. I don't even care. Just don't do whatever it is you're about to do. *Don't leave me!*"

"Request granted. Prepare for transport." The robotic timbre echoed throughout the space. Rolf's stare flickered, searching for the source of the robotic sound. It wasn't his voice and he was damn certain it wasn't Zoey's!

"No!" Zoey jerked her gaze upward. "Wait! He—he can't go with me. He'll die! Raketar, don't—"

A sudden streak snaked outward from Zoey's beams and struck Rolf in the chest. He collapsed to his knees and drew in a ragged breath. His vision blurred and a painful, quick staccato of screeches stabbed his eardrums.

Pressing his hands to his ears, he growled, "What the...hell...was *that*?"

"Rolf! Oh, sweet Jupiter, what have I done?" she cried. She lowered her arms, raced to his side and knelt. The first thought that entered his mind was relief. When she pulled him into her arms, instinct flooded his senses. She wouldn't be leaving him. There was something in her eyes that told him so, that took his breath away.

Her hand came up, warm and tender, and cupped his cheek. "You shouldn't have followed me…"

"No way…" he panted. He was dizzy again, and nauseous, and he vowed silently to forego the liquor for a long time to come. "No way…I'm letting you get away from me."

"But Rolf," she whispered as tears trickled down her cheeks. "Do realize what you've just done?"

He nodded and threw his trembling arms around her. The warmth of her body sent a pleasant shudder through him. "Yes, I stopped you from going…wherever the hell you were going."

"No, Rolf, you didn't stop me. Look," she said on a sob. Her hands gripped his head and turned it down and to the side.

And fear stabbed him raw and black. They were enveloped in a misty capsule, but he could see directly through the wall.

Right down at the receding globe of Earth.

A suction noise popped in his ears. The wall solidified. Earth no longer remained in view. The change left them within a space of nothing but portal holes, bizarre-looking lounge seats, a long slab of sorts at the far end, and a panel opposite that blinked maddeningly within the chilly, silver space.

He inhaled sharply and held the breath in his lungs. His eyes darted to hers. The conglomerate of colors had vanished, and in its place were the sea-nymph aqua irises of the woman who'd peered out at him from the BunnyRanch window that first day he'd met her.

"Rolf… No, *mulera,* no!" Tears streamed down her face. And he could have sworn he saw the light of love drip from her soul just before he collapsed at her feet and darkness enveloped him.

* * * * *

"Blood pressure seventy-four over fifty-two millimeters of mercury, pulse rapid at one hundred forty-three beats per manominute, *respirations thirty per* manominute *and shallow, oxygen saturation eighty-seven percent per* glomera *of blood, body temperature one hundred three point six Fahrenheit-scale degrees. Subject's status declining. Repeat. Status declining."*

"Tell me what to do, for Centaur's sake!"

Rolf's unconscious body completely covered the smooth surface of the *micramed*. Against the cold, black marble slab, his complexion appeared sallow. Zoey watched, horrified, as he struggled for every breath he took. Panic and frustration moved her to tears.

"Remain calm."

"Shut up, Raketar! That's not going to help!" she said to the voice that droned from the micro-speakers. She reached out to touch Rolf then snatched her hand back when he groaned and his head thrashed. "I have a heart, you know. Unlike your complex *botic* innards, I just cannot *remain calm*!" Perspiration beaded over his brow and across his naked chest. She trusted the *micramed's* calculations, which were based on magnetic macular computations, but how could she accept the fact that Rolf could be dying?

Tears brimmed in her eyes. "I can't go on without him." She choked it out.

"You would have done so anyway, had he not stowed onboard."

"But he would have been alive!" She threw herself across his chest and kissed his dry lips. His unique scent filled her nostrils, but the heat that emanated from his body alarmed her.

"Stand back. Warning. Stand back."

"For what reason?" she asked, glaring at the empty space above her. "He needs *somebody* to care, to do something!" Raketar was a computerized, faceless companion, but still, Zoey treated her as an equal. That is, until Raketar made unwarranted demands on her.

"Your own body temperature will make the Earthling's rise. Your weight will disallow for chest expansion, thereby compromising oxygen exchange. Your—"

She threw herself away from Rolf and the *micramed*. "All right, Rake, I get the concept. Now what? And please tell me you have a solution. *Please.*" Her own voice sounded shrill in the open space of the ship, utterly panicked.

The space within the *portalship* was long, angular and capsule-like. With cool silvers and grays, it deflected harmful radiation rays during travel, and provided a protective shield against meteor showers and catapulting random space objects. Even as the craft took hidden chasms and moved stealthily through black holes to reach Dorjan faster than the speed of light, it remained virtually impenetrable. The only risks were that of Raketar malfunctioning, as she had during their break into Earth's harsh atmosphere weeks ago. But self-repairing, Raketar was never down for long.

She now proved that fact beyond truth. *"Stand by and prepare for subject's entry into* medicoffin. *Repeat. Stand by for* medicoffin *initiation."*

Zoey watched and wrung her hands. The tubular *medicoffin*—known as one of the last space-travel resorts to saving a life—rose from the *micramed's* edges and materialized around Rolf. Within *manoseconds,* he convulsed, as all subjects did upon the sudden change in molecular atmospheric conditions of the unit. But he recovered much quicker than most. With relief, she saw that he relaxed, his breathing returned to a fairly normal pattern, and his complexion pinked up.

She paused with her feet glued to one spot, and asked hesitantly, "What are his stats now, Rake?"

"Blood pressure ninety-five over sixty-one, pulse regular at one hundred ten beats per manominute, *respirations twenty-two per* manominute, *oxygen saturation ninety-six percent per* glomera *of blood, body temperature one hundred point one Fahrenheit-scale degrees. Subject's status recovered but guarded. Repeat. Status recovered but guarded."*

Zoey sighed and collapsed into the nearest *nebuchair.* True to one of its many functions, it infused immediate relaxation and bodily repair into her system. Her own heart returned to a normal state of functioning.

"Rake?"

"Yes, Zoey Fabiyan of Dorjan."

"He isn't going to make it, is he?"

A long moment passed as Raketar performed some calculations. Soft varied tones tinkled over the speaker during computations. *"The estimation is that of a forty-seven point nine-seven-two-one percent likelihood."*

She drew up her legs, curled into a ball, and pressed her knees against her chest. The percentage was better than she'd expected, but not good enough. Her heart raced as she asked, "And if he should survive the journey home, what of his ability to withstand the Dorjan atmosphere?"

This one didn't take her long. *"Exactly seventy-six percent."* Raketar paused, humanlike, then added, *"But first he must survive this stellar voyage."*

Zoey dropped her head to her knees. There was no stopping it. Sobs racked her very soul.

She should have been more careful. She should have made certain to engage the *empyral shield.* If only she would have been more responsible, he would never have seen her or the ceremony of reentry with the *portalship.*

If only she'd have followed her strict rules of training, Rolf would be alive and well on Earth, instead of on the way to his grave on Dorjan.

* * * * *

Despite the *portalship's* extreme rate of travel, weeks passed, and still, Rolf did not awaken. Fed and cared for through *osmosis-tech* within the *medicoffin,* his vital signs had finally stabilized. Zoey studied him through the *medicoffin's portwindow.* Quasars, but he was so handsome! She clenched her fists. How she longed to touch him, to hold him, to kiss every inch of his body! Images of their phenomenal lovemaking filled her mind. She moved her gaze from his face, down over the sculpted chest…to his *ketka*. Though it lay nestled and soft within the dark bed of curls above his sac, it still had the power to stir her blood. Zoey inhaled and closed her eyes. She imagined those strong arms around her, the wall of his chest pressed against her sensitive nipples, his sex buried deep inside her. As if he was awake and out of the chamber, she could smell his male scent, taste his kisses.

She had to have him again! He must live! Without him, her life would be meaningless and dull. Clamping her lower lip between her teeth, she once again doused the temptation to go to him in dream-travel. He was gravely ill. It would be utterly selfish of her, not to mention highly dangerous for Rolf, if she were to travel to him while he labored in his comatose state of consciousness.

Please, Lord of the universe, give him the strength to survive my world.

She pressed a hand to her belly and caressed it, knowing his seed thrived within her *nidus*.

Heaven forbid, if he were to pass away, not even King Luran would dare to keep Rolf's seed from her—would he? No. She would have Rolf, one way or another, dead or alive, the man himself or his baby…or, hopefully, both.

And no one or nothing would keep her from it.

"Prepare for Dorjan entry. Repeat. Prepare for entry."

Zoey's gaze snapped upward. "We're home?"

"We have been orbiting for two manodays *now."*

And she had noticed little else but Rolf throughout the entire trek.

"My calculations determine the atmosphere is now stable enough for portalship *entry."*

Zoey crossed to the far *portwindow*. Peering through the circular glass, her pulse fluttered at the sight of the three moons of Dorjan, one oval and bright red, another gray, round and pocked—much like Earth's moon—and the last a pale-green, crescent sliver. She moved her gaze to the right and there, nearly filling the whole space of her vision, hovered the enormity of Dorjan. Round and deep-burnt orange, it took her breath away. Dark swirls of blue seas embraced green-dotted red-land masses. More than twice Earth's size, over half of its surface was determined to be uninhabitable. Opposite this solar system's sun, the other side of Dorjan was one solid cap of ice. With the gravitational pull of its three moons, Dorjan's orbits around its sun, as well as its own rotations, were far different and unique in comparison to Earth's predictable cycles.

Dorjan was a rare planet within the entire universe, in both the astronomical sense and the practical habitat sense. Pride swelled within her chest. Seeing its familiar beauty after months of absence made her long for the comforts of her home and the tranquility of the territory she'd claimed as her own, a right granted her following her last successful space journey. She slanted a look at Rolf, his profile now aglow as the white sun sliced a beam through a far *portwindow* and into the *medicoffin*.

It was simply a miracle he'd survived this far. What would happen after entry into the atmosphere and landing at the king's *Cruxcentre*? She knew the first step would be to quarantine him. Zoey, too, would be placed in special temporary airtight quarters for the purpose of ruling out any foreign disease transmissions brought on by Earthling contact or space travel. Nonetheless, she would be debriefed through protective partitions within the laboratories of the top-secret *Cruxcentre,* and her sterile *nidus* stores would be extracted and set for dispersion.

The dispersion being that for female impregnation in order to replace the large male population that had been lost due to disease—the *whole* reason for her mission.

"Nebuchair *safety recommended during descent. Repeat.* Nebuchair *recommended."*

Zoey obeyed and sealed herself in the protective oval chair. It soothed her and sent warmth and a tingly relaxation through her tense shoulders and spine. Her stomach fluttered at the sudden plunge the craft took. It was a sensation she would never tire of, never dread. But she wondered if Rolf felt the same excitement. Was he comfortable and content within his world of unconsciousness?

As the vessel made its approach to the outer Dorjanian atmosphere, Zoey swung her gaze to his unmoving form. He appeared not to notice the descent or the change in atmospheric pressure, or the return of pleasant scents and sounds and sights that were unique to her homeland.

He appeared to her to be dead.

For the love of Orion, please let him live!

A tear pooled in the corner of one eye. She just couldn't go on without him. How was it possible that she had amassed the strength to leave him behind in the first place? Now that he was with her, though incapacitated as he was, she vowed to never let him out of her sight again—if he survived.

And Zoey knew all too well what he would be up against.

Dorjan's atmosphere was similar in chemical structure to Earth's. Photosynthesis occurred in much the same manner, yet the difference in air quality could be attributed to namely one species of the *jaculondor* tree. A deep-red, massive tree with large bluish leaves, it competed for oxygen with Dorjan humans. Extinction of the invincible tree had been attempted throughout the ages, yet failed at every turn. To counter the problem, Dorjanians kept planted and well cultivated, stores and stores of rich greenery to contribute to the oxygen demands of the people. And while Dorjanians required oxygen as Earthlings do, they could survive on several percentage points less.

Which concerned Zoey. Raketar's estimation of seventy-six percent survival rate for Rolf if he were to endure the atmospheric transition was not as positive as it sounded, given the oxygen issue he would have to contend with.

She chewed on her fingernails as the *portalship* broke through the outer ring, and the walls around her turned translucent and misty once again. At a breakneck speed, the rust-red land rushed toward her. Off in the distance, upon the Great Craggy Rock, could be seen King Luran's mighty castle. Perched above the aqua Dorjan Sea, it had started as nothing more than a huge *zelmur* boulder. Soft yet durable elements intrinsic to Dorjan allowed for *zelmur* rock to be easily etched and hollowed out for shelter. In this case, Mystic Castle's history was such that it was the oldest and largest *zelmur* on the entire planet of Dorjan—with the exception of many more on the Iced-Half that were unattainable.

"Prepare for landing. Repeat. Stand by for landing. Atmospheric pressure within normal range. Land-base notified of approach."

The craft sailed toward the Great Craggy Rock and dove low. "So we're reporting to the Castle's most serious quarantine labs…?"

"Affirmative. Orders have been transmitted to Raketar to deliver Zoey and Earthling directly to King Luran's lowest level laboratory. Repeat— "

"Ah…Rake, zap it, would you? I heard you the first time."

"Once you've both cleared the initial security stages of the Castle's most crucial laboratory, you will then move upward to the main Cruxcentre *in which you will confer with King Luran concerning your journey."*

Her stomach clenched at the thought of that initial meeting with the king. How would she explain her negligence in forgetting to throw up the *empyral shield*? She cringed inwardly. Its use was an elementary tactic that any rookie *astrolage* would utilize. Indirectly, its lack of use was what had put her in this precarious position to begin with—well, that and the forbidden emotional involvement with her subject. Regardless, she would no doubt, be reprimanded in some form or another by Dorjan's great ruler.

"Prepare for debriefing, quarantine procedures and sentencing for improper practices."

"Sentencing?"

"Renowned and esteemed astrolage, *Zoey Fabiyan, has never performed any mission warranting sentencing for unacceptable procedures – with the exception of the current operation."*

She was driven into her seat as the ship hit an unstable pocket of gas. Ignoring the turbulence, she asked softly, "Does…does the king know…everything?"

"All data and relative information are being transmitted to the king per Dorjan codes and Raketar's programming." Though the voice had been announced in its usual emotionless monotone, Zoey could swear she heard a faint note of pity.

She stared unseeing at the blinking data board and dashed a tear from her eye. To finally be home…but the homecoming would be bittersweet, indeed.

The vessel plunged toward the volatile sea. The ship hovered before the closed doors of the lab, designed to be positioned in the bowels of the Castle for near, yet distant and safe control by King Luran's *astrolages*—Zoey's own colleagues. The wall of the Great Craggy Rock jutted upward smooth and steep with various openings, each covered with its own *lazarshield* door. The *portalship* held itself suspended until the lowermost green *lazar* door dissipated.

"Prepare for entry into quarantine laboratory. Repeat. Prepare for entry."

But there was nothing that would ever have prepared Zoey for the sight that met her eyes when the ship rocketed through the open space and landed inside the lab's arrival hub.

Chapter Twelve

She slowly unfolded herself from the *nebuchair*. As she did so, the craft settled onto the landing pad and dissolved around her. All that was left was Rolf in the *medicoffin* as Zoey stood nearby on the silver platform. Surrounding her were hundreds of King Luran's soldiers, all voluptuous females, and all enclosed in protective quarantine suits. With their deadly *bazor* weapons aimed at her, she stiffened, but did not say a word.

The one in front, her eyes barely visible through the slit of the black headpiece, hissed, "Don't move! If you value your life, don't take even one step."

She held up her hands. Her heart stroked her inner ribs with a painful rhythm. Though she moved not a muscle, small beads of sweat trickled between her breasts. She'd never returned to the lowermost bowels of the *Cruxcentre* before. All of her missions had been within their solar system and short in terms of space travel. None had required this sort of strict homecoming, nor clearance in such a secure, threatening manner. Though she was one of Dorjan's most prestigious, highly acclaimed *astrolages*, she'd never before seen or experienced firsthand this particular hub before now.

"There's no need to point your *bazors* at me. I'm not going to attack, nor am I dangerous in any way." She slowly lowered her hands and scanned the many black, one-piece suits. In unison, they jutted their weapons at her. The swish of their choreographed movements echoed in the spacious room. She snapped her hands up in reflexive response and a chill of dark fear went up her spine. It was ominous the way they treated her, as if she were an outsider, an alien invading their planet.

As if she were not a Dorjan citizen.

"King Luran," she called out and raised her eyes to the high, metal-beamed ceiling. Her words reverberated in the massive expanse of the domed room. "What's going on here?"

"Zoey," came the familiar, scolding voice, yet it held a tone of weakness that was uncharacteristic. "You have defied standing Dorjan orders. You know that aliens are never to be brought here unless specifically sought for scientific studies—*and unless prior permission and security clearance is granted!*"

"It was an...accident." She lifted her chin in defiance, but her hands remained in the air. "I called out to abort takeoff. I requested to wait until the Earthling had exited the zone. My appeal was ignored—er, undetected...oh, Sovereign King." She lowered her eyes, knowing what his next words would be.

"Any well-educated, seasoned *astrolage* should know that throwing up an *empyral shield* is the first most inherent security measure to take during *portalship* contact!"

His voice, though somewhat shaky, boomed throughout the lab. Zoey had rarely been on this side of the king's wrath. In fact, she was usually the top captain to dole out punishment and reprimand those in training. But apprentices had the excuse of being in training.

She didn't.

"Yes, my lord—"

"Put your hands down!" he barked. Zoey winced and mentally turned down the volume in her *audiotrap*.

She immediately obeyed and lowered her arms. But she wouldn't allow herself to be humiliated in front of her own associates. It was time to switch tactics. She took one hesitant step forward and lifted her gaze to the lofty ceiling where his voice seemed to hover over her in a black cloud of scorn.

"If I may offer, Your Majesty...I have successfully collected and incubated massive stores of compatible spermatozoa of the Earth-kind. It is highly probable that each and every last one will result in a successful *genetoid* match with our abundant population of fertile *incubot* females. My mission, though altered, has been fruitful."

There was a long pause in which silence prevailed. For one split *manosecond,* she wondered if she'd turned the volume down too far on her *audiotrap.*

"Enough. You will proceed to full quarantine status."

She nodded, and the sweat in her palms cooled a small measure. "Agreed."

"Once you have been cleared, you will report to me immediately."

"Yes, sir."

"That will be all."

She clamped her lip between her teeth. "Your Lordship?"

He sighed. "You have already pushed your rank to its galactic limits, Captain. I said that will be all."

There was no stopping her next words because there was absolutely no way she could proceed to quarantine for any length of time without the answer. "What of the Earthling?"

A rumble sounded to her right. She started, and with a jolt, turned to see the *medicoffin* being showered in a pinkish mist. An ear-piercing suction noise followed. With it came the dissolution of the *medicoffin*...with Rolf inside.

She gasped inwardly. He was gone. And obviously, King Luran saw fit to not disclose his location.

"I repeat for the last time, Captain Fabiyan. That will be all. *Guards, escort her to full quarantine immediately!*"

The soldiers shuffled about and snapped into a foreboding stance with Zoey wedged inside their formation as their focal point. The clomp of their heavy boots upon the metal flooring as they marched in configuration gave her a sense of doom. Never had she thought she would ever be on this side of the king's harsh discipline. Dread swirled in her stomach and ate away at it like a deadly acid.

"To the far cell," one voice said, and immediately she recognized it as her best friend, Phebe. In the full-body suits, it was virtually impossible to distinguish who was inside. But she'd recognize that sweet, husky voice anywhere. Her gaze swung to the soldier in question who stood just behind her left shoulder. Through the helmet slits, she could see Phebe's dark eyes. Was she winking at Zoey?

She sighed and relief flooded her veins. Yes, at least she had one possible ally. Phebe had not failed her since the day they first met at King Luran's academy one galactic *manoyear* ago when the plague had just begun. An instant friendship had been formed, and hopefully, that bond would continue to hold strong despite her current position. Though Phebe had been passed over for various promotions, she'd never been envious of Zoey's status as one of the king's highest-prized scientific warriors.

Or had she?

As she was shuffled through a large portal into a small, medically equipped room, something struck her as odd. Phebe had still been a mere cadet prior to Zoey's trek to Earth months ago. She studied the rank markings on Phebe's upper left chest. Lieutenant Colonel. How was it that she had moved up so quickly in the ranks, and even surpassed Zoey's own status as a captain *astrolage*? Zoey herself had never even known this particular laboratory existed in the lower levels of the *Cruxcentre*. And now Phebe—not so long ago a lowly cadet—appeared to be in total charge of Zoey's fate. In addition, she seemed to be very familiar with this particular quarantine level.

"Everyone out." Phebe motioned to the soldiers. Obediently, the few who'd trickled into the room behind her receded. A *lazar* partition slid shut leaving a silver panel. The odor of antiseptic and metal assaulted her nostrils. Glancing about, Zoey noted rounded walls, the slab table and countless *megabot* machines surrounding it. Soft lights blinked on various panels while clicks, possibly data calculation tunes, sounded from a hidden speaker.

"Strip off your suit." Phebe's voice was tight and emotionless. She stood rigid, her *bazor* aimed at Zoey's chest.

"What, no 'hello, Zoey, how have you been' or even a 'what's up with the alien'?"

Phebe shifted her feet. Through the slot of the helmet, Zoey saw the eyes soften with what she thought might be a shade of guilt. But the voice remained dictator-like. "Remove your suit and lie down on the table. Now."

Her gaze shifted to the weapon. All it would take is one press of the button and a deadly ionic beam would completely fry her entire body. But on the other hand, if she chose to use her training, she could have the *bazor* out of Phebe's hand in *manoseconds*.

"Don't even think about it. We are not alone. You disarm me and we both die. The *megabots* have all been preprogrammed to protect Dorjan from your traitorous activities by releasing debilitating ionic gas levels within this entire space if you should resist. I am protected by my suit, but not for long."

"Traitorous activities?" Zoey heard the note of shock in her own voice. She stared into the dark eyes, and this time, she saw only determination and insolence.

Phebe reached out and hooked her gloved hand at the neckline of Zoey's jumpsuit. In one swift downward motion, she ripped the garment so that Zoey's breasts and abdomen were bared. Cold misty air permeated her warm skin.

"Yes. Selfishly narrowing your samples down to one Earthling, thereby decreasing the broad range of *genetoid* material available to save our planet. Then there's the *empyral shield* issue and bringing the alien with you. In addition, you contemplated staying with your Earth-lover and not returning to Dorjan—oh, yes, all of your thoughts and feelings have been transmitted from your own *compubot* to Raketar, and then directly to the *Cruxcentre*—"

Zoey gasped. She hadn't a clue that Dorjan technology was capable of such intrusion on one's personal life. When had this particular advancement come about? "You've been spying on me the whole time?"

"No, protecting my father's interests," she countered, and jerked one of Zoey's sleeves from her arm.

Cool air rushed over her flesh and tightened her nipples, but she ignored it, only having noted that one particular word that had come from Phebe's mouth. "Your father?"

She swiped the other arm free of the space garment. "For being such a smart *astrolage,* you sure are naïve. King Luran is my father, and I don't relish having to become the ruler if he dies."

"You're...*you're* the Dorjan princess that has been hidden from the world for so long? But you were a cadet."

Phebe snorted. "If *only* that were all I had to be! I infiltrated the academy at my father's insistence to choose one *astrolage* I thought capable of carrying out the crucial mission. *Imputee* that I am, I chose you. Now my father fights for his life while you, in the meantime, had been succumbing to the delights of your own selfish pleasures."

Zoey's heart skipped a beat. "He's truly dying?" She bent and unfastened her boots when Phebe motioned impatiently with her *bazor*.

"Yes, he has the *flekking* plague!" There was the distinct note of resentment laced with a trace of pain in her voice. "If you'd have returned just one *manoday* earlier, he might never have been stricken. Yesterday, he was strong and healthy—today, he's been diagnosed with the deadly disease. And you delaying your stay to have more selfish time with the alien will most likely cost my father his life."

Guilt washed through her, knowing her prolonged stay on Earth had been completely related to her infatuation with Rolf. She closed her eyes with a sigh. Without further instruction, she stripped the tattered fabric from her body and climbed naked onto the slab. Tears threatened to spill from eyes as she stared up into the bright lights.

"I'm...I'm so very sorry. But—but, I fail to see how my return, be it today or yesterday, could have played a role in curing the king or not." She placed her arms and legs in the indentations on the table. Straps clicked into place to hold her wrists and ankles captive.

Phebe set aside the weapon and reached for a pair of shielding gloves. She slid them over the protective quarantine ones she already wore. "In your absence, a highly possible cure has been theorized. With the Earth-male *milt* you carry within your *nidus*, it has been proposed that a vaccine could possibly be developed and used with its *genetoid* material. It has been discovered, as well, that Earthlings are immune to the disease, which is why a vaccine—thought to work for both prevention and curing the active disease—could be the answer." She placed her hands together and ran the gloved palms over Zoey's breasts, then down in a circular motion over her belly. Zoey watched as Phebe's gaze honed in on her flesh, never wavering, as if her eyes could see through the thickness of her skin. A *megabot* alarmed suddenly.

"*Attention.* Nidus *located at your exact hand position. Repeat.* Nidus *located.*"

Zoey shifted with unease. In response, the straps, almost human-like, tightened against her wrists and ankles.

"Lie still. I'm going to harvest the stores from within you." Phebe kept one hand over Zoey's navel while the other moved slowly down her stomach. Swirls of unexpected delight assaulted her. She sucked in a breath in order to ward off the odd sensation of being touched by another woman—a former friend.

Phebe paused, her hand just over the pubic bone. "Relax. This will not hurt—quite the contrary. And be forewarned. Your *sencore* must be stimulated to withdraw the stores from the *nidus*."

The *sencore*! She'd never heard of this procedure to extract from the vital organ before. Alarm bells whistled in her head.

"But—but what of the need to mate after *sencore* stimulation to stop the cycles of bliss?"

Phebe laughed softly. "I will take care of that, as well." She moved her hand down so that the tip of her finger brushed Zoey's clit. Against her will, it instantly hardened and throbbed with a need to be stroked. She held her breath, not knowing what to expect next. Looking up at her colleague—the royal Dorjanian princess!—she watched as Phebe's ample breasts began to rise and fall within the tight black suit. Each deep breath she took stretched the shiny fabric tighter across the full bosom. From this particular angle, Zoey couldn't see the eyes through the helmet slits anymore, but she could feel the woman's gaze move over her flesh like a hot beam from a *lazarshield*.

The slim finger swirled around her hard nub. Phebe plunged it between the folds of Zoey's *pless* and penetrated her damp canal.

"Oh!" she cried out. Fire ignited deep within her sex.

"You must be fully aroused for the extraction to be successful. And you better believe I'm not taking any chances." To emphasize her words, she inserted two more fingers and pumped them in and out frantically. Zoey arched her back, lifted her hips and bucked against the assault.

"I'm…I'm going to…to come," Zoey panted.

"Oh, you're a horny one, all right," she snarled. Phebe withdrew her hand. "You kept your precious Earth-man in an erectile state the entire time you were there."

She ignored the snide comment as an intense baser need for sweet release gripped her. It had been weeks since she'd been pleasured, weeks since she'd left Earth with Rolf in his comatose state. "No, don't stop! Please…" she added softly.

"Don't worry," Phebe replied sarcastically. "Your *sencore* is next." And it was. Phebe lifted her head and looked toward the ceiling as if to draw on some unseen guidance. Her hand returned between Zoey's legs and she smeared her cream over her labia and clit. The torture of Phebe's touch was maddening—but nothing compared to the sudden and expert location of her *sencore*.

Fire combusted in her system. Zoey moaned and bucked against the restraints.

The orgasms went on and on, one after another. Images of Rolf flashed through her mind and she imagined that it was he who touched her, he who brought her to the heights of euphoria. So much intense bliss washed through her that she barely noticed Phebe's other hand as it gradually reached up inside her. Her walls convulsed around Phebe's hand, intensifying the pleasure. She raised her head and gasped for air. In her delirium, she watched as Phebe withdrew a small white sac from her womb.

The *nidus*.

Never before had she seen her own incubation organ. And never again did she want to.

She rode another orgasmic wave as Phebe continued to stimulate her with her free hand. Before the next crest could build, she thought of Rolf again. His seed was within that sac. And she hadn't had a chance to plea her case of custodial rights for some of his *gametes*.

"No…wait…" she begged. "Where…where are you taking it?"

Phebe moved across the room. She slid the *nidus* inside a cylinder cartridge, wrapped a shiny seal around it and inserted it into a hole within the curved wall. She pressed a button and Zoey watched in horror as it disappeared through the gap. "To the medic lab, of course," she replied frostily.

"No! Please! I…I want—"

"What you want is not a part of the plan, Zoey," Phebe said cryptically as she crossed to stand once again at Zoey's side. She yanked out a drawer on the slab below where Zoey lay strapped down like a wild *wofler*. Pulling out a *ketka*-shaped, tan item with shiny, silver straps, Phebe wrapped it over the top of her suit, around her own waist and draped the strips between her legs. She then fastened them so that the contraption settled over her own *pless*.

Mortification swept through Zoey when she realized what it was for. Yes, Phebe had said she would take care of the nonstop pleasure brought on by the *sencore*-induced orgasms. The device was obviously designed to cease the cycle of releases—which even now raged through Zoey's system—if none of the male gender were available to provide that service.

"Release her," she barked to the *megabots*. As she climbed upon the table, the fake *ketka* bounced with her movements. Instantly, the clamps around her wrists and ankles popped open and receded into the table's surface.

Zoey tested the range of motion of her limbs. She warily watched Phebe position herself on all fours, her knees set between Zoey's spread legs. Zoey arched her back as another orgasm slammed into her, this one more intense than the last. She knew the cycle must be broken, but *Mama Luna*, she wished it were Rolf who provided her the relief!

"Just lie back and it'll all be over very soon..." Phebe's suit slid sensuously over Zoey's naked flesh as she walked her hands up until they were planted beside her head.

A spicy fragrance like that of a *frasadil* flower wafted to her nostrils. Though she still wore the protective quarantine helmet, Phebe's eyes, dark as the fudge Zoey had sucked from Rolf's cock weeks ago, stared back at her through the opening. They were glazed with what appeared to be...desire? The shock of it hit her just as a new wave gripped her deep inside her core. Was Phebe deriving some sort of sick pleasure from this? The thought of it both irritated and induced a similar emotion inside her.

"Please," she panted and met Phebe's stare with a newfound bravery. "Just get it over with."

Phebe let out a deep giggle. Simultaneously, she aligned the faux-cock with Zoey's wet pussy just as another wave started to build. Zoey had to hold onto something. Instinct led her to wrap her arms around Phebe's neck. With her legs spread, she braced herself as the *ketka* pushed into her and reached that sensitive spot deep inside her crux. Her eyes fluttered shut. Like an animal in heat, she growled and clamped her legs around Phebe's hips. But in her wild state of desire, she imagined that is was Rolf making love to her. It was Rolf whose body was pressed to her perspiring breasts, it was Rolf who gathered her close and rode her with expert precision.

Rolf, come to me, please come to me!

Zoey heard the gasps for air above her. But she concentrated on making it Rolf, on fulfilling her innermost desire of being with him just once more. Hips slammed against her inner thighs with a male-like force as she thrust her crotch upward to coat the hard device with her sticky cream.

"Ah, yes, *flek* me, Rolf! *Flek* me!"

His unmistakable manly aroma suddenly filled her nostrils. A warm mouth covered hers tasting of sweet ambrosia. Whiskers abraded softly over her cheeks and upper lip. A large hand, hot and practiced, cupped her breast, and the pad of a thumb flickered over one nipple sending fiery sparks to her clit.

Her eyelids, heavy with passion, flew open just as the orgasm started to rise to its pinnacle.

"Rolf…" she whispered. Her arms slid from around Phebe and she wound them around Rolf's neck. He leaned over her, kissing and fondling her as he stood beside the table. Phebe's eyes were closed tightly through the slit of her headgear. She was propped up on her hands, her arms straight, as she drove her own need deep inside Zoey.

"Zoey!" he said on a whisper as he showered her face with butterfly kisses. "Oh, Zoey…"

Then his mouth slammed into hers at the exact moment the final orgasm washed over her. She heard Phebe groan out her own release. That was when Rolf lifted his head and she was able to see Phebe once again.

Phebe's eyes snapped open. She looked down and Zoey knew the precise *manosecond* that the fear and confusion struck her. "What the...?" A scream erupted from her throat as her gaze swung to Rolf then back to Zoey. Her eyes widened with disbelief. "Who...how...?" She yanked the thick *ketka* from Zoey's passage and scrambled from the table. Her hands trembled within the layers of gloves as she fumbled with the straps and undid the sex-toy. Backing toward the door, she flung the device against the wall. It reverberated with a *smack* and slid to the floor leaving behind a streak of clear cream.

"This...this is impossible!" she shrieked. Her voice quivering, she shouted, "Let me out of here! *Now!*" The portal panel flew open. She spun on her boot heel and raced from the lab. The partition closed securely behind her.

Zoey swung her gaze back to Rolf. His image now flickered and faded in and out. "Rolf...don't go. Please."

"Ah, baby, I've missed you." He petted her hair where its long tresses streamed over the edge of the platform. "But I feel it coming..."

"No!" she cried and reached out for him. His warmth touched her for the briefest moment. Then he was gone.

*****

Phebe sat at Luran's bedside. Worry furrowed her brow. The usual rash of the virus had darkened and spread over his torso and face. According to the portable *megabot* stationed nearby in the king's chamber, his internal body temperature neared the danger zone. He shifted in and out of consciousness and his breathing grew more and more shallow with each passing *manominute.*

"Father...?" she said gently, and laced her hand into his warm one.

His lids slowly rose. She watched as his eyes, as deep and brown as a decadent *corfu* dessert, focused on the wispy fabric of the canopy above him. "Yes, *mica.*"

"How are you feeling?"

He coughed then swallowed audibly. "Like *zelmur* rock."

She smiled in spite of the apprehension that curdled in her gut. "I don't wish to disturb you, Father. It is just that..."

Perspiration beaded his forehead. As he turned his head toward her, droplets rolled down and into the graying hairline. "Is there trouble with Captain Fabiyan?"

"Trouble?" She sighed, knowing full well she could not delay informing him of the latest situations. "Yes, there is much unrest."

"Get her here at once," he insisted, rising up onto one elbow.

"No! Now, you must lie down. I need your guidance—I cannot afford to lose you!"

And I need you to live because...I do not wish to become the ruler of this world! Freedom to be me is all I desire.

She pressed her hand into his chest until his head was once again upon the fluffy pillow. When he only looked at her with that expression that meant *I'm waiting,* she reminded him, "She's still in quarantine. Though she'll be cleared shortly, it is still too risky for your own health to bring her here to you."

"Then tune her into the system. I wish to speak to her at once."

"No."

"No?" His silver brows arched with incredulity. "Did you just say no to the king of Dorjan?"

"You must hear me out. Let me finish explaining. This is a highly volatile situation. Things are not...right."

"Not right? Then her *nidus* has not survived extraction?"

"No—I mean, yes, it did survive and is in the lab as we speak." Phebe rose and paced the chamber. "It is just that the entire team of your most skilled *astrolages* have now determined that the vaccine will not work from its *genetoid* material."

King Luran was deathly silent. She turned back to him and saw that he appeared to be in a catatonic state. "So I'm to die after all," he finally whispered.

"I will not believe that!" she said with conviction.

"Regardless, you must at the very least see that the stores are distributed to all fertile women of child-bearing age. I may not survive, but Dorjan will!"

It felt as if a hand had closed around her heart and twisted without mercy. To see him near death, yet insisting on the rebirth of his world gave her both hope and sadness. She lowered herself into the seat and closed her hands around one of his.

Studying him through unshed tears, she kissed his knuckles and said, "You are an honorable man, King Luran."

Moisture formed in his own eyes. He held her gaze and replied, "And you will become my honorable successor. Queen Phebe of Dorjan."

"No…please, Papa, please do not say such things."

"It is inevitable."

She groaned and finally, the tears rolled over her cheeks. "I swear to you, if I could, I would *bazorly* dispose of the captain in a *manosecond*—if you would allow it."

"The plague is not her fault."

"No, but she disobeyed the rules, which delayed her return home."

"But you said the stores would not work for vaccine use, so what does the delay have to do with anything?"

Phebe narrowed her gaze on him. "Because certain genetic compositions of the *milt* were expired by mere *manohours* when the lab finally got possession of it. The samples *may* have worked—if she'd not dallied for so long with the Earthling."

Luran gasped. His jaw snapped shut.

"I know." She sniffed, dashing a tear from her cheek. "And to add further injury, she's playing some sort of games with her dream-travels. She will not let go of him."

"Games?"

"Yes." Phebe just couldn't take it anymore. She rose once again and prowled the suite. "During the extraction procedure of her *nidus*, something very odd occurred…"

Luran shifted in bed. "Phebe, get to the point."

"Her comatose Earthling came to *her*. And she wasn't even unconscious."

His eyes widened. He sat upright in bed. "Are you sure?"

She halted her steps and replied, "Yes, very. I was the one who performed the extraction. I saw it with my own eyes. During the *sencore* stabilization phase, the Earthling male appeared. And what's more, it is unspoken but clear Zoey will not be taking any other mates. I know it's unusual, but I saw something between them…"

"Get me the lab supervisor on the system immediately." He swung his legs over the edge of the bed.

"Father. You're too weak to get out of bed. It's not—"

"I said get me the lead laboratory astrolage *this instant!"*

Phebe startled at his booming voice. He hadn't roared this way in days. "Yes, sir." Heart thudding anxiously, she went to do the king's bidding.

But something told her whatever had struck him with such urgency, may not sit well with Dorjan's future.

Chapter Thirteen

"I was just about to contact you." Lieutenant Thia Zygmont's voice, along with her image, came over the *vistler* screen, her auburn hair twisted into a bun on top of her head. Pulling the thick laboratorial spectacles from her face, she peered into the monitor, her large eyes the color of the massive leaves of a *jaculondor* tree. "There have been some very interesting discoveries today."

"Really? In regard to the Earthling?" In a separate room just off his personal chamber, Luran was perched atop his working throne set before the vast wall of the planet's central *megabot*.

"Yes… And you are going to insist it is impossible," Thia said as the camera performed an auto-zoom on her heart-shaped face, "but we have discovered a *sencore* marking on him between his sac and his anus. Which I'm sure you understand what this could mean…"

Silence prevailed, broken only by the hum of the *megabot's* ongoing calculations and data processing.

"Aha!" His voice erupted as if he'd held his breath for *manocenturies*. Phebe watched, further confused as he raised his finger and jabbed it at Thia's image. "Just what I suspected!"

"You did?" Phebe's mouth gaped with astonishment. Seated at her father's right, she was privy to all confidential information, yet her main concern was the king's health. At the moment, his mental state alarmed her, as well. The crazed, determined look in his eyes in regard to the alien seemed to be a sudden obsession with him.

"Well, there's more…" Thia leaned in toward the monitor. Her full lips curved as if she were a *wofler* who'd just captured and devoured its long-awaited prey. "We've done some extensive *genetoid* blood workups with various *glomera* units, diverse comprehensive *magnetic steilianographical* testing, cosmic *cross-mate* species studies and—"

"Bah! Dispense with the scientific jargon!" The king threw his head back against the headrest and rolled his eyes. His long silver tresses fell over his thin shoulders like drenched rope. He sweated profusely and his blotchy complexion worried Phebe to no end.

"Father...please, you must return to your bed."

He ignored her and barked, "Lieutenant Zygmont! Continue. And for the love of Neron, on a much more elementary level this time."

"Well, to translate, after various tests and procedures, it has been definitively determined that Zoey's alien Earth-man carries various recessive traits of the Dorjanian species. Now," she shifted in her seat, a note of excitement in her voice, "it's been proven that the Earthling portion of his blood is immune to our horrid male-specific plague."

"You mean...?" Luran's complexion behind the rash paled one shade lighter.

Phebe reached for his hand. Her *astrolage* training finally tuned into what Thia alluded to. Hope flourished in her chest. "You've found a cure using his blood?" she blurted out.

Thia grinned smugly. "Yes, Phebe. It is a miracle that the Earthling is obviously a byproduct or descendant of one of our own veteran space travelers, but it is more of a marvel that he ended up here at the precise era when he was most needed. As we speak, I hold King Luran's dose of the vaccine in my hand." She held up a small, blue, glowing tube and wiggled it before the camera for added effect.

Tears brimmed in Luran's dark eyes. He sighed and raised Phebe's hand to his mouth. With trembling lips, he kissed the back of her knuckles. "Ah, daughter, your fear of ruling Dorjan has been conquered, dispensed of."

She sighed and held back the tears that brimmed in her eyes. "But how was it that you seemed to know something before Thia informed you?"

He smiled warmly and winked at her. "When you told me about the Earthling dream-traveling *to* Zoey during the extraction, I suspected as much, since this is a Dorjan trait exclusive to our race. You indicated yourself that things were odd between them. In addition, Raketar had previously transmitted some interesting information to me during the captain's final mating with the Earthling. As you know, it is remotely possible—but highly unlikely—for a non-Dorjanian to be able to achieve euphoric status and rise into our *Miraz Realm* with one of our own *incubot astrolages*."

"He entered the *Miraz Realm* with her?" Phebe heard the tone of disbelief in her voice, but she prayed all these theories were true.

"Yes." Luran grinned smugly.

"Really?" Thia added with a note of excitement. "Well, that further seals our conclusive data."

"And why wasn't I informed of this?" Phebe demanded to know.

"I didn't want to get your hopes up of a cure for our ill male citizens, in case this Rolf Mahoney alien was one of the rare non-Dorjanians who can enter *Miraz*. But the *sencore* marking alone proves his heritage. Raketar and I—and of course the captain— are the only ones who knew of his *Miraz* entry," Luran said to both Phebe and Thia. "I made a decision to keep it from the entire lab in the event you, Phebe, uncovered the news before it was confirmed. I didn't relish you suddenly assuming you were free to pursue your galactic exploration dreams only to have them dashed once again by my death and being forced to take the throne."

"Then it is certain?" Phebe asked Thia. "I won't have to become the queen?"

She nodded. "The vaccine has already been tested on dozens of infected subjects. They are all making miraculous, rapid recoveries. Their stats—blood work, vitals, everything—all show that they are now disease-free. What's more, their immune systems have already developed strong antibodies against future exposure and re-infection. It is all quite exciting."

"Will the Earthling live?" Luran asked.

"Yes, I believe so," Thia said conclusively and leaned back in her *nebuchair*. "His comatose state during cosmic travel was merely his Dorjanian *genetoid* way of shutting his systems down into incubation mode so that his Earth portion could survive the rigors of space. Any other Earthling would have died and disintegrated upon take-off. Our *portalships* are designed for Dorjans, not Earthlings. Also, he seems to be adapting wonderfully to the lower oxygen levels in our atmosphere."

"All of which Zoey will no doubt be relieved and ecstatic to hear," Phebe added. "It is my guess that she's infected as well—with the Earthling emotions of love and the need for monogamy."

"Well…though monogamy goes against Dorjan practices, it is the least I can do. I will grant her rights to exclusivity."

Phebe gasped at that. After getting her shock under control, she asked, "But what of him? I'm certain he wants her, but I'd wager to guess he wants her within his own domain. On Earth."

*****

The last few days since arriving home had been grueling in many ways. Every *astrolage* she came into contact with adamantly refused to inform her of Rolf's condition. Was he alive? And, if so, would he survive?

Fear for his welfare remained uppermost in her heart. She never stopped inquiring, and they never responded to her pleas.

Zoey had undergone safe levels of decontamination ionic gassing shortly after Phebe's extraction of her *nidus*. The process was painless, but it did cause some discomfort. The nonstop fine mist eventually gave her a sense of drowning along with a chilly dampness she was forced to endure until the procedure was complete.

Debriefing had occurred concurrent with refinement. Since transmissions during space travel are typically random and incomplete, debriefing consisted of its conclusion. Data is sent to the main *megabot* through Raketar, and in this instance, with descriptions of all subjects she'd accosted for the mining of *milt* samples. Rationale for this aspect of debriefing was to separate each Earthling's *genetoid* material from all others, then distribute according to compatible female Dorjan recipients. In addition, her own blood *glomera* panels and all bodily function samples were collected for testing—including her reproductive secretions.

She'd been told that Rolf's own reproductive samples—his *milt* contribution—had been substantial.

And she would see that she got a portion of it for herself if she had to breech security to obtain it.

Finally, she had been suction-dried and moved to the next security level up. She now resided in a semi-disc-shaped room—one of many off a central corridor—where windows ran the length of its entire rounded half. With her temporary quarters jutting out over the Dorjan Sea, the view was breathtaking. She stood at the window and watched, mesmerized as white-foamed aqua waters crashed upon the red peninsula of *zelmur* rock in the distance. In the vast yellow-gold, late day sky, two of the three Dorjan moons flanked the round ball of the white sun, its energy flooding through the crystal glass with warmth. She could almost smell the sweet scent of the sea and the sharpness of the soil near her home up the coast. If she tipped her head just so, she could tune in her *audiotrap* to the rush of the great tide, the call of a school of *mergulls,* and just possibly the snort of her beloved *stallisor,* Feenix.

She turned from the window and scrutinized the room. It was comfortable enough with various *nebuchairs* and *nebusofas.* The central *megabot* had tuned the suites into a worldwide system for visual and audio entertainment, though she'd rarely used either. Instead, she chose to be occupied with her own thoughts and wishes. The floor was of a species of soft tan foam intrinsic to Dorjan's seas, the glistening walls made of gold-plated *terel* metals. She'd been provided with all the most nutritious and delectable foods, all the luxuries she stocked in her own seaside ranch home.

But that didn't soothe her unease.

Per the king's orders, she was not allowed to leave. Apparently, sentencing would come down upon her this very *manoday*. Rarely did the king stand in and personally hand out his retributions. But today, she'd been told, he would deal with her in the flesh. Shortly, he would arrive and inform her of the selected punishment for her insubordination, for endangering Dorjan, for compromising his kingdom…for falling in love and desiring one single mate rather than following Dorjan custom by conforming to polygamous practices.

A buzz sounded at the great double doors. Zoey glanced up and stared, waiting for her sentencer to enter. Her pulse thrummed in her neck, choking her with dread.

"May I enter?" King Luran inquired from the opposite side of the closed door.

He was asking her permission?

"But, of course, Your Lordship. Please. Come in."

She bowed her head and fell to her knees. The soft swish and slide of the *lazarshield* panel doors sounded oddly ominous to her ears. The muted rhythm of his approaching footfalls echoed faintly in the suite. Zoey had her hands planted on the floor in respectful worship. Without lifting her head, she glanced up and saw that a pair of booted feet halted directly in front of her. She caught a whiff of his sandy aroma, of his strength and power. And fear curdled in her stomach.

"Rise, child." His deep timbre traveled to her ears in cryptic, undecipherable undertones.

"Yes, King Luran." She rose, unfolding herself slowly. With a trembling hand, she pushed her hair from her eyes, tipped her head back, and took in the full view of him. He was tall yet much thinner than she recalled. His hair hung in long silver ropes over his shoulders. Her gaze met his dark one, and fear such as she'd never felt before, shimmied up her spine. They gleamed like the black of space on a long journey home, cold and vast and infinitely dangerous. There was the unknown to contend with, as well, the uncertainties of what lay beyond the surface of the penetrating stare, the set to the thin lips, the rise and fall of the thick chest. In the black uniform with the silver ringed *botic* neckline for communication with his central *megabot,* and the formfitting *chaizes* that melded into thick boots meant for battle or space travel, he appeared invincible and extremely daunting. Her gut swirled with nauseating trepidation, and she knew, without a doubt, that if capital punishment were to ever become common practice on Dorjan, it would begin with her this very *manominute.*

"Be at ease, Captain." He crossed to the expanse of windows and presented the wall of his back to her.

"I…I'm not sure how to…how to do that."

"Sit." She paused for a moment then obediently fell into the nearest *nebuchair,* welcoming its soothing properties.

"I'll get right to the point, Captain Fabiyan. You've played a major role in altering Dorjan's future." His voice was stern, and she watched as he folded his arms and continued to stare out at the Dorjan Sea.

"I…oh…" She sighed and started to rise.

"Stay seated."

Sinking back into the chair, she replied, "I'm so very sorry for all my transgressions on this last mission, sir. I will do anything at all to make up for it."

"Does that include giving up your lover?"

He may as well have stabbed her in the heart. But if it meant Rolf's safety, then yes, by all means she would give him up for his return to Earth—if he were still alive and if he could survive another space travel. "Y-yes, that includes...giving him up."

"Well..." he said sharply, and spun around to face her. "You're a fool, then."

She stared at him for what seemed like eons. He merely lifted his white brows inviting her to rebut his charge.

"What?"

"You heard me." He rocked back on his heels and glowered at her.

"But—but I don't understand."

"Let me ask you this... If you could have anything in this universe—*anything*—what would it be? And remember, I can gain access to your thoughts if I wish, Captain."

She swallowed a lump of panic. What kind of game did he play? Would she be punished for *speaking* her desires, for *thinking* them, or both?

When she continued to gawk, he sighed, sauntered over and lowered himself into the *nebuchair* across from her. "It's okay, Zoey." His eyes softened to the gold of a warm, soothing fire. He reached out and took her hand in his—and she suddenly realized it was the first time she'd ever been touched by this great ruler. His hand was cool yet comforting. He squeezed hers and said, "You can reveal your true feelings. There will be no reprisals for what is in your heart."

"Well..." she began hesitantly, though something told her this wouldn't end in disaster as she'd at first feared. "For one thing, I'd go back and throw up the *empyral shield* to ensure that the mission would not be compromised."

"You'd do it again?"

"Again?"

He chuckled and patted her hand. "Transcripts just given me by Raketar show that you *did* engage the *empyral shield,* just as your training dictates."

"What? But…no, that can't be. He entered the *portalship's* zone. There is no way Rolf could have seen it with the shield up, much less *entered* the area. Raketar must be mistaken."

"Has Rake ever been wrong?"

It was true. Raketar was designed to be one hundred percent accurate. There was no margin for error where she or her counterparts were concerned. So then, what in lunar lunacy was going on?

"Forgive me, Your Lordship, but truly, I don't understand." She pulled her hand from his, suddenly wary and alarmed, and settled back into the chair so that her nerves could be pacified. Still, sweat dribbled between her breasts. She concentrated on keeping her breathing slow and even.

He leaned back in his own chair, seeming to be neither insulted by her rebuke nor in any hurry to explain further. *Manoseconds* ticked by. Finally, he grinned *woflerishly* and said, "Your Earthling is part Dorjan. As a result, he was able to see through the shield—and enter the zone—just as any Dorjan can."

Stunned, she shook her head profusely. "No. No, that can't be."

"Yes, it can. Apparently, he's a descendant of one of our own—"

She gasped a lengthy, high-pitched squeak, and Luran had the kindness to pause for a brief bit until she got herself under control.

"You already know that we've made frequent past visits to our sister-Earth for research purposes. There have been some who've chosen to stay. In fact, there remain many Dorjan descendants on Earth mixed among the various populations. And your Rolf Mahoney is the child of a male *astrolage* who chose to stay when the Earth-woman he fell in love with abandoned Rolf as a child. Our honorable one couldn't bear to leave Rolf all alone. He worried that the babe would not be able to survive the trek back to Dorjan, so he stayed and reared him on Earth. Our *astrolage* adapted quite well, and, at last contact many, many *manoyears* ago, relayed that he did not wish to return to Dorjan."

Rolf is half Dorjanian?

Zoey inhaled sharply and blew out a long breath. Could it be true? There had always been tales of that sort referring to Dorjanians who'd settled on Earth, but to Zoey, they had been just that. Tales. No one ever really moved to another planet in an entirely different solar system, a portion of a light-year away—or did they?

"How do you know this?"

"Thia and all your colleagues have confirmed it. You, more than any of them, know the laboratory procedures. His *glomera* samples and various other"—he threw up a flippant hand—"procedures and what not, have proven beyond a doubt that his genetics are of both Earthling and Dorjanian descent. Not to mention the…marking."

"Marking?"

"Yes, your lover has a *sencore.*"

Zoey stopped breathing. She felt as if her eyeballs would pop from her head, yet she couldn't suppress the automatic response. A *sencore*? He possessed the one marking of a true Dorjanian?

Her mind spun into rewind mode. The puzzle was almost complete. Things that hadn't made sense before, or that had nagged at her, suddenly started to become clearer with each recollection of her days on Earth. He had traveled *to* her that first day at the BunnyRanch in her office, a trait generally of her species, though it was rumored that some Earthlings possessed the same talent. She recalled his adept manipulation of her own *sencore,* as if he instinctually knew how to use it. And yet, somehow, she'd missed the marking that first night she'd had him spread-eagled. True, the room had been dimly lit, but still, had she already been that enamored of him that she'd overlooked such an important fact? Obviously so, she silently admitted. But there was more ineptness on her part, the *empyral shield*. She'd attributed her negligence at not engaging it, to her distress over leaving Rolf. In actuality, it appears that she'd followed through with protocol as usual. When Rolf had appeared within the zone, she'd assumed she'd forgotten that all-important step.

But she had not.

It all made sense now. Even his survival of the long space trek had baffled her, yet now she could see how his inherited Dorjanian traits in conjunction with his Earthling ones could cause him to teeter on life and death, or, as was probably the case, to shift into protective comatose mode until the journey was ended.

But more so than any of those subtle clues was that of her own heart. From the start, there had been something about him she couldn't quite name. With one look at him that first night she'd located a new client, dream-traveled to him and accosted him, she'd gained an instant aversion to all other males besides him. She must have seen home in his eyes. She must have sensed the connection on a subconscious level.

She shivered. And then there had been the neon blue glow of his eyes when they had entered the *Miraz Realm* during the final extraction of *milt* for her *nidus*.

"When…when we entered *Miraz*, I assumed he was one of the few Earthlings who could achieve that status. I—I didn't even suspect, didn't even begin to assume it was because Dorjanian blood ran through his veins."

Luran nodded sympathetically. "I know, child. I know. And speaking of that blood, there is more news."

She swallowed a suspenseful lump. "Go on."

"This Rolf of yours has provided Dorjan with a cure for the mysterious disease."

"He has?" Zoey's heart skipped a beat.

"Yes, using his natural antibodies. He's immune. Lab developed a vaccine from his Earth-portioned serum."

She was afraid to speak, afraid to shatter the dream, frightened that the hope that blossomed in her chest would be crushed with his next words. "Are you certain? And…he's obviously alive and well?"

"Very—on both counts."

Relief flooded her system. She sagged in her seat.

He was alive! Tears stung her eyes and she didn't even attempt to suppress them, for it was a cleansing she so desperately needed.

Luran rose and held his arms out to his sides. "I'm proof of the miracle. I came down with the illness shortly before your return home. I was nearing death when you arrived. Thia has administered the vaccine to me and already, I feel healthier than I did before I became ill. The fever and rash are gone. *I live because of you, Zoey.*"

"Oh…" She cried the word out. There was a sweet lump of disbelief in her throat and she slowly swallowed it, digesting the king's admission.

"And I am promoting you to Colonel for your unprecedented timing and successful mission."

"Colonel?" She shot to her feet. Her voice was a squeal of delight and awe. The tears fell in a shower of happiness down her cheeks. To be promoted to colonel was a jump in rank by three levels! It also meant she would have more freedom, and much more input in research and travel explorations. And it meant she would be one of the king's trusted few.

His thin mouth spread into a smile. In his eyes, she saw respect and even love. "Yes, and it is well deserved." He raised a hand and wiped the moisture from her cheek with the pad of his thumb.

"Oh, thank you. Thank you *so* much!" Without thought for propriety, she flung herself at him. He was stunned at first, stiffening when she threw her arms around his neck, but then he chuckled, relaxed and gathered her close. "Oh, stars! I'm so sorry," she said, leaning back in the circle of his arms.

He winked. "Not a problem. Does these old bones some good to feel the energy of youth so close to my heart. Now..."

The note of an omen gave her pause. "Now what?"

"There's one—no, two more things..."

Zoey's gaze fell. She slithered from the king's embrace and fell into the nearest *nebuchair*. "I'm still to be punished," she said blandly.

The sudden roar of laughter that erupted from him startled her and she gripped the arms of the chair. She looked up at her great ruler, his large presence so awe-inspiring, and knew that she could not blame him if he chose to follow through with some sort of discipline.

After he got himself under control, he shook his head. "You are a delight!" With a spring to his step, he moved to the door. Over his shoulder, he threw out, "Your lover's seed has been disposed of. I will leave it up to the two of you to contribute to the species."

She trailed along behind him. "You mean you're not going to distribute his spermatozoa among the female population?" It was just what she'd secretly hoped for. She'd wanted Rolf all to herself, right down to every last one of his *genetoid* cells.

The *lazarshield* lifted as he approached. He turned back to her. "His contribution was just under ten percent. The other ninety is more than enough to rejuvenate our population." He grinned wryly. "Besides, I think the two of you can make up for the loss. And you have my permission for monogamy, if you so wish."

She fell to her knees in worship. "Thank you, King Luran. Thank you so very much."

"At ease, *Colonel* Fabiyan. You must remember from this *manomoment* forward that colonels are not required to salute." She snuck a peek at him. He looked down at her with an undeniable gleam of admiration in his eyes.

Her heart swelled with pride. Colonel. She was a Dorjanian colonel!

Zoey rose, unable to peel the grin from her face. "Thank you, sir."

"No," he returned, and spun on his booted heel to depart. Then he paused and turned back to her once again. "Thank you. But know this, Colonel Fabiyan. As Raketar just informed me prior to this visit, you have an alliance to form, one very important to the future of both solar systems, of the entire universe. It is up to you to fulfill this great obligation, to see that your Earth-man is also amenable to this noble duty."

Her smile faded. She nodded and knew that he spoke of the final, sealing phase following the *Miraz Realm* joining.

"Now, go to him. He awaits you in his own Level Two chamber."

Chapter Fourteen

When one suddenly awoke in a strange world, it would seem that likening it to a bizarre dream would be the rational thing to do. But Rolf was beyond prudence. He had seen the strange lights, real and surreal all at the same time. He'd watched Zoey connect to them and could recall with vivid clarity that moment he'd been whisked up into space.

And she had been there with him looking strong and powerful and not the least bit concerned about the peculiar goings on.

Then there had been the recent dream in which he'd watched Zoey being ravished, and by a woman at that, as evidenced by the curves beneath the tight black suit she'd worn. It had inflamed him, turned him on to rock-hard status, yet something about it had nagged at him.

He wanted her all to himself.

He shifted nervously and shoved the thought to the back of his mind.

All that, according to the many oddly dressed individuals who had been attending to him for the last several days, was a definite reality that he'd endured during the last weeks and days. He'd awakened with a whopper of a headache in a freaking capsule with a view. Staring out the window, he'd watched all those people busy themselves in a well-lit, neon-glowing laboratory that was eerily reminiscent of a sci-fi movie set.

And he had been their guinea pig.

They'd poked and prodded and scanned and databased him to the point of near obsession. In their full-body astronaut-like suits, they'd "decontaminated" him—as if he were some sort of rabid, diseased dog! He'd graduated from his tomb into a round room all his very own where he'd been forced to take an all-day cold shower. Each day, he was given a bit more freedom, a bit more information. As he moved from room to room and level to level, the standoffish people warmed to him, and gradually, he was informed about—no, slammed with—"the news".

Yes, the news…

Apparently, he was on a planet called Dorjan in a separate solar system from Earth's—Zoey's home. If it weren't for the fact that he'd pinched himself a gazillion times and still could see, hear, taste, smell and touch all the new sensations, he'd swear he had gone mad.

But that hadn't been all.

Just what did one do when told they were the offspring of someone from another world, another planet? He'd been floored, to say the least. The lab techs had delighted in his awe and denial, and patiently showed him the evidence. The *sencore,* as they'd called it, being one notable mark of evidence. That was when he recalled seeing one very similar tattoo-like mark below the creamy opening of Zoey's beautiful pussy. Something had troubled him then. He remembered a sort of a déjà vu had washed through him when he'd discovered it on her body. But now it all made sense. He recalled why it had affected him so oddly. As a very small child, he'd been exploring his body in a mirror. He'd found the marking, asked his father about it, and been told to forget it and never talk about it to anyone ever again.

And he'd thought being a marred freak, being different, had been what had caused his mother to abandon them.

He snorted then his smile faded. He'd never really known his mother. How could he? He'd been a baby in diapers when she'd left. Rolf had always assumed she'd abandoned him for a life of freedom and men and sin. In his defensive mind, he'd turned her into a hooker. Why else, he'd always rationalized as a young man, would a woman walk away from a husband and her baby boy? It was partially what had prompted him to go to the BunnyRanch in the first place. Like an illness, he needed to make that movie. He had to show her, wherever she was, that he'd survived without her, that he could even make light of her rejection. It had been so important to him, such an obsession, that he'd gone as far as searching for a call girl to portray his mother.

But he'd found Zoey instead.

Looking back, he knew now it had taken one glance, one kiss, and the movie—and his mother—had no longer been a priority. He'd found the woman of his dreams in a cathouse.

And he'd fallen deeply in love with her.

He ground his teeth together. Ha! Imagine that. He was in love with a woman who'd used him like a harlot, who'd stolen his sperm to jumpstart her dying planet and her own career as an *astrolage* captain.

He was in love with a full-blooded alien!

Rolf frowned. Carefully, he reined in his anger and shock. *Save your energy, man. Save it for the blessed moment you lay eyes on her again.*

Lounging at a black table of marble-like quality, he forced himself to think of anything but her, so he gazed out at the sea. The Dorjan Sea. Rolf shifted in his seat, set before the large bay window of sorts, and took in the panoramic view. He'd seen waters and seascapes of the Caribbean, of Mexico and the Greek Isles. But never before had water, land and sky been so crisp and clear, as if someone had poured a huge vat of bright watercolors across the ocean and its lands.

The soil was deep orange-red—fucking *red*!—and he thought of all those Mars photos he'd seen on the Internet sent back to Earth from Rover. Though it had desert-like qualities of patchy barrenness, Dorjan also contained swirled oases of rich green foliage. And then there were the odd trees. Rolf spied one up shore and took in its enormous trunk, the elephant-ear leaves and its massive height. He'd been told, or rather, uploaded with information to his brain's now activated *datochip*—that chip in his brain yet another shocker—that it was a *jaculondor* tree, and an indestructible species that competed with the oxygen stores of their atmosphere. Shortness of breath had been one of his main difficulties in those first hours after awakening, but he'd been assured his lungs would quickly adapt—because of his Dorjanian blood, of course. He inhaled and noted the dizziness was gone. Which apparently meant his lungs had already done just that.

He rose and paced before the window, feeling strangely comfortable in the dark navy, skin-tight suit complete with *chaizes*. The odd pants seemed to fit his hips and legs like a second skin. Any other time, on Earth at least, he'd have felt like a fairy in a get-up like this, but here, somehow, he felt at ease, right.

"Ha! This is fucking ridiculous." Rolf planted his hands on the window ledge and peered out to sea. The sun, a white star-shaped flame in the orange-streaked yellow sky, was just now setting atop the distant waves. Prisms of color shot off the water in all directions, taking his breath away. He thought of her eyes that first and last night she'd traveled to him in his dreams. The white star in the center, the conglomerate of glimmering jewels surrounding it…

What did it mean?

Well, he thought with a snort as he pushed away from the window, since gradual knowledge was even now being transferred to his *datochip*, he was certain that soon, he'd find all of his answers.

A faint drone sounded behind him. He spun around…and there she stood in the doorway. He'd never seen her look more beautiful. And his body tightened, both with swift desire and anger. She remained immobile for a long moment before stepping into the room, her curves outlined by the light of the corridor beyond. The glowing door panel shut behind her. With her lilac eyes locked on his, she glided slowly across the room. Finally, she halted so close to him, he could almost reach out and touch her. Her faint floral scent enticed him, and he could swear he could feel the soft heat of her body permeate the fabric of his garment.

"Rolf…" Her eyes glimmered with shiny droplets of tears. There was a faint pinkness to her cheeks while her full lips shimmered in an iced cherry shade. He licked his own lips, longing to taste her, to feel her voluptuous body against his. With her pale hair swept up into a ponytail atop her head, he thought of a genie. And mentally, he made a wish.

I wish that you would love me as I do you. I wish that you hadn't used me.

Annoyed with himself, he crossed his arms over his chest. "I guess this means you're not going to be doing my taxes for me, huh?"

She blinked. Then dawning sparked in her eyes. Her lips curved up ever so slightly at the corners. "Well, I'm very capable if you would still like me to do them. However, since it's past April fifteenth, and it would take weeks for the IRS to receive your return, you'll still have to pay the penalty."

"Penalty?" He didn't try to hide his bitterness. "I think I've already paid my dues."

She sucked in a breath. "I…I don't know what you mean." Clearly, she hadn't expected sarcasm, or the anger that trembled inside him.

"My stud services." He propped a hip on the window ledge and crossed his ankles. In doing so, he unblocked the beams of the setting sun. As if she were one of his stars on a movie set, light bathed her in brilliant, sparkling colors. His breath caught in his chest and his cock tingled. How he longed to yank her into his arms, to bury himself inside her!

No. He no longer wanted to give himself up without getting anything in return.

She folded her arms under her luscious breasts, the deep cleavage bared in the vee of the snug, pink bodysuit she wore. Every curve and valley of her cunt, every swell of her breasts, was emphasized. And all he could think of was gobbling up her cotton-candied breasts—and ringing her pretty little neck.

"If you're referring to my *nidus* stores for return to boost Dorjan's population, then, yes, I guess I did use your *services*."

Her tone was tight, almost flippant. In response, blood thrummed in his head. His blood pressure rose to a dangerous level. "You *stole* my DNA without my knowledge or consent. You've given it over for other women to become mothers of my—what—maybe hundreds or thousands of children?" He laughed hollowly at the absurdity of it. "Did I *ever* say I wished to father even one child? And *alien* children, at that?"

"*Alien*?" Her beautiful face paled with shock as she planted her fists on her hips in outrage. Those tantalizing eyes glittered with sudden ire, the tears now gone. "You say that with such disgust. I would ask you if you'd been told yet that you are *part Dorjanian* yourself, but I'm much smarter than that!"

"Oh, yes," he agreed, his voice rising as he took one step closer. Her female scent, at first subtle, burst in his lungs and coursed through his system like a drug. "You're smart all right." He forced out a sardonic breath and mocked her by setting his own arms akimbo. "You earned every penny of my money for Madam Ivana."

She gasped. "You son of a bitch!" *Smack*. He flinched at the assault yet didn't move away. Admittedly, he hadn't expected it—that was for sure.

"You're right." He rubbed his stinging jaw and regarded her thoughtfully. "When your mother abandons you, you tend to think of yourself as a son of a bitch all your life. But things are much more clear now. This knowledge pouring into my *datochip* even now tells me she was traumatized when she discovered my *sencore*, which prompted my father to confess to her who—or what—he was. She left out of fear at finding out her husband was from a place far, far away, and the child she'd given birth to, a freak, an *alien*. Somehow, I can see her point."

The turbulence drained from her eyes. Apparently, it was news to her, which meant her own *datochip* hadn't kept her up-to-date on his entire history. She took one hesitant step toward him and pressed her hand to his chest. It was like a brand, scorching-hot and permanent, far more painful than it had been when she'd slapped him. "I'm…I'm so sorry, Rolf. About your mother, your father…and me."

Her head was tipped back and he looked down into the aqua-lavender of her ever-changing eyes, so like the Dorjan Sea behind him, tumultuous and powerful. God, how he loved her! But there was too much confusion, too much to absorb.

"The king has ordered your DNA contribution to be disposed of." She slowly cupped his tender jaw. Her hand trembled, but she held it there, forcing him to feel her gentle touch, her warmth. "The only child you will have is one at a time, and one that you voluntarily wish for."

Relief flooded through him. Not that he'd truly be opposed to assisting the Dorjans in a population boost, but he wanted to be responsible for his children. He wanted to rear them under one roof, which would be impossible with thousands of children—not to mention they would each have a different mother, and there was only one woman he wanted as the mother of his children. He felt tremendous relief at knowing he'd gotten out of a polygamous situation. But more so than that, it thoroughly pleased him that she'd already been concerned with her error. That she'd somehow seen it as a problem for him and resolved it in some manner.

And that meant everything in the universe to him.

"You did that for me?"

Her eyes shifted, but bravely, she moved her gaze back to him. "King Luran did it for us. After the stores were taken from me, I had no say in the matter. To the king, it would be a matter of loyalty versus treason on my part, punishable by banishment from the planet. I *wanted* to keep them all for myself, and had planned to plea for some of your samples. But if the king, in the end, hadn't ordered your contribution destroyed…" She shuddered. "I don't think I could have withstood encountering on a daily basis, your offspring by other women. I couldn't bear seeing your children and knowing they weren't mine."

While he understood her explanation, one point had reached out and grabbed him. "You were going to request some of my sperm?"

She hesitated. Her lips parted with uncertainty but she whispered, "Yes."

Hope warmed his heart. He slid his hands around her hips and pressed her abdomen against his half-hard arousal. He had to hear it from her lips. "Why would you do such a thing?"

Her arms rose and she clasped her hands behind his neck. With her breasts pressed into his ribs, suddenly, he couldn't think. Every ounce of anger drained from his system. His cock throbbed with need to get inside her again, finally after weeks of separation.

"Because, I feared you would die. And…and…"

"Yes?"

"Because I love you, Rolf. If I couldn't have you alive, then I at least wanted to have your child. And, though it goes against Dorjanian practice, I wanted to be the only mother of your children."

His world expanded, encompassing the entire galaxy. "Oh…" he groaned and dropped his head so that his forehead pressed against hers. "Zoey. Do you know what you've just done?"

She shook her head against his, her eyes remaining locked with his.

"You've made me the happiest alien in the universe."

On a sigh, she giggled nervously. "Rolf…I missed you so much!" Her hands stabbed into his hair. With power and passion, she crashed his mouth into hers. Shooting stars exploded in his head. Her mouth, no longer a painful memory, was real and wet against his. Their tongues dueled, mated, teased. In his arms, she felt small and vulnerable, but he knew her to be a great and brave *astrolage*. Pride swelled in his chest, but so did lust.

"Oh, honey…" he panted against her mouth. "I love you. I've loved you, I think, since the very first time you came to me in my dream and forced me to make love to you at the Moonlite BunnyRanch."

Zoey reared back and stared at him, his declaration of love obviously taking her by delighted surprise. She smiled then, an adorable crinkle at the corner of her eyes, and caught his lower lip between her teeth. Moving lower, she devoured his neck. Her tongue did delicious things to his collarbone, sending sparks of heat to his groin.

"Forced? You loved every minute of it, and you know it." With that fact, she plunged her hand between their bodies and cupped his sex.

He hissed in a long breath. "So there's still no talking you into being in that movie of mine, huh?"

She laughed low and throaty. "Well…if it was a sex movie and you were my only stud to mate with, yeah, I might do that."

Rolf threw his head back and roared. "Oh, but wouldn't Madam Ivana love *that* possibility, of a hot movie filmed at her Ranch?"

Zoey stilled her movements and looked up at him with surprise. "Do you want to go back?"

The thought hadn't occurred to him. What *would* he do? Stay here and abandon his life on Earth? "I…I don't know."

"I'll go wherever you want to go, Rolf. My life is with you, no matter what corner of the universe we're in."

Love rushed through him. Her eyes were wide with complete abandonment. "You mean that?"

She nodded, but he saw a trace of apprehension somewhere in her expression. "If you wouldn't mind visiting Dorjan now and then. My parents, my brothers and sisters, I wouldn't want to shut them out totally, to never see them again."

"Well, for starters, I haven't seen much of your homeland. It's difficult to make a decision based on the *Cruxcentre* alone. I would, however, like to at least return to Earth and see my father, to let him know my situation. Who knows, maybe he'll decide to return to Dorjan."

"That would be nice, but first..."

"First?"

She reached for his hand and pulled him toward the door. "You haven't seen much of my homeland *or* my home. Come. We have much lost time to make up for."

*****

They exited the *Cruxcentre* and boarded her personal *robocar*. In the disc-shaped vehicle, Zoey instructed its *botics* to travel at low speeds in order for Rolf to take in the scenery. Across the deep red soil to the right, he could see the outline of purple mountains fading into the dusk light. To the left and down a gradual slope, the tide rose upon the orange sandy beach. The waves crashed in rhythm and echoed musically across the land. Inhaling, he detected the spicy scent of *frasadil* flowers and fresh, unpolluted air. Given that the king's hub was in the center of a main metropolis, the purity of the air quality far surpassed that of Earth's major cities. Though the planet's colors were skewed and somewhat shocking in brightness, Dorjan with its high-mountain, desert-like terrain, reminded him very much of Nevada and the area around the BunnyRanch.

He sat back and enjoyed the ride, the temperature considerably cooler now as the sun faded behind the ocean's horizon. They traveled for a good twenty minutes in contented silence, their hands laced tightly together. He adjusted his *chaises*. Already, his cock was enflamed with need for her, with the awareness of what was to come.

"There it is," she said, and he heard the pride in her voice before he saw the structure.

"That's your home?" He took in every detail of the little round *zelmur* building, and he thought of a southwestern United

States adobe home lopped off and the top replaced with a glass dome. Three moons' light bathed the clear crystal of the roof and sent out a shower of reflective red, silver and pale green lunar light. Acres and acres of lush greenery glistened and arced the home's rear while the front proudly overlooked the Dorjan Sea, its waves crashing upon the beach below.

"Yes," she sighed and laid her head upon his shoulder. "Isn't it beautiful?"

Pulling her close, he hooked a finger to her chin and turned her face toward his. Her eyes were already limpid pools of expectant passion and his breath caught as he stared into their depths. "Gorgeous." He captured her mouth in a whisper-soft kiss. "Just like its owner."

She stared at him in the moonlight for a long moment before blurting out, "Both owners." The hopeful gleam in her eyes took his breath away.

That was when he made his decision to stay with her here on Dorjan.

He swept the estate with an appreciative gaze. "Yes…both owners."

"You mean it?"

"I mean it—um, as long as I can return whenever I want. You know, sort of commute?"

She threw her arms around him and smacked his lips with hers. "I'd love to be your chauffeur!"

A snort sounded from across the estate grounds. Rolf jerked his head around, his protective instincts suddenly sharp and honed. Without further warning, a huge white beast burst from a large wooden building and galloped toward them. Rolf stiffened and shoved Zoey behind him. He had never in all his life seen a more imposing creature. As large as an elephant, it was similar in structure to a horse, only the poor thing's ears were humongous, dragging the ground behind him. Instantly, Rolf's *datochip* told him it was a *stallisor*.

"Holy shit!" he said on a gasp.

Zoey giggled and shoved him away. "It's just Feenix. He's harmless."

"Yeah, well, those ears make me wonder…"

As if Feenix sensed his derision, the long flaps rose and snapped, spreading out in a beautiful array of gold and blue striped wings. The animal took flight, flapped its ears like Dumbo and circled above them.

"Feenix!" she scolded, and obediently he zipped to the ground and hung his head. "Show off." She climbed from the vehicle and petted the beast's long nose. "He's very protective of me," she said with affection.

"No kidding."

"Would you like to ride him?"

"Um, no. Maybe…later." He exited the *robocar* and approached her from behind. Wrapping his arms around her, he hauled her up against his chest. "But I would like to ride *you*…" he whispered in her ear.

"That," she said cryptically, untangling herself from his embrace, "can be arranged." Backing away, she turned and jogged to the front *lazarshield* door.

"Hey, wait!"

When the glowing orange panel dissolved and left a gaping arched doorway into her home, she turned to him and called out, "I've waited a *flekking* lifetime. I can't wait any longer." And she disappeared inside.

Rolf didn't delay to see if she would reappear. He crossed the yard and stepped up to the entrance. Inside, he saw her move through a solarium room, past a scatter of *nebu*-furniture and various pieces of actively lit *vistler* equipment. The walls were curved and red adobe-style with metal-like *terel* joists and raw studs. There was an area off to the side made of *terel*-constructed cabinets and various tables, obviously a kitchen of sorts. From there, through a door leading out toward the ocean, he could see a massive deck made of *ellcore* wood, from a tree in the uninhabited regions—he was now mentally being briefed—

that was virtually indestructible and rot-proof against a constant water environment.

He smiled to himself. *The deck was a definite spot for future lovemaking.*

He strode into the entryway and the *lazarshield* closed behind him with a soft whir. Above him through the clear dome, the navy Dorjanian night sky could be seen. It took his breath away and he watched stunned as a shooting star zipped across his line of vision. The three Dorjan moons could be seen, two in full view, and the third partially obscured by the top edge of the solid walls. Stars blazed and twinkled, their sizes magnified several times larger than they actually appeared with the naked eye. The dome roof was like a telescope lens, and a sudden urge gripped him to take her there under that magnificent show of extravagant astral light.

His gaze drifted lower and he watched as she disrobed in a stream of starlight beside the round *nebubed*. Her naked body glistened once again, as it had in that strange dream during their final encounter on Earth.

The Miraz Realm.

It came to him from his *datochip*, and suddenly he realized why they'd risen there in the first place, why her eyes had changed into a kaleidoscope of mesmerizing colors, and why he'd been unable to ejaculate until he'd penetrated her.

It was an age-old ritual reserved for rare galactic souls destined to be together for eternity. And the *Miraz Realm* was the traditional location, seen rarely throughout the universe, meant to bind the two with that unforgettable bliss achieved by few. Once there, once experienced, it is said that mates have only one last chance to deny the connection. And that is to never mate again.

"Yes, Rolf. Your *datochip* tells you correctly." She nodded and held her arms out to him in welcome. "It's time to unite our two worlds, our two solar systems. Us. Come to me so that we can complete the joining, so that we can be heart-mates. It only takes one final commitment following the *Miraz* joining. Just once more and we will be together forever."

Her voice was calm, soothing and seductive. It seemed to reach into his soul and masturbate it into awareness and acceptance. His loins combusted and throbbed with a need so fierce, he growled aloud, his hands clenched into tight fists. As she stood there glittering in the moonlight—a mirage of every man's fantasy—a goddess came to mind, proud, beautiful, alluring and irresistible. The subtle streaks of gold in her upswept hair now shimmered, falling in cascades over her nude body. And he thought he'd never seen a more perfect woman in all of his life.

With his eyes locked on her, he moved nearer, one step at a time. Gradually, he came into the moonlight below the dome. His gaze caressed the elegant column of her neck, the pert, dark-tipped breasts and the narrow rib cage. A diamond-like jewel winked at him from her navel, enticing him to touch, to taste, to explore. In eager response, Rolf's mouth watered, his pulse pounded in tempo with his quick breaths.

And then there was the valley of her *pless*, the lips swollen and glossy with the moisture of her excitement. Through an open window behind her, the tumultuous Dorjan Sea served as a backdrop to her prelude to love. His goddess turned to mermaid as she caressed her own body, her hand rising to cup one of her generous breasts. At that moment, her lips parted. She moaned in response to the self-plucking of her nipple. Rolling it between her forefinger and thumb, she threw her head back and slid her other hand down and over her flat abdomen.

"Rolf…" she whimpered as her finger found the engorged bud. "I need you."

"You're not the only one in need…" He shoved his *chaizes* down around his ankles and his cock sprang from its confinement. Next, his shirt came off. Impatiently, he kicked off his boots and stepped out of his pants.

He moved closer, feeling much like a stealthy panther cornering his mate. They were now skin-to-skin, their hearts beating in frantic unison. She tipped her head back and stared boldly into his soul. He was certain she knew it would be a swift joining for her hands came up, hot and trembling, to clutch his shoulders. As she did so, red moonbeams slanted over her face lending her an ethereal look. Pride and deep affection swelled in his heart. He leaned forward and forced her to bend backwards over the *nebubed* until they fell together into its softness. Her fingernails raked the flesh on either side of his spine when he forced her legs apart and settled between them. Shuddering at the silky feel of her curves beneath him, at her tender, complete surrender, he positioned himself at her moist crux.

Then he attacked.

With one thrust, he was inside her.

"*Oh God…*" he groaned, burying his face in the crook of her neck. It was a hunger to be satisfied, and yet, he knew he would never be able to get enough of her.

She clawed at his back. "Deeper…" she panted. "Faster…*harder*!"

Her broken cries echoed softly in his ears and boiled his blood into molten lava. He stroked his tool in and out of her tight, slick folds as she clamped her legs around his hips and bucked against him. The fragrance of their joined passion wafted upward, teasing his nostrils. Ducking his head, he captured her parted mouth, stifling her whimpers, plunging his tongue inside in perfect rhythm with his cock. She opened wide and fucked him, mouth-to-mouth, sex-to-sex, heart-to-heart. The flavor of her was exotic ambrosia, succulent fruit, and never before had he been so hungry yet utterly fulfilled all at the same time.

Somewhere in the room, open windows welcomed in a violent wind as it blew inland, carrying with it the sugary scent of the sea. Zoey's guttural moans harmonized with the rush of the ocean, the crash and ebb of the waves upon the shore below. The combination of her wild abandon blended with raw nature brought out something animalistic in him, something all together different than he'd ever felt before.

Something seemed odd, unusual…

A burning fire shot through him, pain and pleasure all at once and yet not quite orgasmic. He tore his mouth from hers. His eyes fluttered open and he stiffened.

"Zoey?" He heard the gruff roar in his own voice. It echoed as if it carried across the space of an untamed jungle. Dazed, he looked down into a face he barely recognized, one just as bewildered as he felt.

* * * * *

Zoey struggled to repress her release as she looked up into the blue glowing eyes of a wild beast. The morphing she'd always heard of in the old legends about those rare Dorjanians finding their true galactic heart-mates, stared her in the face. The *Miraz* joining during her Earth journey, along with their very first mating, had come before this in correct succession. As the legend went, the completion of the two copulations, along with this final mating, sealed their togetherness. Though she'd assumed some sort of bonding was most likely imminent, she'd not known exactly when or what to expect.

Now she did.

Before her very eyes, he shifted into a *zimute*—an enormous, two-legged, upright, golden animal that strongly resembled a lion in Rolf's world, and yet was man-like.

And she transformed, too.

The pleasurable pain of it took her breath away. Her body grew in length and girth, as did Rolf's. A ferocious, beastly surge detonated in her system and she reared up and hissed at him, not in antagonism, but in a feral mating call. He growled back at her, low and throaty. His meaty paws yanked his sex from hers, and he flipped her over in one rough motion.

Then, brutishly, he took her from behind and sank his long, thick *ketka* completely inside her. On all fours, she tossed back her head and growled in ecstasy. His cock grew within her as he changed into complete *zimute* form, and she moaned as it filled her to her very depths.

Celestial bodies of the wide universe directed their light upon them, magnified by the glass dome above. A mist of colorful dust like that of the *Miraz Realm*, glimmered and settled around the beasts embracing them in bliss.

As their tempo built, he wrapped his thick, furry arms around her and drew her close. She could smell the untamed beast in him, sense his determination, and it fed her fire further. Rolf clamped his sharp teeth at her nape, digging his claws into her hide. She shivered, her eyes fluttered shut, and a great howl erupted from deep in her throat. The orgasm, as long and satisfying as a *sencore*-based release, stormed through her. Together they snarled and hissed their simultaneous release.

And together they saw that future destinies were born, fates were sealed and galactic alliances were formed.

As the raging of her blood calmed, she fell face-forward onto the bed panting for air. He slipped from her and curled up behind her. Just before the change reversed, he swished his long tail, slid it between her legs and pulled her body up against his large chest.

"You're mine, Zoey," he whispered in her ear, his voice fierce and husky with the remnants of a *zelmur*. "Mine forever, wherever we go."

"Yes, *mica*, and you are mine, as ordained by the celestial forces."

They twitched together as their bodies gradually shifted back to complete human form. The moons' glow dimmed and the mist faded, leaving them swaddled in faint silver darkness. All that could be heard were the rush of the waves on the beach and raspy breaths.

"But first..." She stifled a yawn and pulled the *zigong* fur over their bodies. "We rest in each others arms, *mulera*, finally without dreams or the burden of *nidal* collections."

"Ah, agreed." His hand, now shifted back into human hand form, combed through her hair sending goose bumps down her back. "But soon we make plans to journey back to Earth to connect with my father."

"If that is your wish," she said on a contented sigh. Taking his hand, she cupped her breast with it.

"Yes, it is, but I do have one other request."

"Anything. I will do anything for you, my love." And she proved it by wiggling her ass into his half-hard arousal.

"Anything?"

"Anything."

"Well, then." He chuckled and the deep timbre caressed her ear as she drifted into drowsiness. "Next trip, I wrap up my movie career on Earth. And in my final showing, you're going to be my leading actress."

Her eyes popped open. She groaned. But then she had to laugh.

Epilogue

A strange light streaked across the night sky above the Moonlite BunnyRanch. But there was no one to see it, not a soul who cared.

Behind the *empyral shield,* three figures clad in one-piece, skin-tight suits, leaped to the ground and fell in a crouch. Together, they slowly rose to an upright position, one clutching a bag of sorts, the other two empty-handed.

"Are you sure about this, Phebe?" Zoey set one hand on the princess' shoulder.

She nodded vigorously. Her dark gaze already searched across the rugged, high-mountain terrain. "Very. My talents are better used here, researching. Much better suited to that than sitting at my father's side praying he doesn't croak and doom me for life." She shivered at the thought. "As I've said countless times, being the Dorjan queen is not my destiny." The corners of her mouth curved and she cupped Zoey's cheek. "Thanks to you two—and to Father for allowing me to give up my inheritance of the crown—I get to live out my dream. And Dorjan has an acceptable alternative…you two as the successive king and queen."

"Well, then," Rolf said, anxious to see his father. "We leave you to your sex research. Raketar will send your *portalship* along when you indicate the need."

"If you should change your mind, we will be in California for an undetermined amount of time. Rake will check on you now and then, until your own ship has contacted you."

"Thank you, but I don't think that will be necessary." Phebe backed from the protection of the shield. She lifted a hand and waved as her body passed through the shield's misty wall. "Travel safely."

And in *manoseconds*, Rolf and Zoey were gone.

Phebe inhaled the spicy mountain air. Her eyes eagerly located the brothel where it sat bathed in the summer moonlight, spread out across an open piece of land. Her stomach swirled with excitement and fluttery nerves. Quickly, she opened the bag she'd been holding at her side and drew out the slinky call girl's costume. Stripping away her travel suit, she stood naked, bathed by the silver lunar light. Then, as if she'd worn that kind of garment every day of her life, she donned it with precision. It felt soft and naughty against her skin. Balmy air stroked her naked flesh where the strips of fabric lacked protection. Her *pless* filled with blood, throbbing in anticipation.

It was time to begin her research.

*****

Inside the busy establishment, business was good, sensual music hummed in full swing and the bartender busied himself serving up cocktails and imported beer. A satellite news channel flickered on the television screen set high above the cash register, the volume turned completely down. Rolf Mahoney's picture flashed upon the screen behind the blonde reporter with the conservative bob cut and big blue eyes. Below her, a red strip displayed the topic of her current report.

Still no trace of the Hollywood producer gone missing months ago. Last seen at the infamous Moonlite BunnyRanch bordello near Carson City, Nevada. A missing persons eight hundred number was displayed.

It was old news. Patrons went on about their sex-oriented business. After all, they weren't there to dwell on an unsolved mystery. They'd come for a good time in exchange for their hard-earned money. One client, just now draped with the bronzed limbs of a sultry redhead, requested the *More Than U Can Handle* party. Another flip-flopped, undecided between the

Slippery Nipples Party, the *Shame and Humiliation* fantasy and *Love at the Y*.

But none had anticipated what was about to walk in the door.

The buzzer rang. Gypsy stepped aside and allowed entry to the next guest. The drone of conversation quieted in the parlor, the only sound that of the music playing softly on the hidden speaker system. Through the arched doorway that led into the lounge, the bartender halted in his reach for a bottle of Louis VIII Cognac. Call girls eyed the drop-dead gorgeous woman with guarded suspicion.

"Hi, I'm Phebe," said the exotic, curvy brunette. "I'm looking for Madam Ivana."

The End

Glossary

astere ~ exclamation for farewell or good-bye

astrolage ~ astronaut/scientist

audiotrap ~ equal to inner ears, but somewhat "robotic" or computer-like in nature

bazor~ a Dorjanian weapon much like a machine gun only loaded with chemicals that will immediately corrupt one's internal *compubot*

botic ~ of or pertaining to robotics or computers

chaises ~ formfitting comfortable pants worn by Dorjans in various forms/formalities as either part of a uniform or for everyday living

compubot ~ portion of genetic makeup that works like a computer/briefer within a Dorjanian's body

corfu ~ a dessert

cross-mated ~ different species of different planets mating

crulo ~ shit, crud, crap, dung

Cruxcentre ~ king's airport

datochip ~ receptor in brain that receives information from compubot, nidus and other sensors/computer-like portions, informing of such things as amount of sperm storage in the nidus, etc.

diona! ~ exclamation for shit! shoot! damn!

Dorjan ~ Zoey's home planet less than one light year from Earth in another solar system

Dorjan Sea ~ great sea of Dorjan

ellcore ~ a tree used to construct buildings or structures in which continued moisture might be a factor *empyral shield* ~ shield thrown up by the portalship (engaged by the pilot—Zoey in this case) to hide comings and goings of the ship from ports of entry and exit

flek ~ fuck

frasadil ~ Dorjan flowers of various colors that can survive in most weather extremes and have a spicy scent

gametes ~ sperm

genetoid ~ of or pertaining to genes—genetoid compatibility

glomera ~ drop (of blood)

imputee ~ idiot

incubot ~ a woman who is capable of sperm-carrying/incubation

jaculondor tree ~ a species of a humongous red-toned, blue-leafed Dorjanian tree that seriously competes for oxygen within the atmosphere (it is opposite of green trees which require carbon dioxide); to counter the problem, excess amounts of green trees are kept planted and cared for

ketka ~ cock

King Luran ~ Dorjan's ruler

lazarshield ~ a shield of light, as in, lazarshield doors covering the laboratory openings

leetah ~ lover

magnetic steilianographical (testing) ~ similar to x-rays, sonographs and MRIs, but of a much more advanced form than on Earth

Mama Luna ~ slang similar to "good Lord!"

manodays ~ Dorjan days

manoseconds/minutes/hours ~ Dorjan time-frame

medicoffin ~ capsule within the portalship that performs medical repairs/cures and seals in a protective travel tube

megabot ~ a machine similar to a computer, but far more advanced *mergull* ~ a half fish, half sea bird that can both fly and swim

metrospace ~ area, linear area

mica ~ hon, darling

micramed ~ medic slab table

milt ~ semen

mina~ honey, sweetheart

Miraz Realm ~ realm of the highest joining entered, in rare cases, during final extraction; holds great significance to their bond

mulera ~ my man

nebuchair ~ capsule-like seat on a portalship or in labs and some homes, with many comfort qualities; promotes sleep, work productivety, relaxation

nebusofa ~ same as nebuchair only long like a sofa or divan

nidus ~ incubation chamber within a female body for storing gametes

osmosis-tech ~ technique by which feeding and bodily functions are taken care of within the medicoffin (or laboratory)

ovus ~ reproductive female egg

pless ~ pussy

portalship ~ spaceship/mode of space travel

portalwindow ~ round window on the portalship or within the medicoffin or the like

Raketar ~ Zoey's personal communicating computer onboard portalship

robocar ~ vehicle void of wheels and motor; hovers on air moving about two feet aboveground, can reach speeds of up to two hundred miles per hour

sencore ~ a second clit or erogenous zone at both male and female "taint" areas

spermatozoa ~ sperm or spermata

stallisor ~ stallion

Stalton Forest ~ one of many rich and colorful Dorjan forests

terel ~ a metal indigenous to Dorjan used to make walls and some flooring

tetrons ~ nipples

vistler ~ monitor/television of sorts, but much more technologically advanced

wofler ~ wild Dorjan beast much like a wolf

woflerishly ~ an adjective for wofler, as in, "he grinned woflerishly"

zelmur ~ red rocks carved out and used as homes and building

zigong ~ Dorjan animal used for its fur, bear-like

zimute ~ wild Dorjan animal much like a lion only it walks upright on two legs, is actually the shapeshifting result of two Dorjanians finding each other as galactic, lifetime mates

About the author:

Titania Ladley began her journey into reading romance at the tender age of 13. Soon, sweet romance just didn't cut it. She craved more detail, more sex, *way* more "creativity" between lovers. By her 20's, she discovered that people actually wrote what she needed to read—what she fantasized about. She then devoured the erotica genre. But, alas, restless as usual, she could no longer tolerate just *reading* about it. In her 30's, Titania couldn't suppress the need, the overwhelming drive to create her own fantasies. She had to write. So she did. Published in erotic romance novels and best-selling novellas, she just can't seem to tame her active imagination. So she writes some more…

Titania is a registered nurse, magazine freelance writer, book reviewer and has penned witty slogans. She resides in the Midwest with her very own hunky hero and three children. She enjoys reading erotic romances, walking, weightlifting, crocheting and baking fattening desserts.

Titania welcomes mail from readers. You can write to her c/o Ellora's Cave Publishing at 1337 Commerce Drive, Suite 13, Stow OH 44224.

Why an electronic book?

We live in the Information Age—an exciting time in the history of human civilization in which technology rules supreme and continues to progress in leaps and bounds every minute of every hour of every day. For a multitude of reasons, more and more avid literary fans are opting to purchase e-books instead of paperbacks. The question to those not yet initiated to the world of electronic reading is simply: *why?*

1. *Price.* An electronic title at Ellora's Cave Publishing runs anywhere from 40-75% less than the cover price of the exact same title in paperback format. Why? Cold mathematics. It is less expensive to publish an e-book than it is to publish a paperback, so the savings are passed along to the consumer.
2. *Space.* Running out of room to house your paperback books? That is one worry you will never have with electronic novels. For a low one-time cost, you can purchase a handheld computer designed specifically for e-reading purposes. Many e-readers are larger than the average handheld, giving you plenty of screen room. Better yet, hundreds of titles can be stored within your new library—a single microchip. (Please note that Ellora's Cave does not endorse any specific brands. You can check our website at www.ellorascave.com for customer recommendations we make available to new consumers.)
3. *Mobility.* Because your new library now consists of only a microchip, your entire cache of books can be taken with you wherever you go.

4. *Personal preferences are accounted for.* Are the words you are currently reading too small? Too large? Too...ANNOYING? Paperback books cannot be modified according to personal preferences, but e-books can.
5. *Innovation.* The way you read a book is not the only advancement the Information Age has gifted the literary community with. There is also the factor of what you can read. Ellora's Cave Publishing will be introducing a new line of interactive titles that are available in e-book format only.
6. *Instant gratification.* Is it the middle of the night and all the bookstores are closed? Are you tired of waiting days—sometimes weeks—for online and offline bookstores to ship the novels you bought? Ellora's Cave Publishing sells instantaneous downloads 24 hours a day, 7 days a week, 365 days a year. Our e-book delivery system is 100% automated, meaning your order is filled as soon as you pay for it.

Those are a few of the top reasons why electronic novels are displacing paperbacks for many an avid reader. As always, Ellora's Cave Publishing welcomes your questions and comments. We invite you to email us at service@ellorascave.com or write to us directly at: 1337 Commerce Drive, Suite 13, Stow OH 44224.

ELLORA'S CAVE
ROMANTICA PUBLISHING